CORPORATE ALMIGHTY: 2098

JAMES OWENS

Helping talented writers publish exceptional books

Corporate Almighty: 2098
Copyright © 2025 James Owens. All rights reserved.

Printed in the United States of America. For information, address
Acorn Publishing, LLC
3943 Irvine Blvd. Ste. 218, Irvine, CA 92602

www.acornpublishingllc.com

Interior design by Nico Seidita
Cover design by Damonza

ISBN-13: 979-8-88528-132-4 (paperback)
Library of Congress Control Number: 2025910087

THE FLY TROPHY

PRINTED ON A LARGE, rectangular piece of manila paper, the following text could be found in every post office where drones drop off the mail, every school bulletin board that nobody likes to read, and on the front page of every newspaper in the country.

It also hung next to the window of Todd Swindell's office at the Flakes Alive Incorporated (FAI) headquarters, where the wily Mr. Swindell served as chief executive officer (CEO). The proclamation marked the beginning of a new phase in stricter governance of the States of the Union.

January 1, 2098

The New America stands poised to prosper. Our new government boasts The Big Seven, that is, seven of the most skilled Chief Executive Officers (CEOs) in the business arena, to guide America through good times and crises as well. This establishmentarian ruling body has aided us in assimilating the good and expelling the bad of previous systems. Just look at the results of fifty-eight years of governing excellence. The loathsome prison system has been abolished, as the new way of serving time involves laboring assiduously for an assigned corporation, while improving oneself for future endeavors.

Meanwhile, we have practically eradicated the black-market drug trade, creating safe places where one can recreate with substances while under laboratory supervision and with the knowledge that an antidote stands ready to be administered any time the user has a bad experience. We have eliminated big religion, with its plethora of money beggars, releasing its grip on politics and business. We have done away with the presidency, political parties and that annoying part of government that spends half of its time on campaigning for the next election instead of tending to its duties. Now the government serves you the full four years of each term. And those four years are ruled over by The Big Seven, who were appointed by the final president of the United States, Ghant Wackersham.

Over the fifty-eight years of Mother Earth's existence, we have removed many distractions from the workforce and the workplace, such as sports and sex. The banning of the latter has ushered us into an era where less than one-half of one percent of the population has a sexually transmitted disease. Soon, STDs will be completely eliminated.

This modern America will shine like never before, as people live productive lives and help the corporate government build for the future. Now then, let the pages of your lives turn, my friends, and experience the New and Improved America here in the year 2098.

At the bottom were the seven CEOs' signatures, as well as a spot for the signature of whomever posted the document—in this case, Todd Swindell, FAI CEO.

Look! There's Todd now! He's having coffee while perusing the pages of the *Wall Street Digest*. Whoops! A fat fly just buzzed past Todd's thin nose. Angry Todd grabs a flyswatter from a hook on the wall and WHAP! He nails that ornery sucker! The tiny creature's brown guts make a smear on Todd's office window.

———

"I refuse to clean that spot until the day Flakes Alive Incorporated overtakes the Great American Flake Company (GAFC) in flake sales," declared a raspy-voiced Todd. "I'm tired of second place, goddamnit! Let those guts rot on that window until we make number one! Let them be a testament to our perseverance here at Flakes Alive Incorporated."

The thin, hollow-cheeked, goatee-wearing Swindell brushed the three scrawny hairs that tried to cover a lot of naked real estate on the top of his bony head and uttered a plaintive sigh. On his office wall, a picture of a sword made in the year 2040 hung proudly. His secret collection of antique swords was only on display in his sumptuously furnished home, out of sight from any earthling who might care to turn him in for withholding merchandise made before 2040, which was against the law. But the rich could bend and stretch the rules a bit.

Todd's office was cluttered with unopened boxes of cologne, candles, chocolates, and other assorted items, the result of job candidates groveling for recognition by bringing gifts when they interviewed. The gifts were carelessly stacked on shelves and on the floor. In the adjoining room sat larger gifts—an umbrella that shouted at you if rain was in the forecast, ultrafast microwaves, and even a fancy new quantum TV.

TWINKLE, TWINKLE, LITTLE STAR

PORING over formulas and chemical tables, Syd Waverly hunched beneath the smoky light radiating from his living room lampstand, unaware of the soft draft that had sneaked into his workspace once Twinkle Deshpande slid open the bedroom window and stealthily slipped inside. Now the smoke tumbled and curled above the Muriel Coronella cigar ensconced in the groove of a shell-shaped ashtray on the tiny, black, round table that encircled the post that held the three glowing light bulbs.

The low volume of the television commercials lent the room the upbeat ambiance of a sales seminar. Oblivious to it all, Syd slowly unseated the cigar, while not taking his eyes off the formulas, raised it to his thin lips, and puffed. He began plugging numbers into an algebraic equation in an attempt to work out the perfect formula for the No-Sog corn flakes that his employer, Flakes Alive Incorporated (FAI), had been coveting for so long.

Meanwhile, Twinkle slithered around the bed like a blacksnake in the dark. As she inched her way toward the door leading into the hallway, she caught a whiff of smoke from the cheap cigar. The poor girl suffered from allergies and tried desperately not to cough. When she felt sure of herself, that she would not cough or gasp, she moved into the hallway with utmost caution.

The flashing lights from the goofy television commercials helped to guide her to the living area, even though she'd taken pains to memorize the layout of the house plus the garden outside.

Twinkle edged her way to the opening in the living room and paused to seek the correct position and prepare herself for the important task before her.

A braided rug underlaid the gold recliner, the lamp and a larger oval coffee table. The rug had become unraveled in three spots, according to Twinkle's keen eye. Each spot represented a small problem in Twinkle's life. She envisioned the loose material of each spot rethreading itself until there were no more ravels. That is how she tidied her own problems, one ravel at a time.

Everything pristine.

A band of tiny square tiles encircled the maple interior of the coffee table. A couple of magazines—one with the title of "Television" and the subtitle of "Get More Out of Commercials"—interrupted the uniformity of the table design. A 75-inch, 3D holographic TV hung on the wall between a set of family photos. A matching gold couch with four gold pillows sat against the only wall without windows. The windows on the side walls had their blinds closed.

Twinkle immediately noticed the wood floor in the living room and dared not move a step closer or risk a creaky old floorboard giving her away. She felt confident that her aim would not fail her at this juncture. She had glided like a feather in a soft breeze from the bedroom window to her position at the end of the hallway, and now it was time to think through her plan. She took a long, slow breath and aimed the pipe. She closed her eyes and imagined going through the motions. Careful not to move her head, she fictitiously blew into the tube and the dart parked itself right in the neck of Syd Waverly. Bullseye! Twinkle had targeted the exterior jugular vein and, in her imagination, succeeded in penetrating just that. She opened her eyes and prepared herself for the real thing.

Suddenly, the worn-out chemist tossed his pen on the lamp-table and rolled out the footrest on his beige recliner, stretching his legs. A flurry of dread flushed over Twinkle's tiny body. She feared Syd might get up to get some coffee or some other beverage. Surely he would see her. But the sage chemist instead relaxed, and the Twinkle's anxiety dissipated. She pulled out a long tube from her slacks and positioned herself on her knees at the corner where the hallway meets the living room. The angle was perfect, allowing for a clear target of the neck area.

The ninety-two pound assassin opened a small canister containing a poisonous dart, which she inserted into the pipe, and aimed it with a steady hand and a most selective eye. Now she blew the dart into poor Syd's neck and patiently watched as the discerning, veteran chemist began to expire. With one soft grunt he barely moved, as the dart tipped with curare did its work in the bloodstream and around the muscles that control the lungs. A bit of drool dripped from the corner of Syd's mouth and his head slumped to the side. The thin cigar still trickled smoke, as the TV man vociferously ranted about some new cleaning product.

Twinkle admired the ambiance of quiet death. She could feel her own chest taking in air and breathing it out. So mysterious, she thought, that such a relaxing moment could correspond to another's demise. Invigorated, her eyes bulged and her soul murmured for the loss of humanity and the coinciding gain in her own mirth. Her bosom tingled at the sight of fresh death.

Twinkle slowly positioned one end of the blow gun on the living room carpet and waited until Mr. Waverly's aspiration subsided. Paralysis had set in. Twinkle checked his nonexistent pulse, removed the dart, and smeared a bit of make-up over the tiny wound. Then she slipped the notepad from beneath Syd's fingers, stuffed it in her pants, put out the cigar, walked into the bedroom and closed and locked the window, finally letting herself out of the front door.

Once she stepped outside, she pulled the plastic booties from her feet, slipped off the plastic gloves and removed the shower cap from her head, tucking them all in a small bag she wore around her neck. Her tiny nipples seemed to swell a bit with excitement beneath the tantalizing moonlight. With scarcely a wisp of dust, she disappeared into the star-studded night.

3

BAD INTELLIGENCE

THOUGH TWINKLE DROVE CASUALLY toward the office, her heart raced with enthusiasm. She glanced at herself in the rearview mirror—a petite figure with medium dark skin, a thin face, and thick lips. She knew her innocent eyes could fool anyone, so she broke into a smug smile. Soon, she would hand the formula over to the lead man of the operation. She could feel her nerves tingling as she approached her destination. She parked her car, went inside the office, and knocked on the door of the meeting place. They were waiting for her. She thrust the document into the hands of her boss, who was an expert in interpreting algebraic expressions.

Silence hung over the room like a wet awning, while the big boss inspected the material on the notebook page.

"Why, this is an incomplete formula!" bawled Chad Scandalman, the corpulent CEO of The Great American Flake Company (GAFC). "What the fuck have you done? It's not finished!"

"Sir," noted Cecil Weatherspoon, vice president of operations at GAFC, "we were under the impression that Mr. Waverly had completed the formula."

"You floundering ass-craps, you fucked up everything!"

yelled Scandalman. "Does this look like it's done?!" He held up the incomplete and scribbled formula for all to see.

"But sir, rumor has it that the formula was completed. The recipe done!" protested Twinkle.

"Don't count your chickens before they're hatched," warned "Cliché" Bob, Scandalman's go-to guy, jack-of-all-tradesman, and golf partner. "You fools!"

"Rumor?" Scandalman commented caustically. "We don't go by rumor, Ms. Deshpande. We go by fact here at GAFC! Fact! Do you hear?!"

"My job," retorted Twinkle rather haughtily, "was only to extinguish, Mr. Scandalman, and that, I have done."

"Cecil," Chad Scandalman asked the shocked vice president, "are you the one responsible for this?"

"Our intelligence," noted Cecil, "pointed to a completed formula, sir. As it turned out, it was bad intelligence."

"Garbage in, garbage out," said Cliché Bob.

"Oh, shut up, you blithering misfit!" yelled Cecil, staring at Bob with piercing eyes.

"I have a mind to hold out on the other half of your payment, Ms. Deshpande," barked Scandalman.

"I wouldn't do that, sir," responded Cecil. "We may need her for another job. Besides, we don't want her to turn on us."

"Just let me remind you of our sworn secrecy," warned Scandalman. "Only us four know about this plan. Make sure we keep it that way."

Each of the four gave acknowledgement.

Scandalman reluctantly handed Twinkle the envelope containing her final payment. "All of you, get the hell out of my office! When I decide the next step, you'll know."

The three schemers filed out of Scandalman's office, Cliché Bob last. Before he could disappear into the hallway, the rotund

CEO reminded him, "Don't forget. Golf tomorrow at Mapleton, Bob. Tee time is two o'clock."

"Right, Mr. Scandalman," Bob confirmed.

The four scoundrels were unaware that Italian American chemist Annie De Luca had already earned consideration as the replacement for Syd Waverly at Flakes Alive Incorporated and was preparing to toil feverishly to create a flake that would remain rigid when soaked in milk. Meanwhile, Twinkle sulked a bit. *I don't have to take Bob's bullshit,* she thought. *And Scandalman is a big hog. I'm a professional assassin, not a spy. They should have had the right intelligence before they sent me in there in such a rush.*

Scandalman sat alone in his tidy office, wringing his hands and muttering his regrets. "Of all the cock-knobbing blunderers, I have the foremost bunglers on the list. Fucking, cock-throttling Goddamn shit, fuck suck muck GODDAMN FUCKERS!" Scandalman pounded his fist on his oak desk and buried his head in his hands. "I want that goddamn formula!"

4

COMMERCIAL SUCCESS

THE HENSON CLAN huddled in the family room, forming a semicircle around a brand new 3D holo-TV they'd purchased at Bold Buy Appliance Store. A seemingly endless succession of cute commercials emanated from the stereo setup. The entire family gazed steadily at the silly commercials, laughing heartily at the antics of the goofy actors, most of whom had given up on the movie industry long before.

There was an insurance commercial with a porpoise driving a sleek new spaceship and another starring an agitated walrus. Then a candy commercial for Dizzy Dots steered the atmosphere into a comic storm in which a cacophony of giggles and grunts by entertained viewers permeated the household. Commercials for intelli-phones and toaster ovens followed when, suddenly, a short clip of the movie *Citizen Kane* drew the family into a chorus of "Oh no's" and "This sucks" announcements. But soon the mood brightened when a cute ad for razor blades elicited *Oohs* and *Aahs* as if the family were watching Fourth of July fireworks.

The father, Herb, was a rather handsome man with a trim build and no facial hair. He had a pointed nose and thick eyebrows. He wore a Newton County School System tattoo on his forehead with the letters NCSS inside an oval. All school systems were now public stock companies, competing for territory and pupilage, and Herb's employer was especially competitive.

The commercials continued for over an hour before a snippet of *The Godfather* elicited more booing from the otherwise lively family. "This is nonsense," cried Herb. "We keep getting interrupted by these boring movie clips."

The Henson family harnessed the spirited fun of commercials to spread joy through the household. The whimsical nature of these brief skits set an ambiance of homey cheer. Their yellow house had a lovely white picket fence around it, a canopy over the front porch, and dormer windows. Inside, the house featured arched doorways, a pair of fireplaces, one in the living room and another in the family room, and two baths with brass fixtures. New carpeting covered most of the floors, except for the kitchen and bath, which had ceramic tile floors. The charming residence felt like the quintessential all-American dwelling.

"Does anyone want to play a game of Oligarchy?" asked Holly Henson, the jolly mother of the crew. She wore her brown hair in a ponytail and had luscious lips that dared not be kissed. Her forehead tattoo matched Herb's, as she relished her role in the Parent Teacher Association. The children all cheered at her game suggestion, and she smiled broadly as she took the Oligarchy box from a living room shelf.

"I do!"

"Oh yes."

"Cool!"

Before long, Herb Jr. raised his cash-heavy hands in the air and shouted "Victory!"

Once the family sat down to eat dinner, the dry-dog-food commercial everybody adored came on the television. The announcer warned against wet food, and, at the conclusion of the ad, a dog was shown rubbing its itchy butt on the carpet. The family members burst into an uproarious laugh, while munching on their meat and potatoes. The TV ads had grown more daring with their toilet humor, beginning far back with cartoon bears peddling toilet paper and so forth, but apparently it mattered not to the average audience.

5

NO-SOG FLAKES

ON SEVERAL OCCASIONS, Annie De Luca thought she had plugged the correct numbers into the No-Sog, Stay-Crisp formula only to be disappointed when each chemical blend failed to produce the prized flake inhibitory waterlogging results. Passionately, she toiled through the hours, her wavy, dark hair shining beneath the fluorescent kitchen light. Her olive complexion reddened a bit with each new disappointment, the birthmark on her left cheek standing out on her tiny face. Meanwhile, her heavy eyebrows moved up and down with hope and then failure.

Annie knew that if she could find the solution at home, she could then replicate the experiment the next day at work. She tried this and that experiment, but the damn flakes turned soggy every time after three minutes of desperate hope. Finally, the hypersensitive lab technician heaved the latest bowl of milk and flakes at the kitchen wall, where the vessel exploded into ten or more pieces, and the creamy solution splattered across the front of the stove and refrigerator.

"Fuck!" she exclaimed, "I can't get it right!"

"What's all the shouting about?" asked her male companion, Anthony Valentino, as he rushed into the room. His already prominent eyeballs grew bigger by the second, as he rubbed his scruffy beard.

"Mind your own business!" shouted Annie. "Go play with your fucking HO trains!" "Well, who's gonna clean this up?" asked Anthony.

"Who cleans *everything* up?" sassed Annie.

"Geez," said Anthony, "what did *I* do?" A glum look fell over his face.

Annie, slightly humbled, but still very frustrated by her inability to make the numbers work, said, "Maybe I have to change the hard-flake formula itself."

"What?"

"Don't stay up for me," advised Annie. "I'm going to be working all night on this project."

"OK," said Anthony. "Goodnight."

And, indeed, Annie fiddled with and juggled the x's, y's and z's of the formula throughout the night. But she just could not crack the solution. Finally, she drifted off with her head on the kitchen table at 2:30 a.m., just in time to gather three hours of sleep before she had to prepare for another day at Flakes Alive Incorporated.

6

"ZIGGIE"

ZIGMUND WEXLER, a German-American pipefitter, fidgeted with his right ear, where the intelli-phone implant rested inside. He wondered whether medical professionals had ever performed an intelli-phone *unplant*. Sure, the device was hands-free, but Ziggie struggled through a constant ringing in his left ear, which he blamed on the device in his right ear. And he just could not get used to the gadget weighing down the right side of his brain.

Other people had no problem with the electronic organ. But most people were phone people, that is to say, they loved to blab over the phone all day while their country went to hell and were not bothered by the inconvenience of metal machinery parked in their ear canal forever. However, Ziggie was no phone person; he did not talk much over the phone. He hoped that one day he could find an underground doctor who would remove it.

And the commercials! One had to tolerate a minimum of two hours and twenty minutes worth of commercials every day. That was the rule. For the unworldly, this was acceptable. But for Ziggie, a veteran intellectual, these blasted verbal ads proved insufferable. Little twenty to thirty-second plugs for this product or that. Inane and dainty laugh-alongs, nerve-grating jingles, and tireless ditties that featured the most stupid humans and animals doing the most stupid things.

One commercial from a major butchery featured a manmade piggie called Porkenflesh who absorbed a bolt of lightning that inspired him to arise from a state of nonexistence and hand out free packages of sausages to the neighbors. That ad was so successful that a follow-up called Brood of Porkenflesh featured piglet children. The piglets left a pork roast on everyone's doorstep. Then, as is the case with all free-market packs of fools, they milked the thing as far as they could, and came out with a commercial for Pork 'n' Poop, a pink litter box for pet pigs, which had become the rage in the 2090s.

Phone implants became available in 2046 but mandatory in 2073, and since then, the gadgets had been embedded in the ears of children as soon as they reached the age of five. As for the implantee, he or she had the option of turning the phone off by verbal command (as long as they had listened to the required two hours and twenty minutes of commercials): recite the phone serial number and the words "phone off."

So, during face-to-face conversations with others, one could disable the phone, though, unfortunately, with that being a hassle, it led people to limit face-to-face communication with other people, a bad thing for a society that already lacked in human relations. One had to leave the phone on at least eight hours a day. Ziggie deplored the entire process of carrying a phone in his head and would pay a sizeable sum to have it removed.

Ziggie fell somewhere between a renegade and a maverick. Over the years, he had pondered restlessly the idea of dropping out of the mainstream madness brought on by The Great Cleanse of 2040. In fact, the seven CEOs that took over the presidency, that is, The Big Seven, marked 2040 as the beginning of time. No one was allowed to discuss anything that occurred before The Great Cleanse.

Ziggie shunned that kind of thinking, labeling it "The Great Sham." Of course, he had to be careful whom he spoke with, as discussing anything pre-2040 was illegal. And discussing anything negative regarding The Great Cleanse was illegal.

He learned all that very early on in the Boot Camp for Business Aspirants (BCBA), which every commerce-oriented student took in the sixth grade. It served as a crash course that taught the fundamentals of mercantilism—how to wear a suit, tie a tie, polish shoes, button collars, shake hands, write checks, and pack a briefcase.

If you planned on college, you had to take a more involved BCBA course during your freshman year in high school. That course entailed even stricter lessons, such as how to wear your hair, make a sales pitch, tune in to neoclassical music, avoid the five o'clock shadow, give pep talks and rally the troops, enlist the art of persuasion, allocate resources, hire and fire, navigate spreadsheets, give praise and admonish, give the authoritative stare, conduct oneself at office parties, etc. All the boring practices of the business world.

One could even choose to specialize in How to be a Corporate Prick. That entailed learning the clean-out-your-desk-and-get-lost methodology for downsizing. These types of business courses, along with math and computer courses, made up most of the high school curriculum these days.

After all, courses in history, biology, geography, philosophy, and even English hardly mattered anymore. Scarcely anyone took them; almost no one went for a degree in the humanities these dreadful days. It was considered a waste. The business moguls of the world wanted you taking computer courses and math courses only. They coveted the business-ready nerds who emerged from the BCBA coursework. They craved the sales candidate who knew nothing of history, but could jump right in and type up a storm on the keyboard, even if their English was beastly awful.

Ziggie despised it all. He had no interest in selling anything.

Ziggie had also once contemplated removal of the ZXR corporation logo tattooed on his forehead. That being too obvious, he abandoned the strategy; however, he soon began to consider a cover-up tattoo over the Dairy Blue Corporation logo on his right forearm. Such "sinful" thoughts tugged at the rebellious thread that coursed through his spirit and mind. He longed to cover the company logo with a tattoo of a tiger.

The scheming rebel finally persuaded himself to inquire about altering the forearm design, though he could not find a tattoo artist willing to break the law. The Seven CEOs and their underlings had so thoroughly molded and shaped society's thinking that folks cringed at the concept of resistance. The Big Seven, as they called them, had a semipermanent roster of four paleo-conservatives and three moderate liberals.

This is the way it was fixed in 2040. That's when the nutcases got in and implemented the maniacal 2040 Plan, a traditionalist doctrine that demanded strict alignment with rigid societal rules and stark loyalty to corporations.

For a guy like Ziggie, who despised corporations, such obsequious behavior as stipulated by a syndicate of business moguls proved intolerable. He simply could not comply.

7

AMERICAN SCOUTING

THE PECULIAR DEMISE of Sydney Waverly warranted investigation, though the detective assigned to the case had failed so far to uncover evidence of murder. Detective Hung Cho Lee knew of the vicious competition and the myriad ill feelings that existed between the two flake giants known as the Great American Flake Company and the Flakes Alive Incorporated. That the GAFC company had surreptitiously poisoned Mr. Waverly was not out of the ballpark of possibilities, yet proving such a devious connection, Detective Lee knew, would abound with difficulties. If only the crime lab could determine whether Mr. Waverly succumbed to poison, and, if so, exactly what kind of poison he had ingested, they would have something to trace back to a source.

Of course, any mysterious death warrants a homicide investigation. Detective Lee did discover a single hair from the front porch of the Waverly residence. It was caught on the corner of an outside doormat. But it would be difficult to link a hair from outside the crime scene to any murder within the residence.

In an intense interview with GAFCs CEO, Chad Scandalman, Detective Lee hinted at corporate wrongdoing, but the idea was swiftly rebuffed.

"As you may know," Lee said, "I am investigating the mysterious death of Flakes Alive Incorporated chemist Sydney Waverly."

"Yes," said Mr. Scandalman, "the poor man just folded up like an autumn flower, I understand."

"Yes, well," explained Mr. Lee, "as your company is an arch competitor of Flakes Alive Incorporated, and Waverly's untimely demise caught us all a little off guard, and he was on the fast track to become a laboratory supervisor, I trust that you might share some thoughts about the matter."

"Well, it's quite tragic for sure," reasoned an agitated Mr. Scandalman, "and I sympathize with Waverly's family and all, but, frankly, I'm just as confused and shocked as you are, detective."

Mr. Lee went on. "Might Waverly's last breath bring a ray of sunshine to the outlook of a corporation that is in direct competition for the No-Sog flake recipe?"

"Now, Mr. Lee—"

"Might even one of your spies—er, scouts—"

"Ahem, yes, we call them scouts—"

". . . have had a hand in it?"

"Our corporation," assured a now pissed-off Scandalman, "would never partake in any such underhanded activity. How dare you insinuate such treachery, detective!" Scandalman wiped his forehead with a handkerchief and directed the eyeballs of his plump countenance right at Mr. Lee's own eyeballs. "Now, if you will excuse me, our corporate lawyers would be glad to answer any further questions."

"You have no secrets?" asked Detective Lee.

"No secrets, sir," replied the perturbed CEO.

"Are you sure?" prodded Hung Cho Lee.

Now Mr. Scandalman grew irate, though he refrained from

yelling. Instead, he adopted a wise-ass attitude. "Sure as getting a hand job at an Asian massage parlor," he said.

It was a wicked insult he hurled at Mr. Lee's heritage.

Detective Lee bristled at the remark, but his demeanor remained cool. "I ought to bust you right now," he said softly.

Now Scandalman became belligerent. "Take your cheesy bow tie and your two-bit hat, Mr. Lee, and get the hell out of here!" barked the heated CEO.

"If I see any of your slimeball scouts creeping around the free-market underbelly, Mr. Scandalman, I'll hook a tow chain to your big fat ass and haul you in like a load of stinky tuna."

"Get out!"

Scandalman said nothing else but boiled inside.

Detective Lee adjusted his fedora, stood up, and exited the office, confident that he had roused Scandalman's anger enough to indicate that the large CEO was lying. Mr. Lee thought that Scandalman's rage indicated that he possessed the kill gene, but the detective figured that the top boss would not commit such a bloodthirsty act himself.

He would have an underling do it.

8

THE TACTICS OF SCANDALMAN

CLICHÉ BOB SERVED as Scandalman's point man, weaving crooked contract scenarios and trying to cheat rival corporate dealmakers. His modus operandi was to annoy them with clichés until they lost focus and allowed themselves to be suckered by his chicanery.

"We've got 'em by the balls," Bob would boast. "It's just a matter of time."

Nobody could produce a worn-out phrase quicker than old Bob. He said, "Have a nice day!" and "Go for it!" so many times each day he could double as a game show host. So when Scandalman recruited him for the Syd-Waverly-snuffing lead man, the rotund CEO knew he would have to endure an almost endless parade of hackneyed sayings and piss-poor platitudes, as Bob kept him abreast of the ongoings of the tiny assassin, Twinkle Deshpande, and VP Cecil Weatherspoon.

But Scandalman never saw a person he could not coerce into dirty work or swindle with low pay.

So, Cliché Bob fervently snatched up the job and set to work with Twinkle and Cecil at once.

When Twinkle accomplished her part—the most critical part—of the assignment and declared Waverly deceased, a river of trite phrases poured out of Bob's mouth as if the supply was limitless. Yes, the clichés rushed forth ineloquently, dizzyingly, almost leading Scandalman into a bout with vertigo.

They don't call him Cliché Bob for nothing, thought Scandalman. *My gosh, if he were ever interrogated by the police, he would put them all to sleep. I'll bet he was a horrid bore in speech class. Should he ever utter a sentence without a cliché, the earth would certainly shake. Why, he could not say his name, rank, and serial number without inserting a cliché somewhere in there. If he ever delivered a eulogy at a funeral, everyone around him would drop dead.*

"Mission accomplished, Mr. Scandalman," declared Bob. "We're home free! Just sign on the dotted line—meaning my paycheck, sir."

"Well, Mr. Bob," revealed Scandalman, "I have been meaning to discuss that with you. You see, the company is a little short on cash flow right now, and I was wondering . . ."

"If I'll take a rain check? Mr. Scandalman," inserted Bob, as if seasoned to appreciate the art of being low-balled by the big CEO. "Certainly, sir. GAFC and I are good. You can take it to the bank!"

By now Scandalman had reworked the Syd Waverly murder in his pompous brain. *Even though the formula was unfinished,* thought Scandalman, *Waverly was surely on the verge of discovering the solution, so it was good that we did away with him before he could make the breakthrough, which surely would have precluded any type of benefit to the Great American Flake Company.*

EFFICIENCY

BABIES with below-normal intellect were aborted in this crazy era of totalitarianism. The Intellect Detector Model II (IDMII) could yield the intellect of any baby in the belly as early as four months after it was conceived. In fact, anyone with a projected cost to develop themself that was higher than the lifetime amount they could produce was eliminated. Projecting a man or woman's worth was no simple task.

Tables and formulas prepared from years of difficult, complex development could now yield accurate figures for comparison, claimed the financial arm of the corporate government.

Economic scientists worked well into the nights for several years to obtain the calculations.

Together they carved out efficiencies in forecasting just how much each human was worth and how much it would take to sustain that person throughout a lifetime. This Sustenance Factor could be weighed against the Total Human Worth, and this comparison determined the fate of the unborn.

Total Human Worth - Sustenance Factor = Life/Death Indicator

If the Life/Death Indicator was positive, one lived. If negative, one died. The capitalist will incur no waste.

THE FLAKE WARS

TODD SWINDELL, business-savvy CEO of Flakes Alive Incorporated, had scoured the internet for Syd Waverly's replacement before settling on FAI's own Annie De Luca. Some old-fashioned sexism played a part in his resistance to the idea, but he soon realized that finding another candidate would take too much time—time they could not afford in the race for the hard flake formula—thus, he would assign the No-Sog experimentation tasks to Annie for now.

Oh, he struggled with his reservations about giving Annie the lead spot in the laboratory. He had thrown his calculator against his office wall in frustration, kicked and dented the steel trash can under his desk, and even shouted imprecations at his spoiled brat of a child, Tory Swindell, one night. But he would give Annie the opportunity, he ultimately decided.

"That fucking Chadwick Scandalman is behind Waverly's sudden death, I just know it," said Todd. And even with Waverly's replacement settled on, Todd wore himself out with his nervous condition, a plague on his senses he could scarcely control.

There was one remedy that would at least mitigate the symptoms of his anxiety: Dream Eruption Formula XX. He reached inside his desk drawer and snatched a tiny bottle of the mental-anguish reducer. The bottle read: "The Concoction that Weaves Dynamite Dreams, Without the Annoying Side Effects of Other Concentrations." He twisted off the cap, tipped the half-ounce bottle high above his twitching lips, and began pouring the solution into his open mouth.

Now Todd laid his head back on the giant leather office chair and seamlessly dozed off. Within seconds, his mind wandered into amusement-park mode, where a multi-colored ringmaster with kooky clowns and energetic white horses played beneath the searchlights. A gold elephant spun a beach ball at the tip of its trunk, while beautiful ladies dressed in glittery bathing suits swung on the trapezes above. Overhead of the roofless stage, fireworks splashed in the sky, booming and whistling and crackling beneath an orange full moon, which seemed three times larger than the moon of which most people are familiar.

Behind the stage, an enormous fountain squirted out brilliant streams amid the colored lamps that encircled it. And every moving item featured psychedelic trails in its wake. Everything gleamed with newfound romance and gleeful adventurousness. Such an invigorating scene could not be duplicated in earthly terms.

In twenty minutes, Todd experienced more glitzy brain treats then a kid with his face pressed against the glass on a penny-candy counter (this delightful experience could only have been enjoyed well before the so-called "beginning of time," that is, before 2040, as penny candy today would be impossible to procure).

Todd awoke energized, contented, refreshed and ready for another day of hoarding capital and issuing orders from his overworked intelli-phone. Articulate but unrestrained, the CEO barked out demands over his brain-nourishing phone implant, while checking the figures on accounting reports. He had embarked upon a second wind of activity that day and sailed through the afternoon with ease. But the thought of Scandalman orchestrating a hit on Todd's innocent lab technician stirred up a burning desire for revenge within his innermost soul.

If I'm going to go to war with that lardass slob, Scandalman, thought Todd, *I'll have to go full force. No bickering over petty shit. I've got to strike back with prompt vengeance. He eliminated one of mine; I've got to eliminate one of his.*

In public, Scandalman and Swindell hurled names at each other. In a radio interview, Scandalman called Flakes Alive Incorporated "the industrial mafia." FAI sued the Great American Flake Company for libel and slander. In an op-ed piece for a prominent Chicago newspaper Swindell referred to Scandalman as "The Demon of Domino." GAFC then sued FAI. They accused each other of having "damaged chromosomes" and "warped genetic codes."

Meanwhile, Todd felt that the fly carcass that had been squished and smeared on the window of his office somehow monitored his performance as a slick CEO. Maybe it was the spirit of the fly. But he felt that it was not there to haunt him, but to motivate him, to guide him. The guts seemed to rally Todd into a mindset for revenge.

THE CARDBOARD WILDS

"YES, KIDS," announced Herb Henson, "we're going to Tanks and Cages Zoological Gardens, but first we must stop off at the Spittoon Factory to leave a specimen."

"What's a specimen, father?" asked young Herb Henson Jr.

"Oh, it's just a contribution, son. You'll learn more about that later in life." "What are you contributing?"

"Oh, well, just a sample of spermatozoa."

"What's that?"

"You'll learn about that once you get older."

"He means jizz," blurted older brother Nolan.

"Huh?" remarked Holly Henson, astounded that one of the Henson boys would utter such vulgar slang. "What did you say? Herb, did you hear your son?"

Herb stopped the car. "Nolan," he said, pointing at the boy with a bony finger and a look of displeasure on his face, "you need your mouth washed out."

"Sorry, dad," apologized Nolan with his eyes toward the floor.

"Don't let me hear that again, young man!" demanded Herb Sr.

Aside from the expletive, the drive to Tanks and Cages

proved more pleasant than the actual visit. For example, the elephant cage was empty, though a giant cardboard cutout in the shape and color of an elephant stood before the bars.

"Father," asked Herb Jr., "do you remember when real elephants roamed the jungles?"

"Ah, well, I'm not supposed to talk about it, son."

"Why not?"

"It's government rules."

"Father, where did all the elephants go?"

"Er, geez, they were harvested for their tusks, son . . . ivory to satisfy the quota. You know, got to keep those machines running. Supply and demand, son . . . that sort of thing. People's livelihoods depended on it."

"They were poachers," added Holly. "That's where the last of the elephants went. To poaching, dear." Holly was uncharacteristically negative, as she did not like those who kill animals.

"But couldn't they spare a few elephants?" wondered Herb Jr. The young lad shook his head as he spoke.

"Well," reasoned Herb Sr., "you know what they say, son: 'Money is the seed of all joy.'"

"So, how do they get ivory now, since all of the elephants are gone?"

"Well, someone invented synthetic ivory." Herb Sr.'s face flushed with embarrassment.

The fish tanks too were mostly empty. All the tuna and Alaskan Cod had been devoured by humans, so pictures of these creatures had to do. The tropical fish only had a few real-life examples, most of them also extinct. And ever since the jungles of the Amazon had succumbed to development, the few animals left there were prohibited from being removed and shown at zoos. That meant that lots of tropical fish, once a high-light of zoos and aquatic centers alike, were no longer allowed.

The mighty tiger was gone, lost to rugs and furniture coverings and hunting trophies, and the birdcages were half empty. A few sickly-looking birds fluttered weakly on their roosts. The snake cages were mostly barren, for most of the slithering critters had been used to make snakeskin boots to keep the markets humming.

After departing from the zoo, the family had a picnic in the Domino, Indiana city park, before returning home to watch commercials and play money games.

ALFI AND ALL THAT JAZZ

ZIGGIE DECIDED to resign from his job as a pipefitter and resolved to go on the run. He finally found a basement tattooist who would dare to cover the Dairy Blue Corporation logo on his forearm with a tiger for $850. But when office worker Miranda Kinny noticed Ziggie's altered tattoo design on the shop floor, she immediately turned him into management, who promptly turned him into the police.

"That goddamn goody-two-shoed bitch," Ziggie muttered as he finished up his work for the day, his last day. In the end, he resigned before they could arrest him or fire him. At quitting time, Ziggie saw the cops waiting at the entrance to the union hall, so he pulled down the beak of his faded blue baseball cap and slipped out the side door.

Jumping in his old beater of a work car, he hit the highway and headed north to the big city. He drove up to Chicago and found a place named Underground Workshop that sold goods and rented sleeping quarters for $800 a week. It did business as a kind of head shop and black-market music emporium. The folks who ran the shop introduced Ziggie to the outlawed jazz music of the 1920s and 1930s, two permanently erased decades, and explained the theory behind the heavily synco-pated music of black people during those times.

Black musicians, they explained, used syncopation as a means of rebellion. Putting emphasis in places unexpected by the listener lent jazz part of its uniqueness. Ziggie, of course, was instructed never to mention the music outside of the modern-day speakeasy. So gracious were his hosts that they offered the renegade a job as salesman and counterperson for the Underground Workshop, where he sold all of the drugs of free trade that had once been illegal.

"You see," said Alfi, one of the shop owners, "all of these substances became legal once the capitalist learned that they could make huge profits by legally peddling them, and, at the same time, eliminate the streetside drug dealers. If it wasn't for the capitalist, they would never have become legal. Drugmakers simply petitioned the government, which is made up of CEOs anyway, and received permission to sell them at prices below the black market prices, though the drugs are taxed quite heav-ily. But, hey, at least you can trust that the drug has the right chemicals in it. On the street, you can't trust the drugs anymore. Especially when meth came along, you didn't know what the hell was used to make it."

"I get it," said Ziggie, pushing up the wire-rimmed glasses that had slipped down his long, thin nose, "if the capitalist wants it, he or she gets it. But why can't they make jazz acces-sible and legal? Surely that would bring in good money."

"Ah," noted Alfi, "but you're forgetting. Anything that happened before 2040 is off limits. You may hear modern jazz but nothing from before 2040. So, you miss out on the heyday of jazz. It's part of the capitalist conditioning culture. So, you see, here at the Underground Workshop, we sell drugs to cloak the selling of old music. Opposite of the way it was long ago, drugs are just a front. That jazz you just sampled for free brings in sixty dollars per listen to non-employees. If anyone comes in with a yearning for outlawed music, we give them their fix for sixty dollars an album. But you, as an employee, get it for free."

"So," said Ziggie, "all those years of sneaking around to acquire intoxicating substances and getting busted—in many cases having people's lives ruined—were for nothing? Some capitalist just snaps his or her fingers and they're suddenly legal. Geez!"

"Yep," said Alfi with complete indifference.

"What about a woman?" asked Ziggie, removing his ballcap and dragging a hand through his light brown hair. "A young supple woman that one could touch and feel. Can you get that?"

"Nope, we don't deal in flesh. The penalty for selling sex of any kind can be life in prison or death."

"But that's so fascist," demurred Ziggie.

"Nope. It's known as *authoritative capitalism*, but you're not allowed to say it. You say 'authoritative capitalism' outside these doors and it's a $1200 ticket . . . automatic, no questions asked." "As for the music," reported Alfi, "we've got everything from Mozart to Mayhem" (a modern brute music band with savage instrumentation and murder-promoting lyrics, banned by The Big Seven).

They listened to someone named Duke Ellington, then another guy known as John Coltrane, whomever that was. The notes glided off the speakers like cotton candy to the mind. They slithered into the soul like a den of friendly snakes and clutched the heart in a vise grip. These were more than just notes in the atmosphere; they represented the full spectrum of human feeling and danced around the spirit like gypsies around a campfire. And every time you thought you understood it, a syncopated note would jump off the platform, toss you off your stilted game, and make you feel alive.

This, Ziggie reflected, was the element missing from the modern world, and it was so wonderful that it made you breathe freely for the first time in your life or for an awful long time if you were older than fifty-eight. A festival of incongruity that teased the passions and smashed the structure of living through the stodgy leadup to the new millennium.

Now Ziggie could see why they outlawed the music. *Those traditionalist ass-cocks suck,* thought Ziggie. *They think people with less emotional ties to art of any kind will perform their jobs better. "Concentration on the corporation," they would say.*

The bastards traded culture for greenbacks; lust for order; variety for control. They diluted every hint of sentiment. They massacred the means of expression. They deviously conducted a full-force rape of memory, forbidding the discussion of recall, smothering joy, crippling curiosity. Now that they had sterilized the mind, they could go on expanding their business ventures until they overwhelmed the earth with greed and materialism; until they bled the soul of mankind dry and led us all into an empty shell of existence, so long as everything was put in place and packaged according to the industrialist's liking.

Those business moguls want everyone concentrating on production, not joy, not creativity, thought Ziggie. They want you to focus on squeezing out every drop, every morsel, every keystroke of energy for the sake of maximum production. Work your life away with utmost intensity and efficiency. A corporate prisoner, you are reduced to a number on a spreadsheet.

And when one of us numbers grows tired of eating and sleeping labor, wasting away for the benefit of the balance sheet, the corporate pricks can tuck him or her away in their cavernous vaults of retirement—the modern nursing home—and find a new soul to strip.

But they had gone way too far, and Ziggie knew it. The Great Cleanse had deprived us all of individuality. And the amendments and laws added since 2040 had virtually neutered us. One walked around as a skeleton of what one should be.

13

A FAT FISH

IF FLAKES ALIVE Incorporated's Todd Swindell had a feather in his cap for every hostile takeover he attempted, he would look like Chief Many Feathers with a full multi-colored headdress. He'd lost count of how many times he tried to side-step management of smaller flake companies that he had felt were undervalued. He would gobble up shares and embrace bad business etiquette in procuring control in order to combat behemoth Great American Flake Company.

Swindell even bribed a shareholder or two into allowing a FAI takeover and served a prison sentence of two years for doing so. He schemed and plotted against number-one ranked GAFC until his overworked paws turned scabby, but he never seemed to make a dent to the customer base of the flake-flying giant. On several occasions he sent scouts to glean secret infor-mation and succeeded at it, only to find that his efforts could not sway more than a handful of loyal customers to trade sides.

Rival CEO for GAFC, Chad Scandalman, had grown used to Todd Swindell's sinister tricks. Once, when Swindell tried to tempt Scandalman's right-hand man, Cliché Bob, into switching sides by offering a $10,000 signing bonus, Scan-dalman countered by giving Bob a $15,000 bonus for outstanding work and loyalty. Swindell then attempted to disseminate false information about Bob, by saying he had underworld connections and that he conducted himself like a scoundrel, but Scandalman scoffed at the sinister idea, and, instead, spread the word that Bob conducted himself like a model employee.

Both CEOs fell into a mudslinging war that resulted in idle cut-lows, bold accusations and even death threats. Swindell told Scandalman that he hoped he would "die in a frying pan like a fat fish." Swindell was tried and acquitted another time, though he spent a fortune on a pair of slimy lawyers to get him off. So, Swindell did everything he could to advance his second-place-in-the-flakes-ratings company into first place, and yet still came out second.

It was time for a retaliatory death.

VACATING HISTORY

WHEN, leading up to 2040, the final president of the United States, Ghant Wackersham, embarked on the scheme to downsize the government by stripping down the federal agencies, the people surmised that he might be doing so not only to render the agencies and departments more efficient but to make it easier for him to wrest total control of government affairs. By firing employees en masse, he would shrink the workforce enough to facilitate the seizure of complete authority. One chops the branches off a fallen tree to make the trunk more manageable, so that one can carry it away, burn it, store it for future firewood, or do whatever one wants to do with it.

Popular protests materialized. People carried signs that read: "Wackersham reduced the government workforce to simplify the takeover." Unfortunately, a certain apathy pervaded society during these years of power concentration. There was simply not enough resistance, and what resistance there was, was crushed by Wackersham and his billionaire buddies' deployment of the military against their own U. S. citizens. Once the uprising was thwarted, Wackersham appointed The Big Seven and handed over the power he had gained.

So, when the year 2040 arrived and The Great Cleanse commenced, government agents had to modify the dates on everything. All buildings had to be dated 2040 or later. All bridge plates older than 2040 had to be changed. All public documents had to be adjusted, even the Constitution of the United States, though that obsolete document became a mere museum piece. Books written before 2040, it was decided, had to be burned. All they could find of record albums, CDs, and DVDs copyrighted pre-2040 also met the flames.

And anyone who dared mention life before 2040 was severely admonished and fined. Persistent mention of such times could result in jail time and even elimination, if deemed bad enough by the courts, unless, of course, one was deemed legally insane, in which case, all of one's rights would disappear and the offender would be relegated to a concentration camp.

All headstones—can you imagine all the headstones in America?—in graveyards had to be re-engraved or destroyed. All old coins had to be gathered up and melted down. The work was endless, but the government's agents, all of them former CEOs, worked assiduously, meticulously, methodically, painstakingly to either redate items or demolish them.

Christianity was abolished. Democracy as we know it was abolished. Anything that had origin before 2040 went bye-bye. And government agents could not discuss any changes outside of addressing them for work purposes. Everyone was required by law to turn into the government any possession which bore a date prior to 2040.

Frumpish clothes quickly disappeared in the flames. So did all antiques. That included an old telephone—a wooden box with a bell near the top and a separate earpiece and mouthpiece. That also included a six-and-a-half ounce cola bottle and an old oil can with the name Permalube written across it. Many heirlooms and keepsakes succumbed to the merciless flames.

Collectors and antique clubs rebelled to no effect. Countless family photos vanished in the flames. Even a forty-eight-star American flag. Even a thirteen-star American flag! For history had no value in this modern society.

The government—that is, the seven CEOs who were in charge of the country—did not expect to change or destroy every molecule of oldness, but expected to change or wipe out all that it could. And explain away what it could not destroy. "It's a fake," "So-and-so is whacky," or "It's a fairytale" were the common explanations for anyone or anything that popped up with a pre-2040 history. Anyone already living in 2040 posed the most outlandish problem, just as anything or anybody who is today fifty-eight years old or older presents the most obvious problem. What was, simply wasn't. They were told not to talk about old times or things. Any old person who did refer to pre-2040 history was deemed "a lunatic." That seemed to be the easiest way to deal with those who insisted on reclaiming history. Just brush them off as "senile" or "crazy," instructed the men and women in power.

Eventually, all those born prior to 2040 would die off, and the need to purge the before-2040 crowd would diminish and then vanish altogether.

A very needy American public longed for dictatorial dominance, it was thought. People needed something to replace the religious figures they had once worshiped, to supplant the history they had once enjoyed. Corporate CEOs became the new Gods, the dictators of peasantry.

Too many wars and too much workforce competition for the mind to digest called for immediate stress reducers, such as Dream Eruption Formula XX and other medicines like it. Stress was a cause for panic, and panic was a reason for control. In order to exert control the government decided to implement a history vacuum. Anything before this time—2040—was mentally and verbally off limits. A most poignant remedy to motivate all idlers, all ponderers of history, was to obliterate everything that occurred before 2040. The country must reinvent itself. Joyous occasions must be minimalized. Sports had to go: too much athletic competition could cripple the corporation. All thought and spirit must be directed for the goodness of the corporation. The corporation must have the capacity to inhale all of which it was capable and exhale its mightiest breath without distraction or hindrance.

Corporation and government and religion became one. The CEOs became ruling Gods of commerce. Of course, the godliest CEO could exert influence on others, but they would all work as one united body for the betterment of American commerce.

Religion would be abolished the same as sports (except for golf). But the different religions would be allowed to set permanent rules before the religions expired. So, religion, before it ended, would have a major say in how the Corporate State was set up. Thus, you have no drinking or drug-taking on Sundays, no sex and no questions as to why not. The corporate bigwigs, it was rumored, had secret sex behind the curtains. But the masses were strictly forbidden to use or practice sex of any kind.

———

"Mom?"

"Yes, dear?"

"Why did they start the years at 2040?"

"Why, I don't know, son. They just saw fit to start time at 2040 and I—I don't think you should be asking about that. Accept things as they are, son."

Later, in private, Holly Henson said to Herb Sr., "You

know, Herb Jr. asks too many questions. I hope he doesn't turn out like your cousin, Ziggie Wexler."

"If he does," said Herb Sr., "we can always turn him over to a reform school or a Government Detention Camp."

GDCs made for notoriously crude reconditioning facilities. Their coordinating officers were callous, vindictive tyrants who treated the inmates with a thoroughly contemptuous deprecation.

Ever since the day little Herb was assigned to them, the Hensons recognized a rebellious dimension the other children happily lacked. If mom would try to turn baby Herb on his side while changing his diaper, he would attempt to turn on the opposite side. Later on, he would refuse to take the direction of elders. He would ignore commercials and watch those silly movie snippets. Anything to be different. And now he was asking questions about origin and even about something he had heard of called "sex."

The Hensons had tried in vain to correct him, to make him "normal" for the state. But he resisted.

He proudly assumed the role as black sheep of the family.

15

BOB'S RHYME

CAPTAIN DORIS MCELVY issued the order to capture Zigmund Wexler and bring him in for Reasoning Exercises. The poor lad had gotten on the wrong foot, mulled the sturdy captain, and must be reconditioned.

"We can revamp his mind," she asserted, "and reset his intuitions in a structured, dignified manner. Do not leave him to scratch through the dust of distant recollection. Reshape his mind and body. And if he still resists, well then, sound the alarms!"

"Captain McElvy," noted Corporal Ivan "Cheeseball" Downey, "surely all traces of good fortune have abandoned him by now. He is probably holed up in a vacant shack, eating roaches. Why don't we catch him, sand down his teeth and make him drink hot tea? And then make him eat ice cream."

"Your ideas are looney," noted McElvy. "But I don't care if maggots are wiggling out of his nose hole, JUST FIND HIM!"

Meanwhile, Todd Swindell, Chief Executive Officer of Flakes Alive Incorporated, placed a retaliatory hit on Great American Flakes Company CEO, Chad Scandalman. He sculpted a deal with Anika Patel, cousin of Twinkle Deshpande, to snuff out the corpulent headman. Anika's father owned a string of old Motel Sevens south of Chicago, and she was practically born with a mainframe computer in her lap. The balding old man sent her to learn newer technology, such as how to create graphical interfaces and such, at Prairieland College. So, her choice of professions seemed plentiful.

But Anika, after meeting Chelsea Gilbertson, a school-chum spy with connections to the underworld, chose to groom herself in the profession of hitwoman in the ripe arena of corporate espionage. And she was damn good at it. Swindell calmly swore Anika to eternal secrecy and the two hammered out a deal that would reward her generously to make the rotund GAFC CEO stop breathing. Only recently had Swindell inked a deal with two-timing Cliché Bob of rival GAFC to rescue what intelligence he had of the evasive No-Sog, Stay-Crisp formula. Bob then furnished Swindell with all his notes about the latest efforts to solve the riddle.

Bob had become a true traitor, a sell-out.

It seemed that Bob had grown tired of Scandalman's innuendos regarding Bob's habits and his faltering position as executive assistant on the GAFC corporate ladder.

"I've had it up to my ears," murmured the corporate renegade. "Scandalman can go take a leap.

Who gives a flying fuck! I mean he went from rags to riches, then got too big for his britches!"

Cliché Bob laughed uncontrollably at his own rhyming cliché, even though it was an accidental rhyme and not an intentional one. Again, he guffawed insidiously, while wiping down his golf clubs.

"I have a golf outing planned with Chad Scandalman," Cliché Bob told Mr. Swindell, "and I'm going to squeeze everything out of him that I can in terms of company secrets, like which direction the company is headed, what moves they might be planning, and how soon they expect to procure the No-Sog recipe and so on. Scandalman trusts me. I'll get the lowdown."

16

BENEATH THE HOTEL BED

DETECTIVE HUNG CHO Lee received a tip that GAFC CEO Chad Scandalman had checked into the Royal Hotel in downtown Chicago while on a business trip. Hung bribed the hotel clerk into giving him a duplicate key card to Scandalman's room. He showed his badge and explained how he was building a case against the murderous CEO and paid the clerk seventy-five dollars for the extra card. Soon, Mr. Lee was rifling through Scandalman's luggage looking for incriminating evidence.

The big CEO had a copy of Syd Waverly's No-Sog formula-in-progress in his coat pocket, and when Hung discovered it, he wrote the unfinished formula in his notepad. He also suspected that the writing was that of Syd Waverly and would send the sample to a writing expert. Just then the door clicked and Hung instantly rolled under the bed. Scandalman entered, patting his big gut as he did so. Once he closed the door, he let out a roaring belch, as he removed his suit and placed it on a hanger. Then he took out a photo and began to play with himself on the bed. He had set the photo on the nightstand next to the King size bed. It was a fully clothed woman, a "business" companion with whom Scandalman often had lunch.

Lee used a tiny pocket mirror from beneath the bed to see

that the large CEO had stripped down to his underwear and was fondling himself. Detective Lee was not about to lie there on the floor underneath the bed until Scandalman could finish his business. So, he quickly rolled out of his hiding place and startled the occupant of the room.

"How the hell did you get in here?" demanded the stunned CEO, his purple-veined pole fully erect and his face dead red.

"I slid beneath the door!" said Lee sarcastically. The keen detective spied the photo and exclaimed, "Ah ha! I got you!!"

"What the fuck!" screeched the hefty CEO, thoroughly embarrassed and angered and covering up his genitals.

"You were getting ready to masturbate, weren't you?"

"You're out of your ever-lovin' gourd!" shouted the big man. "I'm calling hotel security!"

Lee grabbed Scandalman's hand and moved it away from the phone. "You know that's against the law," he said, brandishing his badge.

"What's against the law?"

"Pleasuring yourself, that's what. I should haul your big ass to jail right now." No matter how excited Lee became, he maintained a look of stoic nonchalance.

"Who the hell are you?" Scandalman demanded.

"Masturbating is against the law!" cried Lee, while again flashing his badge. "Detective Hung Cho Lee, Domino Police Department. You're in violation."

"Never mind that. Just what is it you want?"

Lee looked soberly at Scandalman. "I've got the formula you killed Syd Waverly over."

"You ugly creep. You got nothin'."

"Why don't you just admit it," said Lee. "We've got enough evidence to send you away for a long time, you know."

"If you had your imaginary evidence," said Scandalman, "I'd be in handcuffs right now!"

"And I know that Cliché Bob was in on it too," warned Lee.

"You're bluffing," shot back Scandalman, grabbing his pants from the foot of the bed.

"Well," said Lee, "I do have a little info that will make your toes curl."

"What?" blurted the frustrated CEO. "I demand to know!"

"Well, I went to interview Todd Swindell, Flakes Alive Incorporated CEO, and you'll never guess who I saw at his office." Lee wore a slight smirk, the first emotion he displayed.

"Who?"

Lee adjusted his fedora. "First, you've got to tell me who Twinkle Deshpande is."

"I don't know her," lied Mr. Scandalman.

"Take another shot, big man, if you want to know who I saw."

"Alright. Alright. Twinkle is just some girl I hired to run a couple of errands. That's all I know."

"Wrong again asshole!" shouted Lee. "I have reason to believe that Twinkle has ties to the underworld."

"No. No way"

"You sure about that?" Lee annoyingly began playing with a yo-yo he took from his hip pocket.

Mr. Scandalman had managed to slip on his underwear. He wiped a bead of perspiration from his forehead. "Well," he said, "if she has ties to some secret mafia, I certainly didn't know about it."

"Maybe Cliché Bob knows," suggested the wary detective, yo-yo spinning madly up and down.

"Bob is my righthand man," revealed Scandalman. "He knows nothing except my business plans, and about that he is sworn to secrecy. Now who did you see?"

"I just told you."

"Bob?" asked the perplexed CEO. "Why that low-life traitor. That two-timing bamboozler. You sure it was Bob? *My Bob?*"

"Sure as the gorilla shits in the jungle. Bob, of the worn-out phrases."

"I'll fix that sonofabitch!" swore Scandalman, turning red again.

"Like you did Waverly?"

"You can leave now. I have business to conduct."

"I'll be seein' you around." Lee casually let himself out, tipping his hat before he closed the door.

Scandalman thought, *If Bob shares that unfinished formula, he's a dead man. What am I talking about? He's a dead man anyway. He knows too much. He likely plans to get the formula from the first organization who solves the problem, and then sell it to the other corporation.*

And if Hung Cho Lee found out Bob had the formula, and that Bob knows everything about the Syd Waverly assassination, that could incriminate me, since he would offer Bob a sweet deal to turn on me. Bob's gotta go. He's a dead man, goddamnit.

A nervous Mr. Scandalman soon checked under the bed for any other intruders, then masturbated uncontrollably. Finally, he laid there for an hour before he could get to sleep.

17

THE GREAT FALSE NOTION

HERB AND HOLLY HENSON, cruising through the Southtown section of Domino, Indiana on a bright, sunny day, spied a very old man at a bus shelter. But the bus had already gone by. Holly knew it because she often took the same bus to shop at the Domino Mall.

Herb pulled up beside the bus shelter and asked, "Do you need a ride?"

"I'm waitin' for the bus," answered the old man.

"It already came," shouted Herb. "You missed it."

"I'll take a ride then." The old man raised himself with the help of a cane, then wobbled toward the car. "Are you goin' by the fruit market?"

"Sure. Jump right in!"

The old man wore a long gray beard, bushy gray eyebrows, and an old gray jacket. Everything about him was gray. "I'm Gus Jackson," said the crippled old man. "Who're you?"

"Herb and Holly Henson," answered Holly. "How're you doin'?"

"I'm just dandy," responded their new acquaintance. "You know, I haven't met friendly folks like you since I was a kid back in 2018."

"2018? There's no such thing," assured Herb. Herb and Holly glanced at each other.

"Oh, there's such a thing, 'cause I was there."

"That's impossible," said a naïve Holly. "The earth wasn't here before 2040."

"Why, I came out of the Domino orphanage in 2028."

"You know," warned Holly, "you can be penalized for discussing anything before 2040."

"Oh, it's alright," said Gus. "I'm too damn old for punishment. I mean what are they gonna do to me? Flog me? Why, I remember the Chicago Cubs finally won a World Series back in 2016, and our orphanage had pizza night for us Cub fans."

"The *who* won *what*?" squawked Herb. "You see, there is no 2016. The earth didn't exist before 2040."

"You only say that," reasoned Gus, "'cause you were born after 2040 . . . and the government has hammered into your heads the fallacy that before 2040, nothing existed."

"Hmmm," uttered Herb.

"You can drop me off right here. Norman's Fruit Stand. That's where I get all of my fruits and vegetables."

"OK, Gus. Here you go."

"Thank you for the ride. Bye now."

"Bye," said Holly.

Gus got out of the car, but, before he closed the door, he proclaimed, "You know, you at least have to question your government. I know it is uncomfortable to think about it, but things did not suddenly appear—POOF!—in 2040 like the government wants you to believe." With that, Gus shut the door and waved, as he turned toward the fruit market.

"Poor old senile man," said Herb.

"He was almost cute," said Holly, "with his nonsensical stories and all."

Did Gus plant a notion in the middle-aged couple's minds? It was too bizarre to even ponder.

Certainly, Herb, being a schoolteacher, could not risk that kind of thinking. He would be thrust from his job without warning should he reveal an inkling of consideration for such mystery, so he conveniently smothered the conscious idea. And Holly was just too thoroughly delusional to even entertain the idea at all.

Once the last generation of those who recalled pre-2040 events died, the controls on speaking of those heady times would be relaxed. Someday, little need would exist for mind-cleansing exercises and history-erasing efforts by the government.

18

UPWARD VELOCITY

SPEED LIMITS of 100 miles per hour lent the highways a recklessness unprecedented. In Domino, Indiana alone, the highways swallowed about three-and-a-half lives per day on average. The interstates had "Wreck Lanes" reserved, allowing accidents to be shoved over by bulldozers and plows until police and ambulances could get to them, sometimes hours after the event. The gung-ho capitalists needed that elevated speed limit to pursue quick business. "Time is money" went Bob's old cliché.

In fact, the new Interstate 63 expressway that replaced US Route 41, running down the west border of Indiana, became known as "Death Trap Way."

Some corporate-government watchdog groups banded together to fight the 100 mph speed limit with the mantra, "Speed is Greed!" but these types of resistance organizations had been emasculated long ago when The Plan for 2040 went into effect some fifty-eight years before. People just laughed at them, and the speed limit rose and rose, 80 mph in 2060, 90 mph in 2085, and 100 mph by 2095.

Bolting maniacs zig-zagged about and created a menace for other drivers. Scattered across the eight-lane highway from

Chicago to Domino, the skeletons of various wrecks and stolen, gutted automobiles flanked the highway and scabbed the countryside.

Business did enjoy a formidable upsweep.

Another rule change that boosted business involved the federal weight limit and length on semitrucks. The former limit of 80,000 pounds at 80 mph for a truck and trailer proved too sluggish for modern business purposes. The amount of weight allowed was first raised to 100,000 pounds, then raised again to 120,000 pounds. The length allowed for a truck has been stretched out to 82 feet.

These behemoth carriers of American cargo were now so deadly that automobilists were asked to stay away from them. That, of course, was impossible on a busy stretch of highway, but the idea persuaded other drivers to give the trucks the two inner lanes on each side of highways of eight lanes or more (four each way). These rolling mammoths had killed as many as twenty people in one two-vehicle collision.

Got to keep those big wheels a-turning, those supermarket doors a-revolving, those home-center aisles a-swelling, and those big-box stores a-booming. Stacking those landfills one by one.

Every five minutes a tech gadget went obsolete and became another donation to the junkyard, a new one taking its place and howling down the highway in the back of a big, overloaded semitrailer, a virtual mausoleum on wheels.

19

MOUNTAIN OF THE CROSS

CONSUMERS WERE NOW INUNDATED with shopping opportunities. The religious holidays had been replaced with store holidays. What was formerly Easter was now Store Holiday #1 (not very creative, huh?). What was formerly Christmas was now Store Holiday #2. The day after Thanksgiving was still Black Friday and the following Monday was still Cyber Monday.

Magic Marketplace Holidays were special occasions that landed on June 30 and August 31. There was even a Shopping Bonanza Holiday on April 30. Discounts on these holidays peppered the consumer with bargain opportunities.

Even though religion of all forms was banned, rumor had it that CEOs could still sneakily worship the antiquated Christian God and the Son of God behind the scenes and get away with it. In other words, according to rumor, the everyday workforce—formerly the blue-collar workforce, but now the blue-and-white-collar workforce, since some menial retail positions make one dress formally—that is, the peons, proles, or just the little guys—were not allowed to practice religion of any sort in the United States. Not since 2040.

Santa Claus and the Easter Bunny, both nonreligious

figures of folklore, were still allowed until 2043, when it became obvious that these legendary figures yet provoked some into secretly practicing religion. After year 2043 then, old Santa and the Bunny became forbidden figures of folklore. That meant that tiny Santa Claus, Indiana, another place on storied US Route 41, only well south of Domino, had to take down their famous fiberglass Santa statue and change the name of the town to Holiday, Indiana.

But that was okay since other towns and cities had to take down their religious statues and objects. For instance, Effingham, Illinois, said to be the most conservative city in the Prairie State, had to dismantle its giant cross in the year, 2041, after several battles in the rigged courts were lost and all appeals exhausted.

But Effingham was only the start. All crosses, big and small, were prohibited. They had to be turned over to the corporate government by the end of the year 2042. But what would the government do with all of these crosses? They could not burn all the crosses for fear of a social uprising, at least among the fanatics, as that would amount to a most supreme sacrilege.

So they gathered the entire country's crosses and made—what else?—a big landfill out of them. Unlike Putrid Mountain, this place was holy, so the little people called it Holy Mountain, even though such terms were obsolete and violated federal law. So the corporate government renamed the place Mountain of the Cross. And those who still secretly believed in Armageddon no longer thought that such an end-times event would start in the Middle East, but, instead, believed it would start right here at Mountain of the Cross, which was two-and-a-half miles east of Domino, Indiana, and sixty-seven miles southeast of Putrid Mountain, an infamous landfill in South Chicago.

Preachers who were forced to retire with the termination of

all religion surreptitiously sanctified the Mountain of the Cross. There in the mountain were crosses of all sizes, including tiny crosses from necklaces, little hanging-Jesus doo-dads, crosses in picture frames, crosses from church lawns, and, yes, the giant cross from Effingham. Crosses and crucifixes from across the country rested at every angle.

Moonbeams and sunrays played delightful tricks with the silhouettes of the usually gleaming mass.

But in this strange era, generally, the CEO was God and the corporation was the vessel that held the CEO Gods together and delivered them to the people. Replacing monotheism with polytheism was anything but horseplay. It took many years to wrangle the sacred sheep and shift their minds from old-school religion—Christianity, Judaism, Islam, Hinduism, etc.—to modern CEO worshipping.

Hail to capitalism gone wild!

20

ODDS AND ENDS OF THE AUTHORITATIVE CAPITALIST STATE (CULLED FROM ZIGGIE'S NOTES)

THE CORPORATE GOOD Book says that time began in year 2040.

———

The major pastime in America is now shopping. The corporate orchestrators of such have made it an easy, seamless experience. Pick your groceries from an intelli-phone or choose a free ride to pick you up and take you to the supermarket in person, where the car will wait for you outside. Choose a time depending on how busy they are. In the case of ordering by phone or internet, shop the town with one login!

———

The three-minute rock song becomes an endangered species, much too long for the American listener on the go. Twenty seconds seems right and is ideally suited to commercials. The gotta-have-it-now crowd is good with it. One verse and one chorus; no bridge.

———

They finally did away with the Electoral College. In place of that moldy, antiquated system is a new corporate system. Each area or district elects a local CEO who appoints other CEOs to govern the district. The choices for district CEO are right-leaning liberal, moderate conservative, and ultra-conservative. Domino, Indiana gets one vote from the CEO of the Smooth Line Wire Company, which keeps its headquarters there. But Chicago, due to its enormous size, has twenty-three CEO voters. These CEOs then appoint the governing CEOs. Plus, one of The Big Seven ruling CEOs hails from Chi-town.

But they can only attend to minor issues. All of the real decision making is done by The Big Seven, who, as of 2092, are now in place for life.

———

Declining corporations were rescued from the Death Stage by direction of the seven CEOs comprising the government. Once the corporation is deemed unsalvageable, it is dissolved and immediately reincorporated with a new staff. Fired workers will receive unemployment compensation. The new staff is hand-picked by a Committee of Revival, which answers to The Big Seven.

The Revival Committee then sets prices and conducts company business until the new appointed CEO is in place. If the company died because their product had become obsolete, special committees are formed to develop a new product or two. If the company died due to mismanagement, the new staff will correct the old staff's mistakes. This way, the entity's logo never truly dies and all those tattoos people wear remain relevant.

————

In the palmy days of cemeteries one could scan a tombstone bar code, which would give a list of attributes of the person there lying. But they were forced to abolish cemeteries by the whims of corporations, these bold entities saying that "graveyards are a waste of real estate." The corporation needed more space to expand, thus wishing the cemeteries go bye-bye.

"If you want to tend to a rotting corpse," they would say, "do it on your own land. Enough of this human silliness!" So, it was for the corporation to "expand, expand! No stopping us now!"

Corpses were in the process of being reburied or cremated on command. Of course, high-ranking or important figures were transferred to new cemeteries out in the country, but all of the little guys' graves, headstones and all, were destroyed by an incinerator.

————

Central Africa and the Amazon Jungle: both found themselves caving to capitalism. The fancy suits are mowing down trees as if they were blades of grass. There are groups that protest this mindless decimation of nature, but long ago the corporate lobbyists vanquished these pests and had them removed to isolated protest zones, such as underground vaults and remote desert lands. The latter setup was sometimes labelled "calling to the cacti" by critics against the corporations. The former setup was called "objection in a void."

"There are only two choices for our corporate leaders," said noted business champion and provocateur, Alex Stahl: "Accede or impede. And we choose the latter." That meant capitalists would block or repel any protests. "We need complete harmony in our job-creating expansions."

Elizabeth Simmons, consumer advocate, refused to buy in to such destruction of nature. "If by 'complete harmony' he means for all consumers, indeed, all citizens, to rollover and take it up the ass," she said, "he can go eat shit." For that little stunt she earned two swats in public and ten days in the slammer. So much for backing the consumer.

———

A new drug hit the streets during the march to a new millennium. It was known as Cinnamon, a brown, pungent powder. Cinnamon's origin was traced to a basement chemist by the name of Viktor Petrov, a Russian transplant and suspected underworld figure of lower ranking. He had studied chemistry before he dropped out of college and invented Cinnamon as a nasty cousin of methamphetamine. This strange concoction had not yet been accepted and legalized by The Drug Lab. Its ingredients were too objectionable.

When one peaks on Cinnamon, one is said to be "totally spiced." When one comes down from the high, he or she is said to be "spiced out." Viktor eventually got promoted to the middle-level of the underworld organization for his nifty money-making invention.

———

Each morning at school the children are required to say the Pledge of Allegiance to Corporations.

———

In the beginning, to maintain the level of maximum corporate profit, the population needed tweaking. That meant that two out of five male children must be castrated at birth. Later, when the Baby Factory and Spittoon Alley came along, the population could be strictly regulated as to baby production.

———

Spicey, greasy fast-food depots were placed at every corner "to keep the dogs happy," as one government official put it.

———

Fast-paced work took on a whole new meaning in modern society. Sylvester Lakewood keeps so busy that he defecates while eating. He simply does not have time for the two situations to transpire consecutively.

———

Since they outlawed negative product reviews, customer reviews, and criticism of the corporate government of any sort, the little guy had little to say.

———

Posted on the federal government website: "You have little chance in reaching a member of The Big Seven for assistance if you were not in multiple television commercials."

———

To accumulate assets is Godly (like a CEO); may you have bountiful dollars in your lives. To inherit money is human; to expand wealth is Godly.

———

Asset Purge: to have one's property confiscated for financial crimes.

———

Labor unions died a sudden, lonesome death. Wildcat capitalists had dissuaded these worker organizations from forming, then took their argument to The Big Seven, which ordered all unions to disband immediately back in late 2040.

———

Just who appointed The Big Seven? Newcomers to earth's dystopian hell wanted to know. The last president of the United States, Ghant Wackersham, the omnipotent ultra-conservative, appointed them before political parties were outlawed and The Great Cleanse had commenced. From then on members of The Big Seven appointed themselves along with three backups every four years. That way, if a lifetime member dies, a reasonably newly-appointed backup will take his or her place.

———

Unembellished, utilitarian edifices cropped up on every street. Eight corners, four walls, a flat roof, no flair, no outside adornments. The days of colonial, federal, Italianate, and Greek

Revival architecture had passed in favor of simplicity and practicality. No cornices, no columns, no fanlights, no cupolas. Just nondescript, rectangular boxes. And lazy architects.

"Plain and ugly," described Ziggie. "Built strictly for profitability."

COMMERCIAL OVERAGE

IT WAS NOT ONLY that the government became more authoritarian and the advertising industry grew more invasive, but the population proved more receptive to the kind of stupidity that made authoritative capitalism so operable.

The mentality of the average Jane or John shrank to imbecilic levels. The cellphone, especially the intelli-phone implant, in spite of all the information it made available, had somehow made the people dumb, probably because people sought out silly subject matter due to their limited freedoms, restricted pastimes, and overexposure to television and radio commercials.

The country wanted—begged—for more insipid rubbish in people's lives. It was a flavorless epidemic of hogwash the people desired and they got it from the advertising industry. Sure, the commercials got more sly, more sophisticated in their hooks, but soon whacky-commercial overkill drained the excitement from the constant madness. It was like writing with an exclamation point at the end of every sentence: the impact was lost, the message almost meaningless, at least to those with any gumption.

"They have sucked all the guts out of freedom," Ziggie

would say. "All that is left is the American Shell. We are not supposed to disparage any corporation. But look here, they have stripped our minds naked with their bombardment of constant nonsense."

And with most of America's pastimes outlawed, the people worked themselves into a frenzy of bad behavior. Assaults, batteries, and murders have soared to unprecedented levels, since people have nothing to do. "Brute" music materialized in the lowlife nightspots. They cannot play baseball or football or basketball. They cannot enjoy historical music pieces. They cannot enjoy sex. Life was boring and people killed over a cigarette (before they were outlawed), a bottle of pop, a french fry.

Smiling vacuously, corporate think-tank members should have foreseen the utter pandemonium ahead. But they blindly insisted on stripping down liberties, hobbies, and pastimes until everyone hated each other. Everyone simply had too much of each other. The corporate leaders even sabotaged their once-precious free-market trade by adding to the lives of consumers too many restrictions, amendments, and stipulations on every last deal the peons could make. Regulations on consumers skyrocketed, while regulations against corporations vanished.

"Our minds are overloaded with American shit," Ziggie reasoned to anybody who would listen. "Cars with loud-speakers driving up and down the blocks with intrusively high-volume commercials blaring out sales pitches and promotions just so the driver could earn fifty cents an hour extra money. Everywhere you turn an advertisement jumps out and ambushes you. Where can one get relief? I'm tired of tippy-toeing over the remnants of democracy, while the corporate magnates torpedo us with commercialized crap!"

THE MACHINE AND I

WHEN CORPORATE GOVERNMENT dignitaries inaugurated the policy that nixed football, baseball, basketball, soccer, and hockey, the pain grew almost palpable, but as time wore on sports fanatics tucked their chins into their chests and ventured forth in a world without fun. Those who remembered athletic events began to die off, and the job of keeping the masses down became easier. By the late twenty-first century, such vacuous engagements were nearly forgotten and the populous seemed to roam the earth in comas.

Such specimens were known as "humanotons" (emphasis on the second syllable) to the wise. A humanoton was a cross between human and automaton. It seems that humans became so connected to the machinery of their livelihoods that they became machine-like themselves, that is to say, an extension of the machinery. (The Humanoton Disorder was the second of the capitalist diseases, Capitalist Crazy being the first). They just methodically marched about, dutifully performing one chore after another, beady-eyed and soulless, and un-needing of entertainment, just the way the industrialists preferred them. Golf—the bigwig favorite—being the only choice for leisure, it was priced prohibitively to the nonexecutive types. But one could watch it on television, somewhere between the commercials.

Humanoton #1: "Did-you-see-the-golf-tourn-a-ment-to-day?"

Humonoton #2: "Yes-was-not-it-thrill-ing?"

Humonoton #3: "Oh-boy."

———

In the great business center of the Midwest, Chicago, teams of humanotons waited on the walkways for stoplights to change to "WALK." Elsewhere, the robot-like beings seemed so self-involved, but only to the end that they steer all their energy, once isolated, to the corporation and its needs, for the corporation could only be as good as its slowest office-tending enabler.

Therefore, the corporation stood at the top of the food chain, with no predators, save for the hapless few do-gooders who tried feebly to restrain it. These watchdog regulatory persons had been downgraded long ago from legitimate threats to "pesky little creeps." The corporate boosters had succeeded in defanging the corporate policing agencies and dismantling the regulatory machine altogether.

23

THE BRUTE BASH

YOUNG PEOPLE INVENTED brute music to vent their angst in an extreme-stress society. Pretty soon brute music was banned by bar owners on account that too many damaged parties, or, in the case of death, too many families of the deceased, were suing the bar owners. At first, the chaotic tones, the screaming vocals, the relentless bashing of drums drove the practitioners to choose someone and gang up on him or her on the dance floor for a sound beating. Then, at a later date, the screeching vocalist actually began to encourage severe beatings. One lyric went like this:

Gotta have that brutal sound
Gonna make me come unwound
Gotta have that brutal beat
Gonna beat them to defeat
Go on, get him
Go on, get him
Pound him, kick him
Slam him all day
Crush him, thrash him
He wants it that way

Once the bars banned this kind of brutality, the kids started gathering in parks, old warehouses, and anywhere they could charge money to conduct these savage sound sessions and random beatings. It was called the "Brute Bash." Most of the youths experienced the utmost stress in searching for jobs, competing for positions, elbowing each other in interview lines, and knew not how to control their emotions. The world was a tightly wound knot just waiting to unwind in a flurry of violence.

Name-calling became a key component of the barbarity. Brutal epithets regarding race, color, handicap, sex—anything the vicious crowd could attach to the beating—came into vogue. Soon, spitting and urinating on the victim grew popular. The ritual transpired like a biker-gang initiation.

But to fall victim to such savagery became an honor, a badge of courage, a bragging point; like a proud boxer in defeat, it carried a certain dab of fortitude, a streak of mettle, even heroism.

Finally, the government classified brute beatings as a sport, and, as you may know, all sports, with the exception of golf, were illegal. There went the pastime of brute bashing. While it lasted, the dreaded sport made slam-dancing seem like puppy play.

ZIGGIE'S FIRST LETTER TO THE CLANDESTINE JOURNAL

May 10, 2098

HOW ADVERTISING HAS POLLUTED the American brain we must all realize before we can ever hope to work on the problem. Attention has been divided and conquered by the TV commercial, what the discerning public considers a veritable waste product. The mind has been numbed by the cute little ad ditties. Television, radio, newspaper and magazine ads have scalped and befuddled the consumer and re-wired the cerebral circuits. We laugh at the lame, cry over nonsense.

To wean the mind off of junk we must quit commercials. We do this by curbing our TV and radio appetites and by ignoring newspaper and magazine ads. More importantly, cutting down on internet usage is key to freeing our minds of garbage. Severe censorship of cyberspace has hidden the real world from us. Giving over web traffic to intrusive advertising has meddled with truth and reality. Instead of perusing the internet pages, read a book, write a journal, make some art.

—ZW

THE BIG SLUMP: A FREE-MARKET FURROW

THE INDUSTRIALISTS HAD A SECOND COMING.

Following a recession back in the early days after the creation of earth and man in 2040, the economy had boomed. The isolated American crowd had given new life to industry, as America now had to produce its own everything from paper clips to gigantic ships.

The downside to this new way of manufacturing is seen in America's filth—rivers so mucky a brick will float in them; putrid air so thick with smog that one could scarcely see a stoplight through the haze; and greasy earth so saturated with oily grime one could hardly grow a weed in it, much less a scented flower. House plants slumped over and wilted, gardens drooped, and wild animals disappeared.

But the coffers of the supervisor class and their plutocrat friends overflowed with freshly printed $1,000 bills.

Pharmaceutical companies brimmed with legal drug money and teamed up with organized drug dens where anyone could try any substance while under the care of lab personnel. The world was running out of trees, so someone invented synthetic paper. The earth was running out of clay, so someone invented synthetic bricks. No one, as of yet, had invented synthetic water, air or earth.

Fragments of life before 2040 had been buried. The government insisted that life on earth began in 2040. The modern economy had outpaced the production of pollution-fighting methods of the old Environmental Protection Agency, now known as the Environmental Corporate Balancing Agency (ECBA). Riches and poisons had no limit. The money flow was too good to turn back. Stars—the ones that could still be seen through the wicked smog—turned to dollar signs. And everyone in the higher classes rejoiced at the height of newfound wealth. Those who had a 401(k) and could still breathe, that is.

With the heart of the big machine thumping furiously, no company knew when to take a break. The growth was irrepressible. The Federal Reserve, now a feeble body of small-time bankers, did not want to exert much pressure to slow the out-of-control growth on account that they did not want to piss off The Big Seven nor appear to the public as the bad guys, so supply began to stack up, far outstretching demand, and, with warehouses replete with overstocked shelves, and the moment of collapse seeming imminent, the people held their collective breath. The hungry capitalists just could not bring themselves to place any economic controls on the runaway economy and thus wallowed in the revenues of the apparently endless good times, seemingly oblivious to the inevitable downturn.

When the boom times of the 2050s and 2060s were over, Mother Earth descended into a drain-bound spiral. Space for storage ran out, and the swoon commenced with a mighty string of thuds, the economic train locking its wheels in despair. Factories died suddenly in the industrial bloodbath. The homeless population skyrocketed (and never came back down to former levels). Housing sales plummeted. Housing prices moved down. Banks held houses that were worth hardly anything.

But when the nature of the survival-of-the-fittest economy had capitalists on their knees, someone noticed that one could breathe again, that one could see fishes in the rivers again, and one could enjoy the resurgence of the ground critters.

With the blossoming of the indigent population, the critics of capitalism sprang out in numbers.

"Beware of the science of capitalism," one wrote, "the subsidiary, merger, stock split, law of diminishing returns, economies of scale, supply and demand curves, revenue sharing —a science fabricated around greedy profit mongering."

It was then that the government doubled down on the already outlawed criticism of the economic system or the government itself.

Buildings and machinery, including computers, went idle. The humans who operated the buildings and machinery, sat stiff-necked at the computer like robots, had nothing to do and thus became regulars at the organized drug dens and parlors. They were told that a depression was on, and so they ate, drank and breathed various drugs until they were broke.

After that they stood around the airports, train and bus stations, picking their noses and butts until the economy showed some semblance of a spark of life. But the economy stubbornly refused to reignite for some time, so the women and men started to eat stray animals and use up the surplus as fast as it could, to try and kickstart the big but sick machine. So, the machine might as well pick its butt like the humans did.

Ziggie's friend, Alison Renwick, lost her job due to weak production. She was laid off with no severance pay. She had three months to go to be vested in her 401(k), so she lost the employer match. She soon lost her house to slick bankers, just like farmers did back in the Dust Bowl era, which, incidentally, was illegal to mention, since it occurred before the earth had people (2040). Her unemployment compensation ran out.

All she had left was her tattoo stipends and three hungry children. They moved into her parents' home, where she took online classes to learn some new skills. But when her parents died in a horrible, tragic car accident, Alison and her three children ended up in a Crate Camp.

Meanwhile, government flakes began to circulate (just as government cheese once circulated in the chain of recessions in the 1970s—oh, but we are not supposed to mention anything before 2040— sorry!). So, the flake industry slowed, as everything else, but the government purchase of flakes kept the flake makers above water. Now the competition between flake makers grew dirtier than ever, leaving a trail of laid-off flake workers dead or dying in the dingy corridors of the cities around Domino, Indiana and other mill towns.

Assassins flourished, flake workers perished, and the whole rotten system just laid there with empty guard shacks and idle automation devices, and minimal work.

Gradually, with spurts of government assistance and injections of incentives for factories, bored women and men took their places at their old machines. Slowly, computers lit up. A factory whistle here and there played its sweet song. But these boom-and-bust cycles of capitalism make for economic instability. And unequal distribution of wealth posed another great problem. An inordinate number of people skimped or did without, while others lived off their accrued wealth and really did not suffer at all.

Economic instability also occurred as a result of companies playing hopscotch over wages and prices of goods. Originally, Mexico paid lower wages, so many corporations stripped down their facilities and moved there. The workers in Mexico eventually realized their worth and schemed to demand higher wages.

Since America now paid lower compensation, everything was torn down so the corporations could move back to the US, leaving ruins in their wake.

Back and forth it went over the years until it became a great industrial game of musical chairs.

The environments around all companies involved and the low-level worker always got screwed.

Before the system had gotten too clogged up, life was tough but still grand. Now it seemed that misery ruled the day. Finally, a spurt of energy lifted the factories from their doldrums. True, human spirit was lagging, but businesses began to hum steadily again like the cars on a distant freeway. And just when one thought the system was inching back to normalcy, prosperity, another recession restored the air of malaise, the plants laying off masses of associates.

Capitalism entails these troughs, just as it entails the summits. It constantly tries to adjust to growing pains, leaving the worker with old skills to learn new skills while wallowing in temporary poverty. As the factories ground to a veritable halt, no one guessed that this would be only the second in a string of four wicked recessions within fifteen years. Only one thing could deliver the economy from perpetual downturns, from its descent into hell: war.

26

THE MAD MESSENGER

ONE SUN-SOAKED day in the year 2070, a naked man ran down the center of Main Street in the town of Domino with a book raised high over his head, yelling, "I found it! I found it! A 1965 copy of the Oxford English Dictionary! That means we were here before 2040!!!"

Now the suit-and-tie capitalists and the factory engineers and supervisors—the ones who would survive with "Patriot" food samples in their underground bunkers should Armageddon approach—immediately pointed to this poor, besotted creature as a lunatic of the first class.

"Pay him no mind!" they desperately yelled, but the recession-weary population needed some morsel of shocking truth and were too suspicious of the capitalists to let it go.

The cry went up that, "We could start all over again with a new government, a new system!" Why, it would be like a capitalist Phoenix rising out of the gray and white ashes, and moving up, up, up out of the new blazing flames. Then somebody found a copy of *Huckleberry Finn*, and America entertained the possibility of being officially reborn.

Well, at least until the government shut down the entire operation, the new mood of revival. They called in the

National Guard to hush the masses and soon the hoopla died down.

Ziggie Wexler read about it in the *Underground Gazette* and the *Clandestine Journal*, and silently cheered on the rebellious voices, but when the government stepped in, his merry outlook soon nosedived with the rest of the movement. Ziggie thought, *The spirit for a renaissance in liberty and free speech yet exists. You cannot completely bury it as the capitalists have tried to do. It is still there. May we at least imbibe in hope.*

A kernel of suspicion was always there, Ziggie thought, *but now a glimmer of resistance exists.*

Should the population decide to remove its eyes from the television commercials, and examine its own condition, a spurt of action may they take.

The discoverer of the Huckleberry Finn book, by the way, had enough time to read it and bury it in his backyard before the National Guard came in, ransacking all of the houses, ripping apart people's belongings, and otherwise wreaking terror throughout the bottom ranks of society.

IT BEGAN in the mid-2070s with American corporations battling each other over land.

Some of it reclaimed cemeteries. A kind of turf war. Then, there was the stealing of each other's workers. One avaricious corporation enticing the worker of another to "jump ship," as Cliché Bob would put it. This infuriated the HR departments of many companies. Understaffed corporations engaged in recruiting wars. Then they started drafting their employees into little armies that would challenge one another. A few skirmishes broke out and several employees were killed in the ensuing violence.

The heads of companies knew they had to draw the corporations into line, reunite the workforces into a harmonious collaboration for the good of all US companies. So, American companies initiated a gluttonous tariff conflict, in effect, placing exorbitant taxes on foreign goods until they forced a reaction. These international tariff battles morphed into an all-out global war between countries. Corporations were given the power to draft employees into service. A world war had commenced.

During World War One, the Flake Wars slithered into the back seat so the flesh wars could take over. Thankfully, at some point before the horrendous war it was decided by the capitalists that only "normal" weapons would be used to preserve enough humanity to carry on the great capitalist experiment. World industrialists prohibited nukes to safeguard the global markets, the isolated American markets, and the science of profit taking.

Carpet bombing represented old-school war play; drone assassinations represented new-school war play. All those guys and gals who had practiced bombing and annihilating cities, continents and even galaxies in their silly computer war games for all those years could now put their acquired skills to real-life usage. Unfortunately, the vast majority of them cowered and fled to other countries to avoid the draft.

During the great conflict, war-machine-making companies proliferated; after the war, rebuilding companies thrived ubiquitously. Profits for these renovation firms rose to graph positions previously unrealized. Only the biggest flake enterprises survived the war: GAFC, FAI, and Isabella Blake's BFC. Flake rationing had compelled them to evolve into slim and trim profit fountains. And necessarily so, for the almost endless battles downsized the population and thus the customer base.

Now, the flake companies, not knowing which direction to turn with regard to advertising, finally came up with GI Combat Flake Figures—the same as the old Fun Flake Figures, they had faces and wiry limbs, but now updated with helmets and bazookas. And new generations of children embraced the mighty empire and the "necessity" for war. And the capitalist machinery was refurbished and updated for warring purposes, so it could start humming again. And it did.

War museums and War Affinity Clubs bubbled up to the surface of popularity and a new era dawned upon the nation. Bloc I of the great war masters had the USA, Europe, India, Israel, and Japan. Bloc II had Russia, China, Iran, North Korea and Cuba. Bloc III had Mexico, Chile, Venezuela, Peru, Colombia, Brazil, Portugal and Spain.

Vast destruction, of course, took place—the more, the better for those companies whose goals were reconstruction-minded, which were generally branches of the same companies who were tearing everything down with intense bombing campaigns. For instance, the builders of tanks would turn to making railroad cars when the fighting stopped. And stop it did, once the population was down to a manageable level. The guns got quiet and the buildings and machinery went back to making consumer supplies instead of war supplies.

No longer was it just wreath, ribbon, and flag makers (and a very few gravestone inscribers for fallen captains and generals) in maximum production, but now, with the end of the war at hand, the rest of the workforce could join in. A strong and lively business would resume at microwave-oven factories and at car makers and flake companies too. But the depression-and-war-time poverty level of 30 percent remained, after it was discovered that companies would not call back a third of the workforce. So a great number of citizens never did recover from the prewar recession.

Now the people had a whole new group of warriors to mourn and celebrate, patriotism refueled, and so the nasty war served as a means of boosting morale, sisterhood, and brotherhood. Parades and new war holidays followed until the next time 2,500,000 people needed to die (in America alone) and they could do it all over again.

Mankind moves in mysterious ways.

28

AFTERMATH

WORLD WAR ONE was the first war where foreigners partly fought on American soil. One hundred eighty years before the beginning of time (2040) the Civil War was fought on American soil, but no one is supposed to discuss that, and, besides, no foreign countries were involved.

During the current war, in New York City, the Statue of Liberty was blown into many fragments.

The corporate government did not worry much about that, since liberty was not so much celebrated anymore. Bloc II had blown up the Empire State Building too. And in Chicago, the McCormick Place and the old Sears building had been destroyed. In Indianapolis a couple of skirmishes damaged several skyscrapers, though they were mostly protected by the National Guard.

The West Coast was fairly protected by both Japanese and American forces, though Russia did succeed in setting off explosions beneath the Golden Gate Bridge, thus significantly damaging the infrastructure. Hundreds of small towns were decimated by drones from China carrying highly condensed explosives. These towns were mainly on the East Coast and some in the Midwest.

Just under 2,500,000 Americans died, 800,000 on American soil. A total of 1.7 million Americans lost their lives in the European and Asian theatres. This ugly war lasted from 2074 to 2077. The closest town to Domino to incur damage was tiny Euclid, Indiana, about twenty miles southeast from the three major flake companies.

The funny thing about this war (if wars could be funny at all) was that nobody knew why they were fighting. Perhaps to be the highest face on the totem pole, that is, the top country for financial conglomerates. And nobody really won the war, though the various countries claimed victory. It just sort of petered out when everyone got tired of gathering up the dead and cremating torn up bodies.

Surely, it was a cold war, not cold as in noncombat, but cold as in lack of emotion. The dead just piled up and the families who lost loved ones seemed to worry more about the stock market losses than they did about flesh and blood losses.

Money, as the Seed of All Joy, portends a dank, dark century ahead. But that did not stop the street salespersons from hawking "Money: The Seed of All Joy" T-shirts in a vigorous manner. After all, 150-plus years of television had suffocated the American mind, stifled Americans' ability to reason, so money, and the products it buys, was about all that mattered to the average consumer.

The soldiers felt no pain when they came home. They didn't know how to feel pain. In fact, they didn't know how to feel at all. Their feelings had been used up. They were like freshly erased chalkboards. They did nothing, they knew nothing. But as memory gradually returned, anxiety followed.

The first thing they were retrained for was not how to deal with afterwar depression and anxiety but how to make money. And more money. After a week of retraining, they could not tell you their names or their history. But they could give you the ticker symbol for any stock you could name. And they could give you the current price of that stock, how much the stock is up or down on a given day, and how that stock is trending. They could also tell you the value of the Dow Jones Industrial Average, the S&P 500 index, and the NASDAQ Composite, anytime, anywhere.

Good soldiers were they.

Sometimes their intelli-phone implants would have to be replaced. First, they had to be *unplanted*, then exchanged for one in working order, then disposed of so the new phone could be planted. Ziggie, in later days, had heard the rumor that these *unplants* had taken place. He was greatly encouraged.

Some of the soldiers who came home blank-headed were referred to as stumps, on account of losing everything but the root of their minds. Those were the ones who needed a replant.

To prevent the usual cases of post-traumatic stress disorder (PTSD) in returning soldiers who saw combat, the intelli-phone unplant, replant, and accompanying reconditioning of the mind worked fine, if the relatives did not stress out at the idea of losing their loved one. That is because the entire personality changed with each case. You no longer knew the one undergoing the replant. It was a whole new personality in the same old war-scarred body minus a limb or two. Anyway, the person is lost, whether he or she has a replant or dies on the battlefield.

Nevertheless, the war had replaced the old recession-weary country with a brand-new version of itself. Once again, money flowed freely while machines buzzed and hummed their way into full production. The corporate government could now supplant the remaining tent cities with Crate Camps.

29

THINK GREEN

WITH A MISERABLE STRING of recessions and a fresh war that saw almost 2,500,000 Americans die behind them, the languid population simmered in a stew of dejection.

Corporations strived to ameliorate the sorrow. They tirelessly worked to reduce sadness over the loss of human life and the polluted planet. So far unsuccessful in reviving the spirit of the masses, corporations began to bring in motivational speakers. Tom Langston was one such speaker, and he plied his trade at the Great American Flakes Company headquarters in Domino, Indiana. Come, let us listen in at the tail end of Tom's pep talk.

Please imagine all of those good spirits floating around. They lost their lives for the preservation of America, and they now roam around a far better world in spiritual form. They live forever, as the deceased corporate CEO Gods watch over them in another dimension. They transition from corporate bound to heaven bound.

And if contamination of the earth saddens you, just remember that for the advancement of civilization, certain aspects of life must be allowed to decay without worry.

Close your eyes and pretend, if you will, there sits a gargan-

tuan incinerator where we can shovel the contents of all of America's dump sites and landfills and burn them to ashes. Theoretically, these ashes then can be spread over the land to generate and renew forestation. Doesn't your mind feel cleansed?

Now envision that all of those ashes are indeed used to fertilize the foliage that blankets America and the wonderful greenery produces vast seas of oxygen, which offsets the green-house gases in the atmosphere. Blot out those smokestacks and think green, ladies and gentlemen. So green that your eyeballs turn green with chlorophyll!

Are you ready to go back to work? Feel the green, ladies and gentlemen. Forever green! Now go tackle your work tasks with gusto! Long live the green!

Thank you and good night!

Meanwhile, smokestacks spat fumes of doom. Multifarious poisons were pumped into the lakes and rivers. The soils were soiled with filthy muck. And life's clock ticked closer to total ruin. But that did not stop the timeclocks of our industrial institutions! Time must carry on.

30

AN ASTUTE SALES CHAMPION

CHILDREN'S HEROES were the guys and gals in commercials, the future CEOs of the country. Corn flake and wheat flake heroes were among the most glamorous in days of old (2040–2060), but in modern times their luster had faded.

With the end of the war, and the near discovery of new chemical ingredients to make flakes less soggy, that is, the No-Sog Revolution upon us, these adorable flake heroes enjoyed a resurgence of sorts. There was even talk of them becoming computer-game characters. Suddenly, statues and memorial plaques of flake-commercial characters appeared in parks and museums.

Pennant strings with flamboyant flakes in place of flags festooned balconies, yards, and car lots throughout the towns. The flakes had faces with red, white, and blue collars and funny hairdos. One flake looked like he was straight out of a freak show. He wore a blue spiked hairdo.

Fantasy Flakes turned colors when you poured milk on them. "See the rainbow," touted Isabella's new TV ad. She'd hired an aptly named, flamboyant new salesperson, Walter Sale, to push the idea.

They rose with a flash in the marketplace but quickly

fizzled when *Consumers United Magazine* called them chem-flakes, or, chemical flakes. The magazine got into trouble for characterizing the flakes as such, even though it was true. Business tycoons called the magazine's overworked staff "non-patriotic" and several fines were assessed against the magazine according to its financial position.

After the agonies of war, a certain simplicity set in, so those mourning lost loved ones could weep and move on. Isabella took note and dressed down and toned down her homemade advertisements, and thus she stole a glimpse at reaching a mainstream audience in the flake world.

31

THE ART OF THE LIE

ONCE UPON A MEMORY, our national leader found it impossible to tell the truth. Untruths tend to spread like poison ivy. Pretty soon, untruths light up the way, like a torch in a cave in an old Hercules movie.

Lies we call them. Lies became so dominant, nobody believed truth anymore. If you wanted to tell the truth, you had to tell a lie. If you wanted to make a point, you simply said the opposite of what you really meant. Sometimes, these lies were harmless (aside from a lump on the head).

"Dear, did you get your hair done today?"

"You noticed!"

"Yes, it's really ugly."

"It's what?" SMASH! went the cellphone on his noggin.

"I meant it's pretty. Can you pass me the corn, please?"

"Here you go."

"I said corn, not potatoes."

Other times these lies were a bit more serious. "Sergeant Carson, abort the mission."

"Yes sir."

"You fool. Why did you release the nuclear missiles?"

"You said to 'abort the mission.' That means fire!"

After about fifteen years of such confusion, it was decided to go back to literal truth-telling habits. Some refused truth and so continued to lie; some did not. Now, you never know when someone is telling the truth or lying.

32

FOND OF BONDS

CHAD SCANDALMAN and Cliché Bob invented a ghost company through which they could sell phony bonds to raise money "in order to purchase capital," that is, buildings and machinery (computers) for their new scam of a financial services company.

The money was actually used to buy personal toys for the two racketeers, who had no intention of paying it back once the bonds came due. Bonds were also sold to private investors, who sought to "get in on the ground floor" of a new venture in soap-making. The name of the "company" was Squeaky Clean Soap Manufacturing Company (SCSMC). Cliché Bob dreamed up the ironic company name and logo.

Scandalman printed the fake bonds with the fake logo. They advertised the sale of the bonds in *Business Whirl Magazine*. Buyers purchased their bonds by mailing money to a phony PO box.

All correspondence between the two nefarious rapscallions would be purely physical with no allowance of electronics. To carry out the plan, Chad and Bob would communicate via Wolgemuth's Weenie Wagon, a portable hot dog cart in Gatewood Park, just outside of the Great American Flake Company headquarters in north Domino, Indiana. The owner and operator of the cart, Marvin Wolgemuth, would exchange written notes of the two placed in gummed envelopes.

For handling the notes Mr. Wolgemuth would receive thirty dollars per week, plus a lot of hot dog sales between the two artificial-bond dealers. Therefore, no electronic evidence existed. The crooked pair need only send out dividend checks on the first of each month. By the time the first principal was due, the company would have mysteriously disappeared. The first principal would be due in five years, enough time for the two fraudsters to sock away plenty of greenbacks before the company magically dissolved.

This imaginary company would play the Sasquatch of business entities: many think they see it, but it's not really there. It is the beast without a backbone.

33

THE STORY OF TORY

TORY HAD bushy red hair like his mother, an FAI tattoo on his forehead like his father, and two Lakeside Steel Company tattoos on his cheeks. He had a small pug nose and thick lips.

The exalted father, Todd Swindell, got his start in small-time chicanery, like paying to have term papers written for his spoiled son throughout high school and dodging credit card payments until he could file bankruptcy, even though he was not really bankrupt. With his son's graduation he too graduated to a higher level of criminality. His wife had left him when he scammed her out of $20,000 for a business start-up that never started up. He also scammed donors of a homeless charity he had sponsored by keeping the money for himself.

Because he felt sorry for his depressed son, who did not take the divorce very well, he bought him a used Porsche, which the sixteen-year-old promptly wrecked before his old man could make the first monthly installment payment on the loan, a Honda motorcycle, which got stolen through his son's carelessness, and a fake, black-market diploma from Hoosier University for $10,000.

The old man even got Tory a cushy summer position at the Flakes Alive Incorporated headquarters in Central Domino,

Indiana. It was supposed to be a springboard into a better permanent position. Tory quit the job within a week.

Tory then got into trouble with the law, by stealing copper wire from an old factory in neighboring Westmont. "I buy him anything he wants," Swindell would say to his ex-wife, "and he repays me by swiping copper from an obsolete factory." Todd Swindell wrangled with prosecutors and defense attorneys to limit the penalty.

Finally, Tory swiped one of his dad's prized swords and sold it on the street. Todd Swindell could take no more. Nobody messed with his sword collection. He could barely keep up with his son's devilry and the kid had no desire to change.

Now Todd found himself making shady deals with eager young companies, so he could raise more money to keep up with Tory's string of offenses. Finally, Todd forged a new agreement with Tory, stipulating that should he get into trouble again, he would have to turn to his mother for funds, since Todd paid her a hefty sum in alimony already.

It seemed to help for a time, but then Tory got hooked on Pepper, a new street substance that would cause great societal problems in the near future and make its users sneeze a lot. By this time Todd knew that he had created a monster whom he could not tame. Time to pass him off to Mama. With a little compassion from his mother, Tory grew into the role of recovering addict, but he still suffered from depression and anxiety. After all, the expectations of the poor lad to succeed his father had mounted great pressure on his aimless, young soul.

34

GOOEY GLOBS AND SLIMY WADS

"NEXT CASE," said the judge, the Honorable Herman Whistler.

"Your Honor, it's Case 45769 on the docket, Brady Flicker," said the bailiff.

"Mr. Flicker, you're charged with slipping boogers beneath cafeteria tables. How do you plead?"

"But, Your Honor, I wasn't—"

"How do you plead, sir?" said the judge in a louder manner. "I've got forty-seven other cases waiting on me."

"I plead guilty, Your Honor," said a defeated Mr. Flicker in a low tone.

"Thirty days of cafeteria clean-up duty, plus a ten-dollar fine. And Mr. Flicker, be careful not to flick a booger into somebody's eye. Next case!"

"Your Honor, it's Case 32764 on the docket, Chad Scandalman. The accused continually masturbates and wipes his gooey stuff on anything he can grab."

The people in the courtroom snickered at the bailiff's description.

"Your case," said the judge, "violates Penal Code 7, Section 13. It is illegal to masturbate, Mr. Scandalman. I find the defendant guilty and his sentence follows: three days in the county jail, thirty days extra labor at the courthouse, and a hundred-dollar fine."

"But Your Honor," said Scandalman, slightly peevish, "I didn't even get to say anything."

"Have your say, sir."

"Oh, but please, Your Honor," cried Chad Scandalman, "I am such a poor boy who has been relegated to the tawdry premises of an unfinished basement, sir, with no empathy given toward me. Such a chasm has opened between my wife and I that we no longer have common friends, sir, and we no longer attend family outings."

"Enough, man!" blurted the contemptuous judge. "I could sit here all day listening to your woeful effusions about forgotten family and broken dreams, Mr. Scandalman, but it would get us nowhere.

Besides, it says here that you are the chief executive officer of a respectable company. Hardly the makeup of a 'poor boy' as you call yourself. Look here, masturbation is such an ornery act of hedonism, and—do you need counseling?"

"No sir."

"Let me remind you, sir, that we are here on this planet for the sole benefit of the corporation. Let there be no doubt. We live and breathe the corporation—any corporation, Mr. Scandalman, not just your own—and that should be every citizen's first focus."

"Sir, I can quit masturbating on my own," said the embarrassed CEO. "That's the problem, Mr. Scandalman, doing things on your own!" The entire courtroom laughed loudly.

"It says here," announced the unforgiving judge, "that you wipe yourself with kitchen towels, the couch cover, and—do you want me to go on, Mr. Scandalman?"

"No sir, please don't."

"Alright. I am suspending the jail time, sir, but I am adding something else. I sentence you to cafeteria duty, cleaning under tables to be exact. Like Mr. Flicker before you, you should find plenty of matter to scrape and clean. And, if you offend again, sir, I will have you cleaning and scraping beneath theatre seats."

"No—not that!" cried Scandalman.

"That is right. Sticky theatre floors and seats, Mr. Scandalman. I hope I make myself clear."

"Indeed, sir, you do."

"I am going to leave you with one final thought. *If it is meat you beat, you must be neat.*" Now the judge had the entire courtroom in an uproar, as he waxed poetic at the expense of the broken-down CEO. "In other words, no wiping your dick snot on pillowcases and so forth." People laughed with uncontrollable vigor. The judge cruelly toyed with the defenseless man. When the room quieted down, the judge added: "The next offense, Mr. Scandalman, will require a public exhibition of your masturbation."

"Yes, Your Honor."

"Next case!"

"Chadwick, wake up!" shouted Gertrude Scandalman. "You must have been dreaming."

"Huh? What was I doing?"

"Talking in your sleep and flailing your arms around."

Gertrude stacked some clean clothes on the table in the corner of the partly finished basement. "You need to get a dresser down here," barked the callous woman, "if you insist on staying in this cruddy basement."

"Well," said the basement refugee, "I seem to recall that you kicked me out of the upstairs bedroom."

"Yeah, and you deserved it."

35

PHANTOM OF THE WHITE HOUSE

IT HAD BEEN RUMORED for decades that The Big Seven had a clandestine leader, a backstage president, so to speak. Top secret documents only rarely mentioned such a phantom advisor, it was whispered, and such was redacted on any top-secret document leaked or declassified to the public. The whole affair reminded one of the UFO secrecies that predated 2040, dare we mention it. So, this surreptitious being supposedly told The Big Seven when to stop and when to go.

"The phantom calls the shots," Cliché Bob often said.

But no real proof existed of this man or woman's presence, and the possibility of his or her concealment spawned a great debate. The term of the secret presidency was rumored to be for life. Just who it was, if they existed at all, provided another topic for debate. Guesses varied from the defunct Donald Duck to the ghost of Ghant Wackersham, but no one knew for sure.

Zigmund Wexler and his cousin Herb Henson would both tell you that the phantom leader was a fairytale, this being about the only thing the two ever agreed upon.

Ziggie contributed the following to the *Clandestine Journal*:

March 12, 2098

Is there really a mystery being behind The Big Seven? Does this person bark orders, offer advice, or simply monitor like the mythical flying saucer secretly watching over earth? The answer is likely that he or she gives advice. But there are many who give advice. Those of you who think there is a secret President are mistaken.

—ZW

36

FOLDING UP THE COMMUNICATIONS UMBRELLA

SECRECY AND MEDIA control surfaced as other hallmarks of tyranny.

Our corporate government under The Big Seven seriously limited press conferences to inform the people of executive, legislative, and judicial matters. In fact, the current American regime had not held a press conference for three and a half years. Furthermore, anyone caught leaking information not intended for public consumption was subject to termination, criminal charges, and even death, depending on the classification of information and the severity of the "spill."

Janice Minton, secretary for Texas Governor Joey Newhart, earned a draconian punishment in the form of four public lashes and a Class B felony for divulging secret information on account of her telling a news reporter that the governor planned to cut food stamps.

In terms of news outlets, any station broadcasting stories of tolerance or a permissive society or other such "liberal tripe" could and were blacked out or banned altogether. A program that alluded to former freedoms of citizens risked its producers and directors being prosecuted and banished from the industry.

For example, Kelly Brown mentioned free speech and the

now forbidden First Amendment on her radio program *Down to Earth* in June, 2098, and was almost instantly fired and banned from the communications industry.

But that was not all. Her companion, Curtis Mann, was then fired from his gig on the New York Stock Exchange, even though he had nothing to do with the incident. Capitalist politicians, upon seepage of any morsel of truth regarding the way things used to be, panicked as if the sun was burning out.

37

ZIGGIE RUNS OUT OF MONEY

ZIGGIE ENTERED a hamburger joint on Wabash Avenue in the Chicago Loop. He stepped up to an ATM machine and put in his PIN. "Account Not Available," the thing read. Next, he called his credit union and inquired about his funds.

"We're sorry, sir," said the voice, "but your account is suspended. It seems that your assets are frozen until a certain matter is resolved."

"What matter?" Ziggie demanded, even though he knew exactly the matter. "Fuck!"

Next, the forlorn fugitive tried to use his debit card, but found that it too, was suspended. Finally, he tried his credit card and found that they had not gotten to that yet. So he bought some food and procured a motel room on Ohio Street.

"The lousy bastards have me in a chokehold, but goddamnit, I'm not giving in," he said aloud in the privacy of his room.

The next day his credit card would no longer work, so he left the motel, found a used car dealer on the outskirts of the Loop, and sold his old beater of a car for $6,000. His newer car had sat in his garage back in Domino, Indiana and was likely confiscated by this time. *They are breaking me down*, he thought, *but I cannot let them win.*

That night Ziggie slept at a bus station, as he did not want to use his money on bedbug-ridden motel rooms. He laid back on a sordid bench when a most weary wave swept over him. Ziggie climbed up a DNA ladder, turning in full circles as he rose up the double helix design, until exhaustion arrested his progress momentarily. He stood there frozen on a step halfway up, then he looked down into an abyss.

A kind of fog moved up the ladder after him. He lifted his right foot up to another rung, then pulled his left leg up. The strange fog rose to a higher step, as if following the middle-aged fugitive. The fog moved so close that it left the rungs moist with some kind of dew. Suddenly, Ziggie lost his footing and fell deep into the abyss. Flailing and falling, flailing and falling. . .

Then, the weary wanderer woke up. He tried to glean some sort of meaning from his dream. He was indeed falling—his life had gone and slipped into a hidden, dirty corner of the world. He could not get it back. Those days of knowing where he might land had vanished. He was adrift, indeed, in a deep fog just like in his dream. He felt as though he were window shopping at Death's Store. There was no door in the Store as of yet, but finding one felt like an eyelash away. To avert the slide into hell, it was only a matter of discovering in which corner Death was hidden, followed by an effort to avoid that corner.

Then, at his lowest moment, when the great vault of the dark skies seemed to fall down upon him, Ziggie pulled out of his backpack a gift that Alfi had bestowed upon him: a compact disk version of The Jimi Hendrix Experience album *Axis: Bold as Love*. Alfi had played it enough for Ziggie to know that it was the grandest accomplishment of the rock genre ever known to mankind. If only he could hear it now, it might deliver some new insight into Ziggie's life, or, better yet, it might serve up some spark of motivation.

Drifting, dreaming, floating, screaming, Ziggie may yet live again if he could only play it right now in this dingy bus station. But you don't just hear it, you play with it, you feel it, you experience the magical strands swimming through your body like snakes in tunnels. Fluttering anecdotes caress the ears, massage the temples and warm the blood. Mere words could not live up to the majesty of this work.

But the work was so powerful that even just reading the songs' lyrics and gazing at the brilliant colors of the album cover imparted just enough energy and will in Ziggie to proceed with his journeying.

If only I could have been there, thought Ziggie, *in those turbulent times when democracy still had sustainability and freedom offered no bargaining power for a crook behind a suit.*

38

WORKING FOR LESS

A TOTAL of 917,000 U.S. citizens had died from heat-related illnesses so far, this wicked summer of 2098. Corporate government officials feared the body count would reach a million by the conclusion of September.

Cecil Weatherspoon, one of the culprits in the Syd Waverly murder, had had a bout with heat, almost dying from a heart attack when he last attended the Colt "Buggy Whip" Higgens country and western concert at The Hoosier Winds Casino at the once beautiful Indiana Dunes lakeshore resort.

Global warming, it seems, had reached down and strangled Earth; the corporate government just could not refrain from plowing ahead at maximum production, machines growling, smokestacks spitting.

A corridor of industry now stretched from Chicago to Domino, Indiana, straight down the new I-63 highway. Like a great swath of doom, the corridor's engines roared and the smokestacks along its flank poured until the highway could give no more.

The denizens of clogged city streets choked in the smog-laden fumes they called "air." So disgusting and filthy was this effluvium that the average lifespan had shrunk and few expected to live past fifty or sixty years of age.

Cecil moved to the country outside of exurbia, but the drive to work was so long and dreary that he could barely think by the time he arrived at the flake factory. He had one more year to go before he would become fully vested in his measly 401(k), in which the corporation had stopped its matching company funds eight years before and was now fighting to recover the matching funds it had once contributed before that time.

The poor restless man did not know if he could make it through this last year. Fifty-three years old and half-wretched, he felt himself growing feebler by the day. What kind of retirement would he have if he could make it this final year? For his twenty-five-year anniversary they gave him a clad ring with the number "25" on top. Rumors were that for retirement they would give him a booklet of cereal coupons and another clad ring with a big R on top.

Back when overtime paid time-and-a-half he could at least compensate for the lack of a 401(k) match, but then they changed overtime to straight time, and, besides, with the long drive he could no longer work. Herr Nofziger, the pianist, looks about sixty, with a bushy gray beard and a curt, businesslike manner. OT.

Then there was one more thing that badgered him incessantly: his involvement in the Syd Waverly murder. It ran him down like no other burden. He would have to live with it, and try and find a retail job that would allow him to reach social security retirement age and work closer to home.

The corporations were booming but the workers were scrounging for survival. Something was amiss but everyone was too scared to complain on account they might throw you out the door or even arrest you for corporate interference, a charge no one could afford.

Old Ollie Opendyke complained and now he serves time for hindering corporate operations. And old Bert Finney tried to take his company to court because they quit contributing to his medical insurance, and he mysteriously disappeared. His poor wife survives by collecting railroad-yard recyclables and peddling mint gummies outside of Uncle Vito's Italian Restaurant. Add to that the sprinkling of cash received from her corporate logo tattoos, and the old woman could eke out an almost meager existence among her widowed peers.

39

DOUBLE-CROSS

"WHATEVER'S PERCOLATING in that wicked brain of yours," exclaimed Todd Swindell, "let it spill out right here on the floor so everyone in the room can see it, Bob."

"Yes. Let it pour, Bob. Let it pour," instructed Rhonda "Lady Weasel" Yokovich, a bony assistant to Mr. Swindell. When one gazed at her long, thin nose and skinny head, one could imagine a big weasel. "Alright," said Cliché Bob. "Look, Chad Scandalman is a major masturbator. I don't know if he's a sex fiend or what his story is, but I can tell you that he often locks his office door and goes to town in there. Rumor has it that he slinks under his big oak desk and does it there. Now, it seems to me we can plant a camera in there—I can do that—and record him, and then post the video of him going at it on the internet. Folks will go wild over it, major embarrassment will follow, and the cops will bust him for pleasuring himself. This will generate enough negative publicity that it will surely dig into the market share of GAFC. Get it?"

"I get it," said Lady Weasel. "When Scandalman mysteriously disappears, we will go to work!" Her small eyes gleamed with mischief.

"Yes, the humiliation alone will be mortifying," said Mr. Swindell.

"Great!" vociferated Lady Weasel. "When can we start?"

"I'll stop at an electronics store tonight after work, and I'll plant the camera tomorrow. How does that sound?" Cliché Bob's bald head glistened with perspiration beneath the overhead lights.

"Great," exclaimed Lady Weasel, "what else have you got?"

"Well, if the camera thing doesn't work out, we can always consider eliminating Scandalman." Bob wore the proverbial capitalist shit-eating grin when he said this.

Lady Weasel gasped. Todd Swindell had a sort of diabolical gleam in his eyes.

"We can discuss option two," said Bob, "when and if the time comes. First, we'll try recording that big oaf jacking his meat skyward. Again, I must stress total secrecy here. Just us three can know about this."

Bob's risky stint as a dual loyalist brought him more flexibility, he thought, in earning potential. Now he could draw income from the phony bond fund, his regular position at GAFC, and his milking of Todd Swindell at FAI. Without much of a conscience, Bob floated down the river of impropriety until he could paddle no more. It would not take long for his entire world to collapse.

40

EYE OF THE LIE STORM

SOCIETY WALKED a couple of steps backward once the corporate government acquiesced to the business magnates whose Christian roots motivated their anti-LGBTQ stance.

In a paradoxical way this myopic view harkened back to a pre-2040 era where no tolerance existed toward the queer segment of society, proving in an offhand manner that such early times did actually transpire, and thus puncturing the falsehood that the world began in year 2040. Gay men and women had to step back into the dusty closet, and woe to the trans citizens who walked the planet.

"It should not matter what one's sexual orientation may be," said a corporate government spokesperson, "for sex of any kind is prohibited." And in reaction to the accusation that the government was allowing religious influence to creep back in, the government simply reminded everyone that "religion is banned, as it always was."

Afterall, when inveterate liars came into vogue in 2016, and again in 2025, then permanently in 2040, the world had morphed into tyranny. The laws forbidding both religion and sex were quite clear by the latter date. The end of both would lead to a boost in commerce, since everyone's mind would be focused on work tasks only. But mention of the original inveterate liars is prohibited since the introduction of such into government occurred prior to 2040.

Ghant Wackersham, the last president of these United States, lied compulsively. When he was not signing executive orders to curtail freedoms or to make life easier for the corporations, he was whipping up a tornado of lies. He got the lie ball rolling.

And what of the introduction of criminality into the corporate government? That too became accepted in 2025. It used to be that when political leaders were accused, indicted, or convicted of a crime, they resigned in disgrace. But the new way is to elect or appoint such immoral clowns. So, here we are in 2098 with a third of our elected officials and a half of our appointed officials impregnated with criminal backgrounds. The term "squeaky clean" went the way of the caboose.

And what of the introduction of lascivious behavior into politics? For that, we have to go waaaaay back . . .

41

FORE!

CHAD SCANDALMAN COULD NOT HIRE Twinkle to dispose of Cliché Bob. She was "one and done," as the cliché master would say himself. Twinkle operated by a strict code: knock off only one person per company. That way, the assassin minimized the threat of getting caught.

Scandalman figured there was only one person he could totally rely upon: himself. He would invite Bob to a golf outing and figure out a way to jettison him to the land of the dead while on the tees.

First, Scandalman registered with a fictitious name, then led Bob out into The Greens of Destiny. *The Greens will do me well*, Bob carelessly thought, *while trudging down the fairway to hell.* But death's threshold made for a tremendously beautiful scene.

The sharp, heavy smell of freshly cut grass permeated the course. The forests surrounding the course lent the entire scene an air of privacy that other nearby courses lacked. Gorgeous ponds gave the place a serenity unmatched by any other spot on the flat landscape between Chicago and Domino. Ducks and lily pads dotted the waters with a heavenly touch. And a couple of mild slopes completed the view. There existed no better place where the everyday stresses of corporate America could sink into forgottenness in the bosom of Mother Nature.

The game went swimmingly, with Cliché Bob making a few dazzling putts from fifteen feet or more, which only reinforced Chad's desire to end him. Way out on the 18th hole—"no man's land" Bob called it—the pair of corporate bigwigs pondered the moment. Pernicious deeds aside, life was pretty damn good, thought Bob, as he prepared for a thirteen-foot putt. Scandalman had a seven-foot putt.

Suddenly, Bob said to Scandalman, "Why are you taking out your driver?"

Scandalman pointed to the sky, and Bob looked up. Then Scandalman swung the driver with all the strength he could muster and hit Bob with the big end of the club right on the back of his cliché-ridden skull. As blood squirted from the back of his head, Bob momentarily wobbled like a boxer on queer street, then tumbled to the ground. Whap! Scandalman hit him again and the blood sprayed like water out of a hose nozzle. Bob gurgled. Three more whacks and Scandalman thought he was dead.

The blood stayed atop the compressed grass of the green and the puddle widened. Bob then twitched. Scandalman looked around and hurriedly wound up and delivered another, this time Herculean blow to the side of Bob's face. Scandalman was a big man, and, despite being fat and tiring himself out, he had the power of a mad rhino.

Bob's face looked mutilated, but Scandalman did not flinch. He hurriedly wiped his club off with a small towel and placed it back in his golf bag. He looked around again and saw no one who might report him. He wiped his blood-spattered shoes and rubbed his shirt and shorts where the blood droplets were most noticeable. He picked up the golf bag, slung it over his shoulder, and cautiously but hurriedly walked into the adjoining woods.

But what if Bob had already given the nearly finished formula and other company secrets to Todd Swindell? he wondered. He would have to kill Swindell too. He could hear Bob say, "For the love of God!" He now peered through the leaves and branches to make sure Bob was not moving. Satisfied that the cliché King was deceased, he took a big breath and sighed. Then he tramped through the forest and back to his car. When he reached home, he burned all of his clothes in the backyard barbecue pit, showered, and soaked the driver club in the bathtub with generous portions of soap and alcohol to obliterate any DNA evidence.

Before long, he ventured upstairs and relaxed in the living room while watching a string of entertaining commercials on his new $20,000 home theatre system. When a Great American Flakes Company commercial for their "Flakes with Frosting" cereal came on, Chad Scandalman glowed with pride. He had started out operating the machines that produce those flakes and steadily climbed the corporate ladder until he reached the apex and became the CEO of GAFC.

The gushing of pride proved ephemeral, however, as the big man soon drifted off into cozy slumber. Dreams about Bob evoked sorrow and regret in Scandalman's weeping soul. The limping Devil had occupied his heart, he knew, but the engines of progress must move forward.

At the scene of the ugly crime, "Cheeseball" and his partner, Calvin, waited for homicide specialists to arrive.

"This crime is grotesque," said Calvin.

"Only a big, strong man could have done this kind of damage," claimed Cheeseball.

"Yeah," replied Calvin, "show me a woman who could do

this, and I'll show you a man who could pick daisies for a living."

"A good punishment would be to tape a cherry bomb to the killer's balls and set it off." "You come up with some weird forms of punishment, Corporal "Cheeseball" Downey."

42

OFF LIMITS TEAT

HERBERT AND HOLLY HENSON were assigned all five of their children by the Family Services Committee of Newton County, Indiana. Sex was not allowed, of course, so the couple spent their evenings laughing at cute commercials and then sleeping in separate rooms, which was a government recommendation in order to resist any sexual impulses that might arise.

After all, avoiding sexual arousal and any ensuing activity that might break the rules could result in serious charges, if found out by the government. But it was a very challenging feat to abstain from any illegal contact. Hugging was fine, but anything beyond that was forbidden.

On one rather messy but rare occasion Herb decided to stray: he hugged Holly and tried to fidget with her nipples, even though they were squished inside a chest binder and flat as pennies on a railroad track—post-train. Herb felt like he had been caught trying to pick at the turkey before it was done.

"Herb dear, hugs only," cautioned Holly. "Do you want to get us in trouble? You know they teach the kids at school early on about the evils of sex. And if the kids suspect their parents of indulging in such activity, they are encouraged to turn them in to authorities."

"The kids are not home," pleaded Herb.

"Yes, but one of them could walk in at any moment," Holly again warned.

"I heard corporate executives get to do it, so why can't I?"

"The children will report us."

Herb experienced a surge of guilt. He should have known better, his conscience prodded him. *I am a respectable school-teacher*, Herb thought, *and that careless maneuver warrants punishment. How could I have done it?* he fretted. *To save myself the embarrassment and guilt, I will never do it again!*

Sure enough, young Herb Jr. walked in and announced that he was "as hungry as a bear." Herb Sr. would have to resort to fantasy again. Yet, through all of the misery of misconduct and its painful aftermath, a part of him grinned triumphantly at the knowledge that he had gotten away with a feel.

But the feeling of victory proved ephemeral. Again, shame began to close in on the goodie-two-shoe of a man that Herb was, and soon he began nervously mincing about, grappling with a blemished conscience, and whispering for his mother. All for the vestige of a sneaky nipple rub.

It just was not worth it.

43

CAPITALIST CRAZY (THE FLAKE WARS II)

IN THE YEAR 2040, when mankind supposedly came into existence, and after The Great Cleanse, the two flake giants embraced fun competition, trading off with cute slogans furnished by their marketing departments, which consisted of former New York Madison Avenue marketing gurus and a few Chicago independents.

There was the "We've Got Bigger and Better Flakes," slogan of the Great American Flake Company (GAFC). Then there emerged "The Flakier, the Better" slogan of Flakes Alive Incorporated (FAI). Over the years these flake slogans bounced off of each other, one intercepting another, and then another intercepting that. Then GAFC shot back with "Fantastic Flakes," which created quite a stir. Two weeks later FAI countered with "We're All Flakes," and what a campaign that was. Both companies began to press their advertising people to come up with something better, something that would shout out to consumers around the country that their company and flakes were the greatest.

Consequently, GAFC rebounded with the "Formidable Flakes" slogan that sent FAI reeling against the ropes like a stunned pugilist. At this time FAI CEO Todd Swindell grew furious and hired the grandest of all advertising firms, Snelling & Snelling of Chicago, to whip up the *coup de grâce* of all advertising gimmicks. So, FAI launched its "Flaky Fun Figures" toys with one free figure in each box of cereal. This highly successful campaign brought much joy and celebration to FAI and launched many parties at the corporate head-quarters.

Flaky Fun Figures were plastic flakes with wiry arms and legs. Each figure stood four inches high. The first wave of figures included the following:

Freddie Flake

Frankie Flake

Fiona Flake

Fanny Flake

Kids were wild over these silly creatures. FAI basked in the sunshine of an improving bottom line. The Flaky Fun Figures campaign, however, brought tears to the face of GAFC CEO Chad Scandalman. The portly Scandalman said: "That sono-fabitch Todd Swindell wants to brawl, does he? Well, in the words of Cliché Bob, 'I'll fight fire with fire!'" Though GAFC still hung on to its top ranking among flake companies, FAI did threaten to overtake them. So, both sides clawed for recogni-tion, and the fight got ugly. Vicious statements by either company about the other were made by usually unidentified sources. Rumors of landmark lawsuits and Hail Mary mud-hurling exercises brought ferocious thunderstorms roaring past the ears of the public. Strange deaths and rumors of murders even surfaced.

At this point in the year 2082, blood boiling all around, certain players of the heated battle began to suffer symptoms of mountainous anxiety. Irritable bowel disease and panic attacks seized some of the most competitive men and women. A few of them even jumped from office windows to their tragic deaths.

Soon, the term "Capitalist Crazy" emerged from the labyrinths of corporate hallways, meeting rooms, and cube farms. Now Capitalist Crazy evolved into a very real condition, recognized by psychologists and psychiatrists and entered into their books of mind madness. "CC" became a catch phrase in the industry. When anyone did anything beyond expectations, their actions might be ascribed to "CC," even if only jokingly.

The disease was eventually declared a major mental illness caused by competitive tensions in the workplace. Similar to post-traumatic stress disorder (PTSD), CC brings about hallucinations and Delusions of Corporate Grandeur interlaced with acute and horrendous bouts of depression and Episodic Conglomerate Cringing (ECC). The symptoms ranged from "desktop rage" to the aforementioned bellyflopping on concrete sidewalks after having jumped from company headquarters' windows.

Though no cure yet existed, sufferers were compelled to watch endless pickleball tournaments interlaced with insurance-company-history videos in order to relax and become drowsy. This seemed to help with the nervous tension.

Meanwhile, the battle of slogans continued. The annals of flakedom recorded multifarious catchphrases, such as Fruity Flakes, Frivolous Flakes, Fancy Flakes, Freckled Flakes (with teeny candies imbedded), and Family Flakes. To Zigmund Wexler, they were all Phony Flakes.

Thus, two corporate titans locked horns in a vicious battle that left suicides, homicides and mangled lives in its wake. Since then, corporate slimeballs rip and slash at each other's vital organs until one drops and the other staggers away to some dark corner of the global marketplace.

One by one the corporate bigwigs lick dust until the future day when the Supreme Court might place a freeze on advertising and administer "Staying Alive in Corporate America" classes.

44

HOOLIGANS OF OLD HAMMOND

ZIGMUND HAD to return home to Domino, Indiana to retrieve a few things that he had forgotten on his first trip. He knew well the danger of doing so, so he sneaked around through the alleys of the peaceful side of town and approached his house from the back at 2:30 in the morning. Yellow crime tape surrounded the house. He ducked beneath the tape and entered the premises.

Longing to rest on the sofa with a bowl of popcorn or maybe an interesting book, he stood for a moment in the hallway to absorb the tranquil atmosphere. He yearned for the days of old, when he fed the cats outside, washed his car in the driveway, and waited on the mailman. He desperately wanted to sleep in his old bed. He stood there looking at the photos of his mother and father on the wall. There, he pondered his next adventure. Gathering his pure gold bracelet and some emergency cash that he had stashed inside his mattress, he took one more look at his living room, then skedaddled.

Ziggie then found his way down to the railyard, where he hopped on a random boxcar, nestled in a dark corner, and fell asleep. Using his backpack as a pillow, he dreamt away the long, cool hours of the evening in sheltered silence. When he awoke, he ate a hard biscuit and a piece of chocolate candy, then got up and followed the tracks out of town.

He continued down the tracks until the highway began to parallel the iron rails, then he veered off into a vast cornfield and followed a row of corn for about two miles. Then he slipped down a country road briefly, until he came to a creek, at which point he followed the winding, mucky green water for several miles until he reached a vast ocean of corn, wherein he followed the cornfield for miles upon miles, finally staggering into the south suburbs of Chicago.

Ziggie hummed a bawdy blues tune by the legendary Bo Carter, as he walked down the alley of Main Street of some unknown suburb, where newer apartment buildings lined both sides of the road.

Soon the modern apartments gave way to giant old mansions, now compartmentalized to house three or four families each.

Before long he could see a brick corner store with a red awning on his right. As he approached it, he noticed a shabby kid on an old, black bicycle. The kid had a dirty face and chewed on a big glob of bubble gum. The kid stopped his bike about ten feet ahead of Ziggie and asked, "Hey mister, do you have some spare change?" Ziggie reached into his pocket and pulled out a wad of cash, from which he gave the kid a five-dollar bill.

"What will you get?" asked Ziggie, "candy or somethin'?"

The kid squinted in the dirty sun and said, "I want a pop." Ziggie asked, "What town is this?"

"Why this is Stathem and yer headed for the bad part of town."

"That right? Where's the good part?"

"Ain't no good part in Stathem, mister," said the boy. "The good folks all moved down to Maple and Bregman. But yer goin' the wrong way for that." The kid stuck the five-dollar bill in his shirt pocket and remarked, "You see, this used to be Hammond, Indiana. But things got so bad here, with the junkies and thieves moving in, that everyone moved to better parts. Then the city officials renamed it Stathem, after some guy who opened a warming center for the homeless."

It seemed that the entire south suburbs of the Windy City were now "bad." Smokestacks and guard shacks surrounded one vast ghetto, and those places were now inactive. Trains still shot through town on their way to Chicago, not even slowing enough to get robbed, should some modern-day pack of hoodlums choose to stop one of them. Even though industry had faltered, filth impregnated the air and left the sorry citizens begging for rain enough to offer some type of relief from the asthmatic conditions.

"Well," said Ziggie, "you're still here, so it can't be that bad of a town."

"Anyway, thanks mister," shouted the kid as he rode up to the corner store, chained his bike to a bike rack, and went inside.

Ziggie strolled down the street, wary of gang members and rogue individuals, and came upon another set of railroad tracks running to the north. He quickly decided to follow them into the big city, where gentrification, he had heard, had rescued part of the area from the perils of urban conflict and thuggery.

No sooner had he rounded a sweeping curve to the northwest and began to cross a street known as Calumet Avenue, when a small group of young but seasoned hoods began to walk and ride in a circle around him right in the middle of the highway. He could easily fend off two or three of the ruffian vultures, but a count of five sparked a bit of trepidation in him.

"What do you guys want?" said the perspiring wanderer, trying to sound tough.

"We want yer money," announced the obvious gang leader, a kid about six inches taller than the next tallest young scamp.

Ziggie gambled on as tough of a look as he knew to put on. "You juvenile delinquents go on home now," barked the Chicago-bound fugitive, as he waved his hand in the fetid air. "I hear your mothers calling."

"Should we jump him, Peatie?" said a nervous kid to the gangly leader.

Ziggie struggled to find a strategy that might work to repel the little gangsters. "Maybe if you guys asked instead of demanding, I might have given you a couple of bucks."

"How so?" asked the leader.

Ziggie relented. He was careful to only pull out a small portion of the cash wad he had in his pocket. "Here's a twenty and a five (not much money in 2098). Go get yourselves a candy bar or somethin', you sorry-assed hoodlums." There he went again with the tough-guy attitude.

The leader, sensing that Ziggie wavered in his attitude, kicked a pop can off the side of the road. But he too revealed just a slight sense of fear. So, the five of them reluctantly waltzed off and headed for the nearest market, while the sun, made opaque by the dreariness of the place, began to dip westward.

45

A LUBE FOR HERB

HERB HENSON PARKED his car and entered Spittoon Alley. A friendly receptionist checked him in and a nurse who conducted herself like a higher-up, perhaps a doctor, escorted him to a long, narrow room, known as "The Alley." "Please take your place at A16, sir," said the smug nurse.

Herb obsequiously stepped over and stood in front of the A16 stall. "The doctor will be with you in a moment," said the pretentious nurse.

Herb stared at the colorful scenery painted around a hole in the wall where he would soon park his member. There were trees and mountains and fluffy clouds painted around the hole. The art rose a little from street graffiti but nevertheless looked a bit amateurish. A spittoon, Herb knew, sat on the other side of the wall, elevated by a small wooden stool.

"Mr. Herbert Henson?" spoke the doctor, holding a note board in his left hand. "Yes, that's me," replied Herb.

"Social Security number, please," said the business-like figure.

Herb rattled off his number, his date of birth and anything else requested by the dry physician. "Now then, unzip your trousers and pull them down to your knees, sir."

Without much humiliation, Herb did just that.

"Insert your penis," the doctor ordered, "and bend forward a bit. We'll apply some lubricant . . . it's cold. Insert instrument. A little pressure . . . and there we go."

"A little pressure, huh?" Herb mumbled, "it felt like my friggin' eyeballs were going to pop out!"

The stern doctor had administered an electrical stimulator by inserting it into Herb's rectum and tapping a button when the device rested against the prostate gland, causing Herb to ejaculate into the spittoon on the opposite side of the wall. The mild electrical current barely stung; in fact, it felt rather good, though it was certainly short-lived pleasure. But, to anyone besides Herb, the humiliation always introduced the most pain.

"There then, we will send your sample to the Baby Factory, where it will be examined and possibly used to aid conception by way of artificial insemination, that is, in vitro fertilization." The doctor then handed Herb some tissue to wipe himself in both the front, where a drop or two of semen may have strayed, and back, where the extra lubricant used in the quick process had gathered.

Herb pulled up his drawers and zipped them shut.

Absent of mortification, Herb gathered himself and exited the semen clinic, hoping for a game of Oligarchy with his assigned children when he got home. Spittoon Alley, for most, was a dreadful experience. But Herb, who always followed the rules, had no problem bending and grunting at the doctor's wishes.

46

CORPORATE EDICTS

POLITICIANS ROUTINELY DIPPED into the corporate cookie jar with no fear of exposure, snatching money to lobby other corporations or political higher-ups to approve laws that were favorable to the original corporation. Only a few were ever prosecuted, and of those, most were content to launch their next campaign for reappointment from a prison cell.

They shamelessly lobbied the CEOs who made the decisions about laws—and secretly to ensure that they would be selected again during the next round of political appointments. But it was illegal to use corporate money to influence appointments, and, though lobbying for laws was legal, lobbying for appointments was not. The appointing CEO was supposed to choose on his or her own knowledge.

Moreover, the criminal element so seamlessly saturated the ruling class that one could scarcely distinguish the good from the bad. And the line between politicians and corporations had blurred so much that laws governing the association were hardly enforceable.

Merchants of doom presided over the political class with careless abandon. The original criminal element recklessly downsized the government during The Great Cleanse of 2040 to make it easier to seize total control, and now the authoritarian collusion among politicians and corporate executives was so thoroughly woven into the fabric of governance that, minus revolution, it can never be *dethreaded*.

Thus, the politician and the corporation could both propose new laws. The corporation commonly proposed new rules to the legislature, which would translate the code into *lawyerspeak*, then send it back to the corporation so it could issue the final edict. Some of the edicts were ludicrous like the following:

Corporate Edict #3567. All passersby must now salute any Corporate Headquarters edifice.

Others signaled dire and momentous changes, like the following:

Corporate Edict #3592. Thou shalt not covet riches outside the aegis of the corporation, meaning that private enterprise is now illegal. All businesses must conduct themselves under the sphere of the corporation. Entrepreneurs are compelled to incorporate. Private businesses will no longer be allowed.

Ziggie laughed when he heard about Corporate Edict #3567. "They can kiss my ass if they think I'm gonna salute every time I pass a corporate headquarters building. I mean that's an audacious demand and who the hell is going to enforce it? Just think, some image-conscious corporate prick probably received a hundred-thousand-dollar bonus to come up with that stupidity."

Ziggie sat at a table with a couple of cab drivers and homeless men at Jody's Café in South Chicago.

"That corporation across the street," joked one ragged guy between sips of coffee, "is lookin' for your salute, Joe!"

"Yeah, if they're lucky, I might wave my dick at 'em," snapped one brawny fellow who must have been Joe.

The entire table cackled at the comment.

47

THE WRONG MAN

THROUGH THE GRAPEVINE, Detective Hung Cho Lee heard hints that management for FAI had ordered a secret hit on the lab technician in charge at GAFC. Unbeknownst to Mr. Lee, Anika Patel, Twinkle's cousin, would carry out the operation.

"There has been a change in plans, Anika," said Todd Swindell, CEO of the booming FAI company. "We have decided to hold off on targeting Chad Scandalman. Instead, we want you to exterminate the lead lab tech, Gary Stein."

Meanwhile, GAFC had embarked on a new slogan campaign to mark the ages: "Rake in the Stay-Crisp Flakes." In truth, the Stay-Crisp Flakes only stayed crisp for about four-and-a-half minutes, an improvement on the three-and-a-half minute average, but hardly enough to call them "Stay-Crisp Flakes." For that celebratory title, the flakes would have to remain crisp for at least ten minutes, and everyone in the industry knew it.

Therefore, Todd Swindell called it an "outrage" that GAFC had made the false claim and outright cheated. It was a rather bold move on the part of GAFC management. But there it was, and it put up a pretty good fight against FAI's slogan and

Flakey Fun Figures campaign. More than ever before, FAI had to make sure that the true secret formula, rumored to be almost finished, would not wind up in the grimy hands of a GAFC employee.

It was all settled. Anika Patel would bump into Gary Stein at the Shoppers' Miraculous Mall at Grandview Avenue and Century Street in the city of Domino and inject him with a lethal dose of sodium pentothal. Afterwards, she would make a rapid exit and hide out for at least a month in her apartment.

Todd Swindell handed Anika an envelope containing a photo of Gary Stein and half-payment of $50,000, the other half to be delivered at the conclusion of the devious act.

Anika canvased the parking lot of the GAFC headquarters until she identified the man in the picture as he left work one afternoon. She then followed him home. She found a spot across the street from Mr. Stein's home, a spot from where she could watch for his movement. She now had him under full surveillance.

For three nights, Gary Stein did nothing but go home from work, eat dinner, watch a few commercials and go to bed. He was a single man and had a strict bedtime, as the lights always went out at nine o'clock each evening. At that time Anika would go home and come back the next night.

On Friday, the fourth night of surveillance, Gary went to the grocery store, Fabulous Foods. Anika, tired of waiting for Mr. Stein to visit the Shoppers' Miraculous Mall, walked into the store and followed him around. But she could not catch him alone.

Too many people crowded the aisles. Anika tried to isolate him in the soft drink aisle, but other bodies browsed the different varieties of pop, snatched up the cases and lifted them into their carts. She tried the coffee aisle, but again, there were too many consumers just milling about and examining the coffee labels. Finally, Gary entered the aisle with cooking oils and such. It was empty!

Anika walked straight to Gary, bumped into him, and simultaneously stabbed him in the stomach with the syringe, while pushing in the plunger, all in one slick move. She did not stay for the show, turning and walking briskly toward the meat aisle. She heard the victim fall but did not look back. No one had seen her, she was sure.

She grabbed a package of chicken, went to a self-checkout aisle, paid with cash and walked out as nonchalantly as possible. Meanwhile, her victim squirmed about the shiny floor of Fabulous Foods and went into convulsions. A shopper finally visited the aisle where the victim lay and immediately called 911.

The only problem was that Anika had inadvertently snuffed out the taste tester, Archibald Stevens, and not the lab technician, Gary Stein. That's because the picture she had been given was of Arch Stevens and not Gary Stein. Soon the news made it back to the top. In fact, it trampled the stunned FAI CEO.

"What good is a taste tester, goddamnit!" cried Todd Swindell when he heard the terrible news. "Goddamn fucking son of a ball bustin' bitch!"

"Cosmic fucking cheese farts!" moaned Arthur Stemwhistle, Todd Swindell's architect of sneakiness. "How did she possibly mix up a taste tester with a lab technician!?"

"I injected the man in the photo," Anika insisted.

"Let me see that damn photo," demanded Arthur.

Anika slipped it out of the bent envelope and handed it to Arthur. He released a big breath and put his head down.

"What?" asked Todd Swindell.

"I inadvertently gave her the wrong photo," admitted Arthur.

"Well," said Swindell, "of all the goddamn fuck-ups, Arthur, this one outclasses them all for stupidity! What the fuck were you thinking!"

"I guess I wasn't thinking at all," said the embarrassed architect.

"You're fired, you sonofabitch!" Swindell threw the bag of money at Anika. "Fucking people. You're all driving me goddamn crazy!"

Lady Weasel snapped, "Well I didn't do anything wrong."

"No, you didn't," cried a frustrated and angry Mr. Swindell. "We're going to have to lie low for a while, but we're still going after Gary-fucking-Stein . . . and this time, Lady Weasel, you'll be in charge!"

PUTRID MOUNTAIN

SLEEPING under the abandoned railroad bridge over the Little Calumet River rendered no inspiration to the now tattered Ziggie. He sprawled upon oily mud and mentally wrestled with the stench of fresh sewage, which kept his sinuses closed and his appetite in check, thus saving him food and tissue paper throughout the fog-laden night.

When he awoke, his sinuses, joints and mind all aching, he fished in his backpack for his intelli-phone screen, so he could utilize its flashlight to help him find his way back up the steep embankment to the railroad tracks, for the sun had not yet sprung daylight upon the foul scene.

Ziggie thought about how the river might have looked three hundred years ago—crisp, clear water replete with ducks and other foul—and almost instantaneously he grimaced and seized up with terror, a raw combination of angst and dread over his wrongdoing, his daredevil act to think back before the beginning of time, for he had been conditioned to feel extreme guilt for daring to entertain such thought, as it was against the rules to delve into anything before 2040. He tried earnestly to shoo the guilt away, and struggled in doing so, until, at last, with one final cursing of himself for bending to guilt, he was ready to resume his journey, hoping to make great progress before any other hoodlums awoke.

A chill ran through the fugitive's sore body. He almost laughed at his miserable predicament. He thought, *once you make the bad list, like Zigmund Wexler, your life changes forever.* Your house would be ransacked by the corporate-government police. They would tear through your drawers, ravage through your papers, turn over baskets, even check your book collection, refrigerator, and the back of your toilet. Your cars would be searched and even your work desk.

Nothing was put back in place. They simply left your belongings in shambles. The same kind of shambles my life is in, thought Ziggie. He remembered his old friends as he walked. Russell Evans, Jack Phifer, and Dan Weiss used to come over and listen to music and drink beer and shoot the shit. He recalled the tender relationship he had with his girlfriend, Gina Waggoner. She approached him at a Tastee Freeze ice cream stand, and, for a while, the two had been inseparable.

Does she even know I'm gone now? he wondered, as he hiked up a wooden bridge above Hartz Ditch. "Shambles," Ziggie whispered. "My life is in shambles."

It was the big machine. This massive machine was built to ramble on without a care, to stop for nothing. There existed nothing to insulate you from its hungry gears or cogs. It would just eat you right up, chew on you for a moment, and spit out your bleeding guts without so much as a blink. You had no choice but to stay on the run.

Having moved on from his acute guilt and rabid disgust, he now set his mind to racking up some mileage. By noon he had made it across the state line into miserable Calumet, Illinois, where the go-go girls had once danced upon the stages of seedy mom-and-pop clubs all along the State Line Road and State Street, and, by late afternoon, he stumbled into South Chicago, where a humongous landfill, so tall and mighty that it resembled one putrid, sunbaked mountain in the middle of what was once pristine prairie, towered over him like a mausoleum would a toddler. Unchecked capitalism, he knew, had driven life away from these abysmal lands, and no gentrification of even the highest order could save it. The houses nearby were all abandoned and beyond repair.

Later on, with darkness approaching, he again hid himself away from the criminals, poachers and vagabonds of the nightlife. This time he rested beneath an old Interstate 57 bridge, next to where a newer bridge had been constructed. He ate a couple of biscuits, and he thought about the Putrid Mountain again and the junkyards that surrounded it. All of those disposals held the contents of what were once consumer dream items, state-of-the-art products and all of their splendid packaging and technology-driven makeup.

Ziggie winced as he imagined all the shiny showcases of department stores, then shopping-mall shelves, then big box store shelves that sold these items without inhibition, without caution or foresight. Now those items were part of Putrid Mountain, just multiple decades worth of discarded junk and rotting food. Putrid Mountain, thought Ziggie, belches forth enough methane and stinky gases to suffocate a herd of rhinoceroses.

Soon Ziggie slipped off to sleep and dreamt about homeless trolls who lived under the bridge and decided they did not appreciate his presence and began harassing him and chasing him about and robbing him, where some of them held him down while others reached into his backpack and yanked out food and gadgets, such as his razor, his watch, and other assorted objects and fidgeted with them and chortled as Ziggie resisted to no avail. When they began punching him, he woke up startled by this nightmare. He was shivering in the cool morning air, so he chomped on a biscuit, hoping to generate some kind of body heat.

Finally, he set off on what he figured to be the last leg of his journey to the downtown section of Chicago, the famous Loop, and about all that was left of the old city, besides some refurbished houses along the rim of the business district. Almost the entire metropolis had crumbled in decay.

Within the next hour Ziggie finally reached those gentrified neighborhoods he had heard about. They formed a belt around the downtown. Mostly, he was out of danger, but it took him all day to reach the Loop. In the morning Ziggie found himself lying on a bus-stop bench with TV commercials blaring in his ear. Since the corporations who run the government installed TV screens at bus stops, the intrusive commercials peppered the ears with mindless nonsense, at least from the sagacious Ziggie's gutsy perspective. Of course, most shoppers loved the televised ads and despised when the controllers saw fit to insert a movie clip or some such boring material.

Ziggie stretched his limbs and staggered sore-footedly down the new sidewalks, noticing the beauty of the flowerbeds—he had not seen a flower since leaving Domino, Indiana—and the variety of statuettes lining the walkways up to the doors of the revamped homes.

Finally, between a couple of businesses he spied the skyscrapers of old Chi-Town. He had made it at last. So, he ducked into the Underground Workshop and resumed his duties as counter clerk and salesman.

49

HELP FOR THE HOMELESS CRISIS

IN AN EFFORT TO avert the preponderance of tent cities, a committee was formed by America's metropolises to explore a solution. Following the Great Cleanse, many African Americans filled prominent roles as heads of financial affairs, presidents and vice-presidents of mammoth companies and even a few chief executive officer positions; but most of them were still seemingly glued to the ghettos— always growing larger—from whence they came. What had started as ghetto pockets grew into ghetto collars and then into ghetto cloaks, taking up massive yardage where regular suburbs once sprawled.

In the great year of 2098 seven CEO's ran the government and two were black, never letting the white CEOs forget about the poor neighborhoods that needed assistance. Before the cold set in on the dreary landscapes of the largest cities, the committee appointed to deal with the homeless problem proposed the issuance of wooden crates, called on the street "Capitalist Crates," or CCs, to help house the indigent souls. Any cluster of such "housing" earned the name of "Crate Camp," also otherwise known as CCs (depending on the context, "CC" could mean Capitalist Crazy, Capitalist Crates, or Crate Camp).

There were Crate Camp Blacks (CCBs), Crate Camp Latinos (CCLs), Crate Camp Whites (CCWs), and even Crate Camp Others (CCOs) for small groups of usually foreign minorities not quite large enough for their own camps. A Crate Corridor existed between Chicago and Kankakee, Illinois and along routes between smaller cities and other big cities.

The crates were eight-by-six-foot pine boxes with a door at one end. A body and a few essentials would fit into a crate. These Crate Camps were fast replacing tent cities. Now the government thought itself very generous for issuing these pine crates to the homeless population, which had by 2098 reached an astounding 29 percent of the total population.

Citizens of the Crate Camps wanted to expose the homeless crisis by locating crates along interstate highways, but The Big Seven wanted them placed in isolated zones away from traffic and the public eye. Crate Camp denizens ignored the effort to silence them and created linear villages along freeways, such as I-57, I-80, and I-70.

Originally, the government planned to make the crates just three or four feet wide but thought that they would too much resemble coffins, which would not generate much praise for the operation and the government. They thought that the depression of the poor might be compounded by the expectation to sleep in their own coffins. Such a droll policy might cause criticism or inside jokes being made about The Big Seven.

50

COIN WITHOUT A STORY

ONE NIPPY BUT SUNNY AFTERNOON, little Herb Henson walked home from school, cutting through the Gibson Farms property—fallow for the last five years—when he came across a 1903 Liberty Head Nickel in the dirt, which, seemingly, had just been turned in preparation for a new crop. The coin was all rusted but one could barely make out the year. It had probably laid in that field for almost two hundred years.

Herb Jr. took it home and showed his father what some olden-day farmer must have dropped— dare he say it—two centuries ago.

Herb Sr. immediately confiscated the antique coin. "I must turn this in to the corporate government," he said.

"But dad," cried Herb Jr. "doesn't that prove there was life before 2040?"

"No, son. The mint must have made a mistake. It's probably a stamping error." And Herb Sr. really believed what he had explained.

"But dad—"

"Just forget you ever found it, son."

Private coin collections were purchased by the government in 2040. And any coin with an earlier date was turned in by citizens on that date as well. And though the government tried to wipe out all old coins, they found it impossible to totally eliminate them. Had either Herb pushed for answers to the riddle, they would, of course, be passed off as "loopy."

But savvy Herb Jr. suspected the entire cover-up. Seeds had been planted in his mind. What if he refused to play the corporate government game? Would they "disappear" him? He decided to hold his feelings inside for a while.

51

THE CLANDESTINE JOURNAL

ALL INTERNET PROTEST sites were blocked as of 2043. Occasionally, a new one squeaked by the censor programs but was quickly discovered by the secondary programs and citizen watchdogs and eradicated. The only thing resembling an underground communication was a hardcopy of the *Clandestine Journal*, to which Ziggie Wexler sent a letter to the editor entitled "Corporate Almighty." His short piece follows:

The founders of America, whoever they are, would cringe at modern corporate fealty. They wrote a constitution to declare and uphold our now forgotten freedoms. Like layers of the onion, our rights were peeled away, our Gods were zapped, until the almighty corporation stood by itself as the sole object of worship. The corporation's operators are now the lone subjects of our admiration. May some independent God swoop down and save us from our own folly.
—ZW

Detectives and cops knew exactly who "ZW" was. They had been searching for him. They figured he was hiding out somewhere in Chicago. His incendiary writings made him a wanted man. His defacing of a corporate logo rendered him eligible for a spot on the top ten most wanted list. Any visit to a post office would reveal that the clever agitator was up to number four on the list.

52

THE FLAKE FAIR

A TRADE CONVENTION of sorts took place at the New Chicago Expo Center during the hot, steamy month of July 2098.

Todd Swindell, CEO of Flakes Alive Incorporated, stretched his thin, pale hand out to shake with Chad Scandalman, plump CEO of the Great American Flake Company. The two had met before at a Flake Festival in Indianapolis, but since that time competition and the accompanying bad blood had heated up, so neither corporate bigwig stood ready to engage the other in conversation.

Farm Cooperatives, wholesalers of wheat, corn and oats, along with vendors of all sorts, lined the walls of the giant complex. The place was packed with business barons.

"What a fat, ornery hog that Scandalman is," muttered Todd Swindell to his secretary, Dalia Habib, once he thought the big man was out of earshot. "He's got shoulders like an ape and a fat ass like a hippopotamus." Dalia placed a hand over her mouth and snickered.

"That bony little gimlet-ass," whispered Chad Scandalman to his preppy female intern, Star Ann Wilkenson. Star giggled cautiously as Swindell shifted his attention toward a new arrival.

Now the master of ceremonies, the prim Ms. Helen Oglethorn, approached the two CEOs with a forced smile. "I assume," she said, "you two have met each other?"

"Yes, I know him," disinterestedly admitted Chad Scandalman. "And *I* know *him*," smugly acknowledged Todd Swindell.

At this juncture the two engaged in a childish back-and-forth.

"He's a fraud."

"He's a fake."

"Two-penny Todd."

"Cheatin' Chad."

"Waffle head."

"Banana lips."

"Rump warmer."

"Zit licker."

"Your mama dreams of toad butts."

"You mama kisses warthogs."

"Your daddy juggles dog nuts."

"Your daddy nibbles titty farts."

"What the hell's a *titty fart*. There's no such thing."

"Your--."

"Alright you two," admonished prissy Helen. "Can we have a break here?"

Soon the Chief Executive Officers all lined up for photos, each of them showcasing that big, phony, America-Can-Do-No-Wrong, capitalist smile, good for little more than toothpaste commercials. It was the brand of smile that the two aforementioned CEOs had worked years to shape. The kind of artificial smile they ask a salesperson to make with each new customer.

One other CEO that few recognized was Isabella Blake, an African-American entrepreneur who had just financed the building of a small competing factory on US Route 41 in Domino, Indiana. The wealthiest moguls laughed her off as the head of some weak start-up company that would surely fold within the next three years.

Just when the final photo snapped, Mr. Scandalman noticed a familiar face in the crowd, one that he was shocked and angered to see. It was the assassin, Twinkle Deshpande! The tiny figure floated about like a lone moth, not getting too friendly with anyone. What the hell is she here for, thought Chad. According to code, I can only hire her once, so what does she want? Then Scandalman seized up with horror. Is she here to follow me? What if some other company hired her to dispose of me?

Immediately, Chad hurried to the restroom to masturbate, but all of the stalls were occupied. He had to release the pressure in his groin, so he ducked into an empty conference room, locked the door, and jerked himself into panic-soothing ecstasy. The perspiring CEO pulled up his pants and zipped the fly. Then he noticed that he wore a bit of semen on his suit coat. Oh no! He spit on his handkerchief and tried frantically to rub out the spot. By God, it was as if an act of terrorism had spoiled his evening, thought the over-excited corporate head. Pretty soon a big wet spot had formed where he had wiped his coat. He waved desperately with his hands trying to dry it. Finally, when he thought it had dried enough, he unlocked the door and exited the room.

"Mr. Scandalman, why are you perspiring so much?" asked Star. "Maybe you should sit down, sir."

Just when Scandalman was ready to scoop up his nosy intern and bolt out the door, Twinkle approached him. The mercury rose up his spine as he heated up. A bead of sweat had rolled into the crease between his nose and cheek.

"What the fuck are you doing here?" whispered the anxious CEO, now feeling a bit bold.

"I'm here on another job," replied Twinkle.

"For whom?"

"That I cannot say."

Scandalman fidgeted with his tie and collar.

"But I do know one thing, Mr. Scandalman," noted Twinkle, with a glimmer of naughtiness in her brown eyes. "I know you have been secretly masturbating."

Now a bolt of lightning flashed up Scandalman's spine. He looked down in shame.

"So, you are a spy."

"No. I'm an assassin. But I have to scope out the job, don't I?"

Another bead of sweat rolled down Scandalman's forehead, where he brushed it with his shirt sleeve.

"But I won't report you," said Twinkle, "if you pay a bonus for my previous work for you."

"But you failed to get the formula," said Scandalman.

"It's not my fault that you issued the go-ahead before the formula was finished."

"How can I trust you?" asked the big man.

"Nobody ever found out who killed Syd Waverly, did they?" Twinkle smiled briefly, the only time Scandalman had ever seen her do so. "It will be the same for this."

"How much?"

"Fifty stiff $1000 bills," said the demented assassin. "And you'll never see me again."

"You said that the last time." Scandalman gave Twinkle the laser eye, the same look he gave to business partners when scrutinizing them and trying to look shrewd. "You won't report this to authorities nor anyone else?"

"That's correct, Mr. Scandalman," she said softly.

"Where do I send it?"

"Here's a post-office box number," said Twinkle, while scribbling it on a notepad. As she tore out the page and handed it to the hefty CEO, she stated, "Have it there by next Monday, sir."

Then Twinkle did an amazing thing. She moved up close to Scandalman and licked his earlobe. With a wry smirk, she whispered, "And don't get any syrup on it."

"Ha-ha. Real funny," Scandalman said sarcastically. "Don't get any curry on your sari." Frustrated that his remark maybe lacked the bite of Twinkle's one-liner, he stared down at her condescendingly. Then, with a flash of paranoia, he quickly surveyed his suit to make sure no semen spots were visible.

Scandalman gave her a parting dirty look, then motioned for his intern. "Wait just a minute," he said to Star, holding his arm out so she could not move forward. He felt so nervous that he experienced an unyielding urge to demonstrate his pomposity. Suddenly, with a flash delusion of grandeur, he told the intern to "bear with me," and he rushed to the front of the giant room. He jumped up on the podium and with every cell in his strained body, yelled in the microphone "I AM THE GOD OF ALL FLAKES! IS THAT UNDERSTOOD YOU FLAKELESS FUCKERS! YOU WIMPY BEDWETTING NEOPHYTES! YOU IMPOTENT BONELESS WEASELS! I AM GOD!!!"

The outlandish tirade earned Scandalman a place in the ranks of the "Capitalist Crazy."

Though a spatter of heckling seized the tense moment, it quickly dissipated and suddenly all fell quiet, so much so that the big room was overwhelmed with silence. Poor Helen Oglethorn floated somewhere between exhausted and flabberghasted.

Todd Swindell thought: I hope Mr. Scandalman recovers from his mental illness, but I also hope his company does not.

The rest of the shocked audience just thought: what an audacious, pompous maniac!

Scandalman sent the money, and, as promised, he never heard from the diabolical Twinkle again. For such a flimsy little body, he thought, she sure is a queen-sized wretch.

53

THE EDUCATED CONSUMER

A FLYER RECEIVED in every mailbox:

There was once a day when people resisted advertising, eschewed commercials, hid from annoying salespersons. This is no longer the case. We have learned to embrace such activity, for it is at the very heart of our industriousness. Ceaseless circulars, interminable bargaining, boundless promotions all vie for our attention, and we, the savvy consumer, must interpret these friendly aggressions and act to the best of our reasoning ability in purchasing quality services and merchandise. We must view the advertisement as a courtesy, a blessing even, to inform us and guide us to an educated choice in the purchasing of products from our highly specialized offices and manufactories.
—Sponsored by the American Commercial Club

Ziggie saw one that came to the Underground Workshop. He scoffed at the stupid thing. *They are invading our space with ads and commercials,* he thought. *According to this nonsense, we should consider receiving advertisements a privilege. When does it stop?*

"Do you know," he said to Alfi, "the other day I called the

bank to get the time and temperature. I was ambushed by the most irritating sales pitch before they would give up the information I sought. Here, let me dial the number and you listen."

Alfi took the phone as Ziggie tapped the numbers.

"Hi! Clearance Clarence Here!
We Have Barn Burster Sales! Red Hot Deals Fresh Off The Semi Beds! Eye-Popping, Heart-Throbbing Super Buys! Just Wrap Your Limbs Around One Of Our Bargains Today! Boys And Girls, Moms And Dads—We've Got Something For Everyone! No Gimmicks Here! Just Our Pledge To Please! Come On All You Binge Buyers! Big Boxes And Big Savings! At Clearence Clarence's Shoppers' Galaxy! Where Your Purchase Won't Hurt Yas!
The time is 7:42 pm. The temperature is eighty-seven degrees."

"All that just to get the time!" Ziggie shouted.

"Yeah," said Alfi, "last week I picked up a newspaper at the bus station. All of the stories were buried in the back. The first ten pages were pure ads. Talk about pathetic ad overkill..."

MEMORIES

PHYSICAL ITEMS CAN BE BURNED, torn to pieces, disintegrated. But the intangibles have a way of surviving as long as the human mind can conjure up visions. Authority despises certain ways of the mind.

The totalitarian corporate government's worst fear: memories. Namely, memories of the way things were before the takeover, The Great Cleanse. Memories of free speech. Memories of lush liberty.

Those born before the fateful 2040 purging carry thoughts of old like change in the pocket. One pro-autocratic-government, arch-conservative radio talk show host, Doug Wimplehorn, nailed the dilemma to a guideboard for all the world to hear: "In thirty years they'll all be dead and we won't have to worry about memories at all."

But old Doug forgot about word of mouth. Those memories can be translated to anecdotes for the next generation. They don't have to die. Ziggie certainly knew it.

He said: "So fuck Wimplehorn and the tribe of Nazis he rode in with!"

DEAD FLY'S WATCH

"MR. SWINDELL," said a soft voice over the telephone, "a Mr. Hung Cho Lee is here to see you."

"Send him on in, Dalia," the CEO directed.

Todd Swindell straightened up a few magazines, sat in his plush office chair, and interlaced his fingers. Mr. Lee knocked three times and Todd invited him in.

"Mr. Swindell, I'm Detective Hung Cho Lee and I'm here investigating the death of Archibald Stevens last Friday."

"Yes, Arch was a good man, I understand, Mr. Lee. GAFC is down a good man and for what? I understand law enforcement believes he was injected with something—some kind of poison?"

"Yes, the full lab report has not yet come in, but that is our belief, sir. Do you know much about it?"

"Not really," responded Swindell, "Just what I told you."

"Is there anyone in your company who might have reason to end the life of this man?"

"Now Detective Lee," reasoned the thin, raspy-voiced CEO, "why would anyone in my company kill a lousy taste tester?"

"Lousy?" repeated Mr. Lee, "We're talking about a human life here, Mr. Swindell."

"I'm sorry," apologized Swindell, "please forgive my unfeeling remark. It's just that no one here would do away with a taste tester, sir. What would be the purpose?" He looked up at the fly guts smeared on his office window as if for some kind of morbid guidance.

"How's Syd Waverly's replacement coming along?" asked Hung Cho Lee.

"Oh, she's just dandy. Annie De Luca is a real up-and-comer, Mr. Lee. A dedicated trooper."

"You know," Detective Lee reported, "I interviewed Waverly's companion, Colleen, and she could not imagine why anyone would have a beef with Syd. From all accounts, he was the nicest of guys. Indeed, Colleen is scared for herself and her children's lives."

"Well," said Swindell, "the company is taking care of her, Mr. Lee. We raised close to twenty-five thousand in donations and she gets double indemnity from Syd's life insurance. We even offered her an office clerk position here at FAI."

"Why do you keep looking up at that window, Mr. Swindell?"

"Oh, that. It's just a habit of mine."

"But there is nothing there, Mr. Swindell." Lee studied Todd Swindell's fidgeting and twitching.

"Oh, I know," responded Mr. Swindell. "It's just a bad habit."

"What's so bad about it?" Lee asked in a stern manner. This remark signaled a turning point in the conversation.

"Just—nothing." Todd Swindell thought that the fly remains have seen everything that has gone on it that little office. *Wouldn't you really like to know?* he wondered smugly. *Heh-heh-heh.*

"Mr. Swindell," Lee baited him, "I think you are lying. I think you do know something about the taste tester's sudden death."

"That's fucking outrageous, Mr. Lee! And I think this conversation is over!" Swindell got up and opened the door for Lee, who stared up at the office window, as if looking for a camera or something.

Satisfied that nothing was there, he tipped his hat and began to leave. "We'll be talking again, Mr. Swindell," said the stoic detective.

56

THE PANHANDLER'S CINNAMON

ANNIE DE LUCA, lab technician for Flakes Alive Incorporated, set off on a stroll to the park.

She usually went there on her day off and relaxed in the sunshine. But on this fine Saturday someone asked her if she wanted to buy some Cinnamon, a brown, somewhat pungent chemical used as a super amphetamine and mild hallucinogen. The dismayed chemist warned the seller of the bad chemicals with which Cinnamon was made and moved to a different park bench. She enjoyed the birds and the squirrels for a moment when a female panhandler, who happened to be one of the seller's customers, approached her.

The money beggar was thoroughly "drenched" with the new street poison. She spoke so rapidly that Annie could barely interpret her words.

The panhandler spewed the following: "Madam, can you spare a couple of dollars I was stripped of my sales license because I did a bad thing I criticized my corporation and now I cannot earn a living and I am desperate you see because I lost my husband and my children are hungry and they walk around with no shoes and I have apologized but they still won't reissue my license and I don't know what to do and I beg you madam please spare me a couple of dollars or some change since I am ruined oh madam please they abridged my free speech and have cast me as the fool of the street the clown of the town I am an imbecile a scoundrel I stole the money from my daughter's stash she had hidden it in a flashlight battery compartment and I stole it swiped it like the filthy common thief I am and bought drugs with it and indulged in Cinnamon and my life is a dismal mess I am no good but can you spare me a dollar or two I have no place to go and I'm feeling sick bilious and I don't know what to do with myself and . . ."

Annie felt sorry for the young hag and wanted to help her. "If I give you money," said Annie, "how do I know you won't march right out and buy more drugs?"

"Oh thank you God thank you madam I promise I won't buy drugs I am high enough please forgive me God thank you . . ."

So, the passionate Annie reached into her purse, took out a twenty dollar bill and handed it to her. She wished her better times and the poor wretch continued to talk, even as Annie got up from the bench and walked away. Annie fretted about the homeless population that had swelled so strongly over the past two decades, which happened to be most of her young life.

This park has always been such a wholesome place to hang out, Annie thought. If this place goes bad, then you know this economy has failed us. Failed the human race. But am I the only one to question this dichotomous financial state where some are so rich and others so poor? Anytime you have to keep in check your views about such a dysfunctional arrangement, there exists at least a strand of authoritarian rule. Oh, my, are we fascist? There are too many sad characters like that girl not to question the American system.

Annie wiped a tear from her sunburnt face and went home.

57

THE HENSONS GO TO HOLLYWOOD

ONE KNEW that autumn was about to set in. Even on the warm days, the heat was just not as penetrating as summer heat. A slight chill lingered. Maybe it was the lack of humidity. The sun shone brightly enough, but a few floating leaves released their hold on the trees and let the population know that cold weather was near. Dormancy was at hand.

The Henson family had just returned from their last vacation before the back-to-school days commenced. They had visited The Museum of Television Commercials in old Hollywood, California.

There they viewed The World's Funniest Commercials booth and The Oddball Commercials Auditorium and the special History of Commercials section that showed TV ads since 2040, the beginning of time. When the pesky movie clips would embark on their intrusive displays, the Hensons dutifully went up front to get popcorn and root beer and other edible delights.

But now they were home and the kids had started school. Herb resumed his job as a fourth-grade teacher and Holly reopened her Kiddie Kare daycare center, which proved quite lucrative for the all-in capitalist family. Both adults recalled

those halcyon days when they attended school back in the
2070s. Now they barely had time to play, though they did
manage to call for one of the fifty-four types of Oligarchy
games.

There was, of course, Oligarchy for Children, Oligarchy for
Entrepreneurial Upstarts, Oligarchy for Sporting Venues (golf
was the only surviving sport), Oligarchy for Grocers, and
Oligarchy for Factories among many others.

Though the real fun was over, the Hensons could antici-
pate next year's planned vacation to The Museum of Window
Shopping down in lovely Naples, Florida.

58

SLAPPING THE DUCK

CHAD SCANDALMAN MADE his fortune by dealing shrewdly.

He was a no-nonsense, skilled negotiator of the highest rank. He could battle it out with the best.

His only weaknesses were food and masturbation.

As soon as Scandalman closed the deal with any business, he would lock his office door, grab the lubricant from his briefcase, crawl under his desk and masturbate, often so furiously that the knick-knacks on his polished desktop would shake and move until they fell off the edge and onto the carpeted floor.

PLUNK-ETY-DUNK they would go like the fictional lemmings off a cliff. And just as the excitement peaked, he would have to stuff his handkerchief in his mouth with his free hand so as to muffle his guttural vociferations. Upon his completion, about the time the grunting had wound down, he removed the cloth from his mouth and began wiping himself clean.

Those wild business dealings always piloted a wave of delirium from his mind to his midsection. He could sign a contract to supply a small chain of grocery stores, or ship flakes with a new carrier and he would have to urgently pleasure himself. Sometimes he would go number two and then mastur-bate. But any kind of business excitement always launched some kind of banned sexual urge in the poor man.

On those really edgy days he would fondle his meat over anything, even a mild stimulus like a business call on his implanted intelli-phone or an encounter with a peddler of magazines at the front-office entrance. His wife, Gertrude Scandalman, grew weary with all of the stiff hand towels and handkerchiefs she had to wash. She also harbored some little bit of resentment that Chad did not involve her in his antics.

Chad jacked himself so often during these ultra-stimulated episodes that his prostate gland began to ache. The poor thing was simply overworked. These kinds of emergency masturba-tion sessions, he supposed, arrested his full development into the foremost business figure to which he aspired, but he knew not how to stop them.

59

ISABELLA BLAKE'S FLAKES
GAINING MARKET SHARE

ABOUT THE FIRST week in September 2098, a third competitor entered the flake arena.

The two foremost flake czars had spent so much time battling amongst themselves that they hardly noticed. The tertiary player was the Blake Flakes Company run by Isabella Blake, a whirlwind up-and-comer both of glitz and substance, a flamboyant African American queen who had the jewels.

Her corporation had existed for fifteen years but had just made its first big splash into recognition by introducing "Sun-Baked Flakes" in a market dominated by male business magnates. Isabella, the CEO and president, loved to soak in the spotlight of the TV world, and, seeing that the public had tired of the bickering of the two major flake firms, seized her opportunity to shine.

She was a one-woman wrecking crew who did all her own marketing, releasing flashy commercials, wearing flashy outfits, and boasting of her flashy logo, a colorful five-point star with BFC in the center. She had unleashed a flurry of television, radio and magazine ads aimed at putting deep dents in the two leading flake firms' armor. Those two giants could no longer ignore the progressive Ms. Blake.

The emerging star, an outspoken entrepreneur, an astute financier, the head dragon of the modern corporate blueprint, was a firm, sometimes brash, go-getter, and her aggressive attitude was out to weave nightmares for GAFC and FAI. Isabella was a scholar and philanthropist. But mostly, she was, as Cliché Bob would have described it, "driven to succeed."

Now the showy "Dynamo of Domino," as one local paper put it, unveiled her most prized physical advertisement, a giant twelve-foot-high fiberglass flake with a smiling face that stood out on the street on US Highway 41 at her corporate headquarters and factory. Road junkies loved the camera-ready showpiece. The whole town embraced the attraction. And the large cable and satellite companies deemed it "The World's Biggest Flake." Not only had BFC eked out a niche in the cereal industry, but Isabella had boldly boasted: "This puts industry leaders on notice: We're coming for you!"

All of this fearless promotion would only rachet-up the stress that already existed in the industry.

Chad Scandalman, already jittery and restive, would advance into aggressive psychopathy. As already demonstrated Mr. Scandalman had definitely secured a slot in the realm of "Capitalist Crazy."

Isabella had American flags painted on her fingernails, a large BFC logo tattooed on her forehead, and rainbow-colored pants suits that hollered out her presence. And Isabella Blake was already rumored to have a scout or two planted in the workforces of the two flake giants, GAFC and FAI. What sneaky parasites the industry had unleashed, and of the spy games too, Isabella was a player. And, it would not be long, now that the two flake giants had taken note of BFC, before some scouts would infiltrate Isabella's workplace as well.

Isabella had a very small marketing department. No Madison Avenue marketing sages here, for she did all her own company commercials with a gleaming smile and a charismatic presence.

Following is a glimpse at the commercial status of the different flake competitors:

2098 Market Share of Flake Companies
<u>Wall Street Report</u>
GAFC had 42 percent of the flake market
FAI had 38 percent of the flake market
BFC had 14 percent of the flake market
The rest had 6 percent of the flake market

True, Blake Flakes Company had a rather small share, but the true indicator of its growth was the trend of the company. Let's look at same table of market share values a year earlier in 2097:

2097 Market Share of Flake Companies
<u>Wall Street Report</u>
GAFC had 47 percent of the flake market
FAI had 38 percent of the flake market
BFC had 6 percent of the flake market
The rest had 9 percent of the flake market

The trend upward for BFC and downward for GAFC had caused such an ugly stir that the CEOs would not talk to each other at future conventions and fairs. Chad Scandalman was, of course, agitated and absurdly restless. Todd Swindell was hopeful, as FAI's market share remained neutral. Isabella Blake was focused and hungry.

The spread of 41 percent between the well-established market leader, GAFC, and the young snapper of a company, BFC, had shrunk to only 28 percent over just one year. Intolerable for Scandalman and favorable for Blake. In fact, Isabella dreamed of the day when she could overtake GAFC and trounce Scandalman's operation. "Pounce and Trounce" Isabella called it.

Those latest market share statistics shattered Scandalman, and he became even more disturbed, unbalanced, with blood on his mind, terror on his hands, and vengeance in his heart. The highest-ranking flake boss felt abused, so he bit his lips, grinded his teeth, and schemed to eviscerate his competitors.

As time moved forward Isabella practically owned the black consumers of cereal, but she figured out the need to dress down, so to speak, and take on a homier and more casual persona. If she expected to gain more market share and overtake the industry leaders, she must appeal to the white cereal eaters. She must go mainstream.

But that is a story for the future.

60

THE LONELY HAIR

DETECTIVE HUNG CHO LEE had recovered one item of evidence from the scene of Syd Waverly's death.

It was a tiny hair, thick and black but without a root. He found it beneath the weekly sales paper on Waverly's front porch. Now he ventured into a hair comparison campaign among Sydney's friends and acquaintances and fellow workers. Mr. Lee knew that without DNA from a root, he could not isolate the culprit but he could eliminate many suspects.

He had the hair analyzed at the police headquarters lab, and they determined it was of Arab or Indian origin. Now his list of suspects shrank to a very manageable size.

The wise detective knew of Twinkle Deshpande and her cousin Anika Patel and their daring careers. But gathering more evidence and finding out where they live would amount to a great challenge.

As for Cliché Bob's terrible death, the brutality of which left a mark on Detective Lee and a number of first responders, was a horrific, grisly scene that stuck in one's mind like a knife in a pumpkin. But Detective Lee had a good idea that the "Capitalist Crazy" Chad Scandalman was a key player in that heinous incident and the ruthless fiend was close to being arrested.

The more Mr. Lee learned of Scandalman, the more abominable his character appeared. The witty detective knew that both Cliché Bob and Chad Scandalman were avid golfers. Golf partners, in fact. He suspected that Bob could only have been beaten with a heavy golf club. The balding trickster, as he would say himself, was "deader than a doornail."

Finally, a counterperson identified Scandalman as a person who had visited the golf course on the day of the murder. Detective Lee just needed more hard evidence.

61

DOMINO GROWS; ZIGGIE SHRINKS

GOLDEN FLAKE CRUMBLE Nut cereal was the first foray by GAFC into mixing candy with cereal.

The flakes were frosted and powdered with sugary speckles. Mothers howled over it, calling it junk food. Free stickers with every box only exacerbated the problem, as mothers whined that their furniture was being ruined by these adhesive labels with different corporate logos.

Anyway, the healthy-flake craze had waned, and a new era had begun. In fact, FAI announced a sugary competitor of its own by the name of Sweet Glazed Flakes. Never outdone, Isabella Blake introduced her Chocolate Sugar-Bomb Flakes.

So, while doctors and fitness gurus griped about an impending new diabetes epidemic, the three major flake companies profited mightily. Meanwhile, Domino roared with business activity; the lights, the bustle, the scurrying people all mirrored the boom times for the once-little town. With two theatres (for commercials only), six motels, and a thriving new airport, Domino grew into the most popular metropolitan destination between Indianapolis and Chicago.

Soon the town became a city. And all the gloomy features of a city followed the hubbub. Shortly thereafter, mini-ghettos formed and crime multiplied. In the seediest of areas housing prices plummeted and poor, single-parent families moved in. The kids ran wild.

The same old story played out just as it did with other prairie boomtowns one, two, and even three hundred years ago. Domino was claiming its spot in the big leagues.

On Maple Street in the central part of town stood Ziggie Wexler's old house. Corporate government officials had sold it along with his car and kept the funds to root out other "evildoers" of Ziggie's caliber.

When Ziggie discovered the confiscation of all his assets, he was, of course, livid. But he was also hurt. Hurt that the capitalists he was supposed to worship had stolen from him. Was he being forced to respect capitalism? Fear capitalism? Worship the all-powerful billionaire class?

Nonsense, he thought. *I will not have it. The capitalist money suckers have raided the vault. I am now naked, stripped down like a tree in a forest fire. Like a whittled stick. Like a stolen car on the shoulder of a New York freeway. The thieving sonsabitches have left me dry. Alone.*

62

MURDERING WITHIN ONE'S OWN COMPANY

THE SERIES of corporate murders plaguing the country also included in-house murders.

For instance, a jealous forklift driver at GAFC slayed his colleague for picking orders faster, shrink-wrapping pallets of product more rapidly, and being all around more attentive to his work tasks.

A disgruntled accounting clerk at FAI killed his boss for hounding him to go faster.

A pissed-off payroll specialist at a steel mill snuffed out a timekeeper for reporting him late.

It seemed that Capitalist Crazy was not just an executive disease, not just an intercompany condition, but also an intra-company illness of diverse origins.

Someone like Ziggie could see the disease spreading through the aisles of the corporations.

Others could not. Swindell saw it but knew not what to do about it. Swindell even knew that he suffered from the disease. Swindell's son, Tory, even had a touch of it, though he had merely labored for two weeks in the corporation.

It was the expectations that affected Tory. The people around him applied pressure on him.

Living in the shadow of his dad's riches and success, boiling beneath the pressure of his dreaded mother. He just wanted to exterminate her, extinguish her wicked flame, and wipe the chalkboard with a wet cloth.

63

SQUIRREL HOLE

IT SEEMED that the combination of capitalism and liberty made for a society of violence.

Prior to the Great Cleanse of 2040 (even though no one was supposed to mention it) and the onset of authoritarian rule, reports of violence saturated the news. At that point social and political scientists were rather sure that strict, rigid living by the rule of law would curtail the abject violence, but the combination of boredom and jealousy further ignited the ferocious propensities of human beings to hurt each other.

Yes, the placement of tough, inflexible rules and regulations curtailed the violence at first, but eventually, it only made the violence more common. That left capitalism alone to absorb all the blame. In a capitalist economic system, what somebody has, somebody else wants, and this envy stews and bubbles, until virulent behavior results. There is always some unthinking rich person flaunting his or her toys among the poor. Enough to cause serious resentment.

Large numbers of capitalist worker bees were buzzing about, trying to ascertain how to swipe wealth and property from the bosses and other people above them. The highest echelon of property owners had almost total protection from the hungry masses in the form of state-of-the-art alarm systems, beefed up security personnel, and isolated country estates.

But the middle layer lacked those protections and had to mingle with the violent worker bees.

Thus, the middle ranks provided padding for the higher ranks, that is, the wealthiest citizens.

So, with the poverty-stricken masses at a touch above 30 percent of the total population now, an almost 20 percent rise over the past 58 years, and the middle-class serving as a buffer for the rich, the top 10 percent of the highest earners amassed untold fortunes, as the calls for a socialist movement mounted.

Where these calls originated the uppermost echelon could not pinpoint, but underground sources like the *Clandestine Journal* were laden with heavy blame and closely monitored. The Journal, the corporate government knew, operated out of New York, Chicago, and Los Angeles. Their presses were constantly on the move from one defunct warehouse to another.

The corporate bigwigs and the authorities who protected them desperately needed to silence this potentially volatile arm of the public, so they began creating more strict controls on the low-income people, specifically, the bottom 30 percent. Tough laws regarding poor people's right to assemble ensued. In addition, a raid was planned for the Chicago printers of the Journal, if they could isolate it, since the Midwest Command of the FBI thought top-ten-most-wanted-list operator, Zigmund Wexler, communicated through the Chicago branch.

But once their latest location was disclosed and after the raid had transpired, they found no information on Ziggie. In fact, to try and throw off corporate government officials, Ziggie sent most of his submissions to the New York office of the *Clandestine Journal*. But most corporate intelligence correctly pointed to Ziggie hanging around Chicago. The corridor between Chicago and Domino, Indiana would be closely scrutinized. But just to piss them off Ziggie quickly sent a short note to the Journal's Chicago office. It read:

The business smile; all capitalists wear it; all phonies share it.

Once the FBI and the cops realized the message had come through the Chicago office of the Journal, they were incensed that this "pesky little rodent" could be so close and get away with it. They redoubled their efforts to dig this agitating derelict out of his ground-squirrel's hole.

64

PLATE OF GOO

WHEN THE GREAT American Flake Company expanded so quickly in the 2060s, tiny Domino, Indiana flourished.

Then, when Flakes Alive Incorporated decided to move a few blocks south of GAFC, the place boomed and Domino grew into a formidable mid-sized city in the northwest portion of the Hoosier State.

Guard shacks and factory gates lined West Industrial Drive in the northern part of Domino. Out of one eight-by-ten foot shack walked Security Guard Paul Adolfo. He followed the red brick sidewalk that led to the offices of the Great American Flake Company. He began his round by plucking a piece of hard candy from a decorated jar on the first desk he saw. He circled around the south side of the building as usual.

Suddenly, brutal terror inundated his mind and body. He stood half-shocked and half-amazed before a display of sheer horror. There, slumped over her desk was marketing specialist, Megan Sally, her deep black hair aglow with the blood that surrounded a gaping hole in the back of her head. Blood had sprayed all over her cubicle and then poured from the mortal wound.

Paul stood frozen, mouth agape. Then, he noticed a note

taped to her arched back. It read: "Ms. Sally has marketed her last flake, schmoozed her last sucker."

The guard read it without touching it, then called 911.

"Megan was a real go-getter," as the salespeople say. She talked practically nonstop, annoying some, persuading others. She had worked at a Madison Avenue marketing firm in New York, before coming to tiny Domino and its surrounding cornfields. Lured by reasonable pay and a quiet country dwelling, she leaped at the chance of owning prime real estate outside a growing city.

She possessed all the tools of an advertising guru and the supervisory skills to lead her crew. But now she lay on a veritable desktop slaughter block, where splattered blood and stringy veinous materials dripped and hung from the inside of the cubicle walls.

"She was better than the best carnival barker," lamented CEO Chad Scandalman in a meeting later on that day.

A few feathers from a pillow that came out of Cliché Bob's old office attached themselves to blood spots. Cops figured the pillow served as a silencer. No gun was found, but it was discovered that the murder weapon was a 9-millimeter handgun.

"She will be sorely missed," said a thoroughly disappointed Scandalman, reminding himself that he must have sounded like Cliché Bob. He wondered whether anyone from Flakes Alive Incorporated had been responsible for the gruesome deed.

"Poor Megan," muttered Scandalman, though all he was really worried about was satisfactorily filling the vacancy left by her. "Who's going to direct our radio and television commercials? Who's going to generate our advertising copy for magazines and newspapers? Woe is us."

Corporal Ivan "Cheeseball" Downey and his partner,

Calvin, were among the first responders to the hideous scene. "Boy," said Cheeseball, "they left us one big plate of goo."

"Yes, they did," said Calvin.

"I think I'd like to stuff an M80 up the culprit's rectum and light him or her up!"

Within two hours after the elimination of his star marketer, Scandalman had been on the phone calling marketing personnel from several other cereal companies to see if they were ready to "take the flake" and become the new marketing top dog for GAFC.

Megan Sally's blood had not completely dried and the shrewd, shameful Scandalman was soliciting the open position. "The wheels of progress must keep turning," Scandalman would say. "No breaks for flakes."

When the rapacious CEO stirred some interest from Warren Thomkins, principal marketing agent for tiny Porter Cereal Company, he nervously, daringly locked his office door —even with all the cops hanging around—scurried to a spot beneath his desk, and promptly whacked himself into orgasmic rapture.

65

PROBING FOR CLUES

DETECTIVE HUNG CHO LEE carefully examined the scene of the heinous murder, uncovering several potential clues, including a fingerprint from the side of the cubicle and a shell casing of a 9-millimeter gun. He gathered what he could and then drove to the offices of Flakes Alive Incorporated to discuss the sudden rash of killings with CEO Todd Swindell.

"First," noted Mr. Lee, "we have the suspicious death of FAI employee, Sydney Waverly, in his own home . . . and then the possible retaliations in the deaths of GAFC's Cliché Bob and Megan Sally." "Now just wait a minute, Mr. Lee," protested FAI CEO, Todd Swindell, "you're not insinuating somebody from this company committed such a brutal crime as the Cliché Bob murder . . . and then Megan—what's her name —S-Sally's murder, are you?" The skinny CEO was irate. "If so, I think this is a matter for one of our corporate lawyers, sir!"

"Such a hasty lawyering-up would result in a poor reflection on you and your company, Mr. Swindell, don't you think?"

"Look here," said the frustrated CEO, "we at Flakes Alive have nothing to hide, Mr. Lee. Now, what can I do to assist you in your investigation?" Swindell pulled up on the suspenders that held up the pants around his skinny ass and twitched. He had a very thin body and beady little eyes. "Perhaps you would like a tour of our manufacturing facilities?"

Detective Lee stared at Swindell for a moment then began to look around his office. A golf trophy stood high on a table, the statuette in full swing with a driver in gold. Family photos flanked the golf trophy. A large plant occupied a spot next to a window. Mr. Lee stood up and looked outside, where a fountain stood among some park benches and a few trees.

"I will call you if I have any further questions," said Detective Lee, as he moved toward the door.

"I will escort you out," said Mr. Swindell.

"Just one more thing, Mr. Swindell."

"Shoot."

"Did you know of Ms. Sally before today?"

"I knew of her, Mr. Lee. And my marketing staff knows her work. You see, marketing is quite the competitive business, sir. In fact, it is the very heart and soul of our flake business."

"I should like to talk with your lead marketing person, Mr. Swindell."

Todd Swindell glanced up at his fly guts trophy. It seemed to hint that cooperation was in order at this point.

"Perhaps I can arrange that Mr. Lee. Give me a call. HR may want to sit in on this." Todd Swindell handed Detective Lee his business card as they headed toward the exit.

66

GREED IS THE SEED

HUNG CHO LEE'S first interview with Alicia Gomez of FAI went swimmingly for both parties.

No surprises surfaced from their discussion until Alicia informed the detective that the lead marketing engineer, Lucinda Talbot, harbored a special hatred toward Megan Sally. In fact, the two had been quite envious of each other's work.

"Did Lucinda and Megan know each other very well?" asked Detective Lee.

"I'm not sure," Alicia responded. "But I do know that Lucinda sent one of our corporate scouts to check out Megan."

"She sent a spy?" asked a now amped-up Detective Lee. "Well, we like to refer to them as 'scouts.'"

"Who was the scout and what did he or she find?" asked Lee.

"You would have to talk to Lucinda about that, Detective," said Alicia. "I think it had something to do with GAFC's new marketing slogan."

Ten minutes later, Lee had pulled Lucinda Talbot into a small conference room. "That lying bitch!" exclaimed Lucinda, as she turned her head in astonishment.

"How so?" he asked.

"She was the one that hated Megan Sally, not me!" emphatically claimed Lucinda. "You see, Alicia is one of those desperate people who would do anything to get ahead. She wanted a promotion, so she asked for a scout to be sent to GAFC to garner intelligence. That's how we learned that GAFC was working on a new slogan. Alicia's scout told us."

"So you harbored no ill will toward Megan Sally?" asked the detective.

"Well, I mean, I would have loved to know what she knew, but that's part of the business competition. But I certainly wouldn't *kill* her. God almighty no!"

"What else can you tell me about Alicia Gomez?"

"How 'bout that she shared a boyfriend with Megan Sally?"

"Oh," responded Detective Lee, "now this is getting really intriguing."

"Yeah," said Lucinda. "Alicia tried to get him to tell her the new slogan. But he claimed that Megan would not divulge that information."

"So, Alicia never got her promotion?"

"No. Well, she might have earned some Brownie points by informing management that GAFC had a new slogan, but that's it. She didn't actually know what the slogan would be."

"Who is the double-agent boyfriend?" inquired the detective.

"Donald. That's all I know him by. He's an independent marketing agent."

With that information, Lee thanked Lucinda, then drove back to GAFC's headquarters. He browsed through Megan Sally's notebook and found the phone number of Donald Noble. From Donald he learned that Alicia owned a 9-millimeter pistol. He also learned that Alicia wanted to "hurt" Megan Sally.

Now he had enough to arrest Alicia Gomez, but he decided to wait for more corroborating evidence. Meanwhile, Detective Lee obtained a warrant to search Alicia's house. There they found a 9-millimeter pistol.

The gun, the incriminating remarks all pointed to Alicia Gomez. Later, the ballistics test matched the slug found in Megan's head to Alicia's gun.

Lee decided that he must arrest Alicia and find evidence that either Flakes Alive Incorporated ordered the hit on Megan or that it was simply a personal rift that motivated Ms. Gomez. He supposed the enmity between the two peers could have caused Ms. Gomez to slide into the world of Capitalist Crazy.

67

ON THE RUN AGAIN

ZIGMUND WEXLER RECEIVED a special treat on Halloween, 2098. His employer, Alfi of the Underground Workshop, called him into a cavernous room in the back of the big shop and spun for him the 1966 Beatles classic album, *Revolver*, purported to be the greatest rock album of all time by many critics. Alfi handed him a joint and played the record. Ziggie was mostly delighted, though a few of the most psychedelic strands he did not totally understand.

"I knew I had heard of these Beatles somewhere before!" he nervously exclaimed. "What right did the bastards have to conceal one of art's true gems?"

"My great-grandpa buried this copy on our property," said Alfi. "We dug it up last year, along with several other rock masterpieces. Isn't it wonderful? Oh, just wait till you hear it a couple times."

But just as the B-side had begun, someone rang the bell of the closed shop. Alfi lifted the needle from the record and instructed Ziggie to keep quiet. Alfi then closed and locked the door to the room and went up front. He saw two police officers at the front door.

Unlocking the door and opening it, Alfi said, "Can I help you?"

"Yes, this is Officer Hertz, and I am Captain McElvy. We were wondering, have you seen this man in the neighborhood?" Doris McElvy showed Alfi a photo of Ziggie. He had short hair and a well-shaved, clean-cut look, but Alfi saw that it was Ziggie right away.

"No, I don't recognize him," said the jittery store owner, concerned that the cops might take notice of his nervousness.

Captain McElvy stared at Alfi for a moment, then said, "Well, if you see this rascal, he is wanted for defacing a corporate logo and disparaging a corporate entity."

"I'll sure keep an eye peeled for him," assured Alfi.

"We'd appreciate that, sir. We'll check back with you. Good day."

As soon as the cops dismissed themselves, Alfi ran to the back of the store and notified Ziggie that a rapid departure must occur. "I think the cops were suspicious," said Alfi, "on account of my being so nervous and all."

"I'll be gone in five minutes," assured Ziggie.

"Listen," said Alfi, "I've got a friend in Newton County, Indiana. He helps out those who go against the system. His name is Ned Pagorski. He used to work in the steel mill in Gary and you can totally trust him." Alfi wrote down the directions to Ned's ranch and handed the paper to Ziggie.

So, Ziggie packed his clothes and toiletries, accepted some cash for his last week of work, and showed himself out the back door of the boutique.

68

SCANDALMAN GOES BYE-BYE

CHAD SCANDALMAN, the corpulent CEO of the Great American Flakes Company, leaned over the deluxe pool table (an abolished sport) and shot the cueball at the eightball, which ricocheted off the side and found its way to the corner pocket.

The arrogant business mogul, seized by delusions of grandeur, then gathered all the balls and arranged them in the triangle for another game with himself. As he lifted the triangle, a sudden shot to his head caused him to drop like a misplaced pallet of concrete blocks. A dark figure dashed from the scene, ran upstairs, and presumably let his-or-herself out.

When word leaked, everyone feared The Flake Wars had graduated to the snuffing out of CEOs.

Hung Cho Lee leaped into action, dusting for fingerprints, checking for DNA, sending the bullet for ballistics testing. Could Flakes Alive Incorporated have fought back? he asked himself. Could this be retaliation for the Syd Waverly killing? Could this be the culmination of the twenty-two-year-old Flake Wars? Is there yet more to come? They cannot go any higher nor stoop any lower.

Several cops were put in charge of the upstairs. A couple had ventured down to the basement.

One of them was Corporal Ivan "Cheeseball" Downey and his partner, Calvin. Cheeseball shook his head upon viewing the bloody crime scene. "For killing a CEO," he explained, "the punishment should be public disembowelment on a Tilt-a-Whirl."

"A Tilt-a-Whirl? What the hell?" said Calvin. "And don't you think that disembowelment is kind of barbaric? And what's the purpose of the carnival ride?"

"Well, a Tilt-a-Whirl is brought to the public square. The offender is strapped into one of the seats. The Slicer, a special device for slitting, opens the abdomen, then allows the guts to flow out. When the intestines are fully exposed, the Tilt-a-Whirl is turned on. Now the intestines are pitted against gravity, and, therefore, move in every direction as the machine tilts this way and that. Once the person passes out from the excruciating pain, he or she is awoken with smelling salts. This keeps on till the guilty one perishes. Then the prisoner's heart and lungs are cut out. Starved pigs are then allowed to board the Tilt-a-Whirl and feast upon the remains."

"Cheeseball," said Calvin, "that is gross and unnecessary."

"Oh yes, that will appear in the book I'm going to write when I retire: *Tortures by 'Cheeseball.'*"

"How'd you ever get to be a cop?"

Detective Lee questioned Chad's wife, Maureen Gertrude Scandalman, who had been sleeping upstairs. "I was startled awake by the blast," she reported. "I got up and ran downstairs, but before I could find out what had just occurred, a strange, dark figure bolted out of the front entrance. Oh, Mr. Lee, do you think poor Chad felt anything?" A quivering Mrs. Scandalman sobbed openly.

"No," said Lee, "death was almost certainly instantaneous, my dear Mrs. Scandalman. Do you have a place to stay for the evening?"

"Why, yes, I could stay with my daughter, Christina." Gertrude showed Detective Lee a picture of Chad when his face was intact. "He was such a grand leader, a fair boss," she cried. "Who could do such a thing?"

Lee fell into intense thought: First, FAI chemist Syd Waverly; then, GAFC frontman, "Cliché" Bob; then GAFC marketing lead, Megan Sally; and now GAFC CEO Chad Scandalman. Could FAI have done a three-for-one deal?

Hmmm, we will see.

69

WILDEBEEST BURGERS

IN THE NEW Capitalist America (NCA), individuals could not sue businesses.

The courts were instead tied up with corporate transgressions against other corporations, individual crimes against corporations, corporate intrusions, and corporate nuisances. But complainant John Doe always lost, since he no longer held power to take anyone or anything to court. Even for many years before NCA, the little guy had little chance in holding a company accountable, for John Doe against the great corporation almost always went to the mighty corporation.

For example, the Cuckoo Cola Nut Company (CCNC) offered consumers a "supercharged" cola drink with 400mg of caffeine and a sprinkle of methamphetamine. It seemed that Grandma Sloakum ingested two bottles of the wicked stuff, went crazy, and shot up seven family members with an AR270, relative of the ancient AR15.

Poor old Walter Sloakum, one of the grandsons and the only one to survive the slaughter, attempted to sue the cola corporation for malpractice and was almost immediately shot down by a fervid Judge Markham for being a nuisance to the company. The charges were laughingly dismissed. The entire courtroom guffawed at the hapless, disfigured plaintiff before he could exit the building.

Walter Sloakum cringed as he heard the verdict and the last stinging words of "Jolly" Judge Markham: "The moral of the story is 'Don't meth around with Cuckoo Cola Nut Company.'"

In another rude example, the Gougemore Oil Corporation (GOC) commonly blended nitrogen with its gasoline to give cars more pep in helping them reach the 100 mph speed limit. But Scott G. Winfield was blown to smithereens when his Hondo Rocket was rear-ended by a panel truck. The volatile fuel mixture instantly turned the car into an inferno and its driver into charcoal.

The Honorably Ornery Judge Campos III awarded Winfield's wife, Jenna, one penny and issued the following advice: "The Gougemore Oil Corporation relieved you of the expense of cremating your husband, Mrs. Winfield. Be thankful!"

Even a class action lawsuit could not penetrate the corporate armor. A massive suit brought by over two million parties against hamburger giant, Bold Burger, claimed that the sandwich meat used by the company was none other than wildebeest meat! And the doomed plaintiffs proved their case by tracking backwards the meat supply of the company—straight back to Africa.

To fight the suit the audacious company did not deny the claim, but instead, brought in a sample for the fiery judge to try. His Honor daintily lifted the sample to his thin lips, tasted it, and chewed on it ravenously. "Mmmm," he attested, "delightful." Then he banged his gavel and proclaimed, "Let us feast on wildebeest!"

The little guy just had no chance. And now, with the program of the NCA in place, none of these cases would even make it to court.

70

EUREKA ANIKA!

UPON ENTERING ANY CORPORATE BUILDING, one's DNA was taken and instantly uploaded into a mainframe system with a massive database that was monitored by agents working under The Big Seven.

Detective Lee had scoured the grocery store aisle where Archibald Stevens' life had been terminated and picked up a few specks of evidence. They all but one tested negative for human DNA. The one exception was a speck of glitter, which yielded a trace amount of DNA. It was Anika Patel's DNA!

It seems that the Indian American executioner had attended a birthday party for an FAI employee the morning of the assassination, where glitter had been used by some of the participants as a fashion statement, and, although Anika did not partake, one lonely piece of glitter had found its way to Anika's scalp.

That one speck fell off at the crime scene when Anika bumped into Archibald, and the modern, highly sensitive, instant DNA-detecting device used by Detective Lee registered the find. The cops had Anika's DNA on file, since they had started to collect the DNA from every baby in 2070, and Anika was born in 2074. Coupled with intelli-phone data that placed Anika at or near the scene and a one-time payment to Anika by FAI of $50,000, the evidence exposed the nefarious plot.

Detective Lee needed only to find Anika. She floated around the Chicago area, changing residences about every three or four weeks, renting out a cabin here or there, but mostly staying in different motel rooms. One month she would stay at the Palomino Motel off of I-294 and the next month she would stay at the Golden Nugget on I-80.

But she did not yet know they had discovered her DNA on a particle of glitter. She only knew that in her business one must stay on the move. Her father's motel rooms had become too risky and her man friend, Deepak, had already had his apartment searched once.

Deepak warned Anika to hide out at some remote place. He advised her to change her name, cut her hair, and live with him in some rural setting. He had a sexual attraction to the beautiful Indian maiden, but Anika dared not allow him to pursue such a relationship.

71

A SPLINTER OF HOPE

ZIGGIE WEXLER STOOD in front of the 95th Street bus station in South Chicago with a coffee can and a small sign that read: "Need money for bus ticket."

He intended to take a bus to Peoria, Illinois and start out fresh. He knew he was taking a huge risk of getting caught, but he had spent the money he had withdrawn from the Domino National Bank when he first left home, and he had used up his last cash payment for working at Alfi's Underground Workshop. In addition to that the government had frozen his assets, so he could not cash out his 401(k) plan.

So far, with a most woeful expression and dingy clothes, Ziggie had collected a bunch of pennies and a few clad coins. But just as he was about to surrender his can of change to the local bank, Isabella Blake, the flake up-and-comer, walked up and gave the tattered fugitive three twenty-dollar bills. Ziggie turned ecstatic and emphatically thanked the cereal company executive, whom he had never before met.

"Why so glum?" asked Isabella.

"I'm on the run," said Ziggie, feeling that he could trust the generous donor.

"Uh-oh, for what?"

"For disparaging a corporate logo tattoo." He rolled up his sleeve and pointed to the tiger design on his forearm.

"Oh my," said a surprised Isabella. "You would think that the law would have something better to do than chase down people who have altered their skin designs."

"I'm also an outspoken critic of our corporate government structure and our unfair economy," admitted Ziggie.

"Well," said Isabella, "I certainly cannot complain, as my situation is pretty good, but, on the other hand, we should all have a right to complain if we see fit." She studied Ziggie's tired eyes with pity. "You might want to keep your ideas to yourself, though. You know, to stay out of trouble."

"You know, there was once a thing called 'free speech,'" noted Ziggie.

"Is that right?" Isabella said. Then, she admitted, "Well, yes, I have seen hints that there was such a policy back in the day."

"Yes, you can read about it at the museum here in Chicago. They posted the old Constitution, though parts are heavily redacted, including the date it was signed. It was the First Amendment—the very *first*, mind you—that gave the right of free speech."

"I'll have to go there one day," said Isabella. "Tell me, where are you going, sir, if you don't mind me asking."

"Well, I've been thinking about Peoria as a destination. But I may wind up in Newton County, Indiana. I'm not sure yet."

"Instead of Peoria, why don't you try the northside of Chicago? I have a friend up there who might be able to help you." Isabella looked at the forlorn Ziggie with earnest concern. "He hires people down on their luck. He pays cash, so they won't be able to track you."

"Hmm, maybe I'll eventually give it a shot." Ziggie sighed,

then added, "I just don't want to stay in Chicago right now, as I think the authorities are on to me."

The exuberant Isabella took out a pen and paper and scribbled down the name and address for Ziggie. She then smiled and wished Ziggie success.

"Thank you so much!" said an encouraged Ziggie. He looked at the piece of paper and it said: "Robert Casey, 17611 Armitage Ave."

72

"DARKMERICA"

IN CONJUNCTION with the FBI and state police, the corporation probed into every citizen's background, phone calls, and internet activity.

But now that 30 percent of the population was homeless and 80 percent of that figure was without a job, keeping track of them had grown quite difficult. Crates were portable, so they had no stationary status, no addresses. Some Crate Camp dwellers did have intelli-phone implants, which assisted the monitoring officials in tracking their whereabouts and activity. Others, born before 2070, did not.

Ziggie's mom and dad had resisted the implants, though his sister, Elizabeth, had allowed it.

Ziggie's parents spoke little of the control the government had exercised over the years, though they did occasionally talk about their parents—Ziggie's grandfathers and grandmothers— and their lives before The Great Cleanse. Ziggie's grandfather on his dad's side did curse the stringent rules of the government on occasion, but Ziggie's dad used to caution him against doing so.

Somehow this planted a seed of resistance in Ziggie's soul. Meanwhile, Elizabeth's obeyance to authoritative capitalism sometimes irked Ziggie. She was an all-American cheerleader in high school and a steadfast government supporter, no matter the capitalist intrusion they condoned.

For resisters, that is, people like Zigmund Wexler, the FBI and other intelligence agencies kept especially meticulous records. In the case of Ziggie, they'd watched him since he was a third grader, drawing pictures of women and men shedding their skins to become newly enlightened people, political criminals breaking out of jails and mental institutions, and baseball players hitting, tossing, and fielding their way to stardom.

In a high school art class, he drew some of his most outrageous, rebellious work. And he was closely monitored by both high school officials and law enforcement. His high school counselor worried obsessively about his future. These were all indications that his wayward activities might mar his reputation for all time. They were warning signs that Ziggie might stray from good-living principles and even dip his young toes into criminal waters. More transgressions would surely follow, authorities thought, and they did.

When Ziggie was thirteen, signs of his sexual inclinations roused his watchers into hauling the young man in for a lecture on the no-no's of sex. At that point they put him on anti-sex meds.

At sixteen, Ziggie wrote a high school essay on "The Dark Side of the Dollar." A fine money-hoarding critique it was, until his teacher gave a copy to his watchers in the FBI. Other papers he wrote touched on how to think independently, how to shun the usual lifestyles, and how to be a maverick. By the twelfth grade, to avoid the pestering of the FBI, and schoolteachers and parents, he learned to keep his unorthodox ideologies to himself. He refused to succumb to the hounding of the liberty thieves.

The whole experience of being prodded and probed was

like holding a lap cat that was nervously flexing its nails through your pants and in and out of your skin. Enervating. They were blithering, impotent custodians at best.

Everything in this society is a lie, thought Ziggie, as he grew up to despise authoritarianism and despots. *The constantly "robust economy" is a lie, overlooking the fact that 30 percent of us live in crates of poverty. Passion without sex is a huge lie. It's all lies upon lies, overlapping even more desperate lies.*

How do we escape this lie trap? Ziggie had been wondering about this for the last few decades.

Ziggie continued to roll thoughts around in his head. *Bone-chilling capitalists with frozen personalities, ice cubes for eyes, and blizzards in their souls set out to shape everyone into that same cold-clay image. The financiers keep producing and the landfills keep rising. What can halt it? The race to hell seemed unstoppable. They want tight control, tight control on every-thing except the slop we leave behind. The putrid, rancid waste of capitalism. There was no control on that.*

Oh, Mother Earth, what have we done to you? Raped, sodomized you, and made you eat the earthlings' toxins. They tell us: build more houses; plant a tree. Build another car; plant a tree. Build a new refrigerator (even though you do not need one); plant a tree. The money grippers will make it right. Well, the money grippers have not made it right. They leave debris wher-ever they trod.

It is known, thought Ziggie, *that America dropped into darkness in 2025, but one is forbidden to speak or write of it.*

And Ziggie was right, for it was such a foul and odious fool who delivered the darkness that the shapers of the 2040 Plan had to leave him behind even though he laid some of the groundwork for the present system. They buried his tainted legacy along with that of slavery, the Vietnam War catastrophe, and the illegal invasion of Iraq. They had erased the littered chalkboard and could start all over again.

Then they applied strict control over the people, discarding liberties of old, acting like they never existed. "The people wanted it," they said in private chambers. "They needed it," said the overzealous capitalists who had corralled the masses for the purpose of applying strict rules for society and stripping away leisure activities so that all could concentrate on advancing the corporations.

And, though no one dare reference it, they all knew that 2025 marked the end of true, unthwarted liberty. There had been hints of fascism leading up to the moment, but in 2025 the official building of the foundation for total control began. From there it took fifteen years to hash out the 2040 Plan.

"The people want something to have control over them," noted the corporate government, "since religion has been abolished." And perhaps they were right. People just did not have the spirit to overturn authoritative lies. They just rolled over and played stupid.

Soon, pondered Ziggie, libraries were overhauled. Resistant librarians were arrested and tortured, according to certain credible sources. Mountains of books were burned. The capitalists of 2025 allowed the Christians to write intolerant codes to block freedoms, and, when 2040 arrived, they turned their backs on religion by banning it altogether.

What a bizarre irony: the churches had set the all-time rules, then they themselves were back-stabbed, abolished. Our leaders of the time were void of scruples, and, therefore, their iron hands of doom shattered the republic. At first, you were allowed to worship who you wanted individually, but religious organizations and their tax-free statuses were outlawed. In some cases, religious fanatics had to be liquidated. Then came the mandate that traditional Gods must be abandoned, that only corporate

CEOs could be worshipped. At first, it was dead CEOs. Then it became all CEOs. This polytheistic paganism scrapped the religion of old.

A distraught Ziggie ruminated on America's fate. America has disappeared, he thought. They shouldn't even call it "America" anymore. Perhaps "Darkmerica" would be a name more fitting.

73

ISOLATION BINS

THOSE CITIZENS DEEMED "void of entrepreneurial zeal," that is, not good capitalists, were compelled to enter concentration camps, mostly out in the desert wasteland. Perhaps one was deemed to have a "lackadaisical business-promoting attitude," or a "lazy sense of commerce," or a "weak eye for trade and bargaining," or maybe one was considered to be a "dolt in dealing,"—they too would have to spend time at a concentration camp.

And should a person espouse admiration for any form of socialism, he or she would be shipped to isolation bins built inside concentration camps. These isolation bins were so removed from humankind that severe loneliness overcame most captives within a matter of weeks and led to unrecoverable depression, which often led to death. The only human contact was seeing a hand leave a tray of food through a tiny-hinged door two times a day, outside the cell but within reach.

Finally, those caught in conspiring to spread concepts in socialism were and are still put to death.

This deranged concept had its origin in the mind of Ghant Wackersham, America's last president.

On the reverse side of the coin, citizens who exhibited enough vigor to please the corporations fell into a miserable lot as well, for they suffered from company attitudes toward workers that lacked in vitality.

Having tossed employee loyalty in the shitcan several decades ago, upper GAFC management now proposed to bring it back. This royal joke was an attempt to rebound from the Cliché Bob betrayal and the ensuing loss of confidence of the stockholders, who began selling GAFC stocks and buying safer bonds.

Faithful employees like Annie De Luca were gobsmacked by the idea of renewed loyalty, though few trusted the corporation to follow through with the declaration of this renewed loyalty.

74

THE PATH TO CEO

LIKE THE SIGNS that used to say, "Support Your Local Sheriff," the newer version of such said, "Worship Your Local CEO." They sat along highways, at entrances into the different towns, and, of course, in the factories and offices of corporations. The chief executive officer and the corporation itself demanded your reverence.

In fact, your employer, a great corporation, as they all are, demanded that you attend services— not during working hours —in the auditorium or cafeteria to worship the CEOs, present and past, three times a week. The corporation also required employees to wear the mission statement on the back of your corporate-issued blouse or shirt.

A mother explained the position of CEO to her child at a local restaurant. "But, mom, CEOs can't be Gods. They're too flawed."

"Those flaws are there to teach lessons to the common folks, son."

"My CEO at the newspaper (Billy cleaned floors after school) is a good guy, but they say he's a drunkard."

"Don't believe hearsay."

"But I thought you can't see God?"

"God manifests himself through many and various means. The body of the CEO may serve as a mere vessel for God to occupy."

"But, mom, how do you become a CEO?"

"You have to pay your dues making commercials before you can be a CEO."

"Yes, I know."

"Son, mercantilism has to be ingrained in your mind."

"But how do you get in commercials?"

"Your Uncle Thad spent ten years in retail and ten years in manufacturing. Then he earned a college degree in film and video. He also earned a degree in business management. Top of his class. Then he worked ten years in commercials to become a CEO. Oh, he made some dillies. He played in a shampoo commercial, a couple of fast food commercials, a furniture store commercial, he's seen it all."

In fact, Billy's Uncle Thad had just wound up one of the biggest benefit-slashing undertakings of all time, as CEO of Brandon Machine Company. In response, many other companies had instituted several of the same cutbacks. "Austerity" the mills and factories called it. Following is one company's New Plan for the Year 2100:

- No laughing on the job.
- Breaks cut from fifteen minutes to five minutes.
- Reintroduce the six-day work week.
- No more two-week vacations.
- Cut in hourly pay, Phase 1: fifty cents per hour. Phase 2: one dollar per hour.
- Deduction of thirty dollars per check for Corporate Welfare Donation (fund to help curb effect of last recession).
- No more corporate-sponsored parties.

- No day off on your birthday.
- Twenty minutes for lunch.

If these cuts and new rules did not piss off a few workers, the government cuts would surely do so. And when the recession ended and America crept back into prosperity, the corporations gave none of it back to the workers.

———

Editorial rejected by *The Domino Times:*

No one saw a reason for it. The corporations were doing swell. A trimmed down workforce had rendered the offices and factories of this great nation lean and ripe for profit taking. A robust business cycle had commenced. Yet the companies and the government cried from the rafters, "Austerity!"

What few benefits had been spared to workers must now endure more cuts. Road and bridge repairs must also welcome the knife. Rising wages must be curtailed. Social welfare programs sliced. All excess drained away. Everything cropped except executive bonuses.

Then, once the corporate government had milked the workforce for all its worth, they commenced upon a "Law and Order" campaign. True, such muscular declarations had bolstered every politician's quest for office since the beginning of politics itself, but this time nobody was running. Most of the government was appointed these days, and this dire announcement came between appointments. So, the corporate government flexed its biceps and the helpless populace cringed, the days inching by in languid waves.

Corporations and the government have always been fused at the hip, but now the two have been absorbed into each other. By some sort of weird, dual osmosis, one took on the character of the other, and the two blended into one obscene monster. Now corporations officially rule the people. A piece of paper, an intangible entity, an invisible, hideous giant tells you when to eat, sleep, and render your services to the world. You must not curse it, bend it, nor feed it falsehoods of any manner. Just act in accordance with its dominion.

    —Anonymous

Not only did the subservient editorial staff reject it, but they turned it in to the corporate government with a description of the person who dropped it off. The description of the crafty messenger matched that of the notorious Zigmund Wexler.

75

DIFFERENT TASTES

"CEO GODS BLESS AMERICA!" exclaimed Herb Henson. "May the corporations never die!"

"What's all the celebrating about, dad?" inquired young Herb.

"It's the blessing of a new martyr, son. CEO Chad Scandalman of the Great American Flakes Company has passed away."

"So, what did he do that's so great?" asked Herb Jr.

"Why, he practically invented America's favorite breakfast flake. He's an all-American Hero!"

"Big deal," shrugged an unimpressed young Herb.

"What do you mean, 'big deal,' Herb Jr.?" remarked Holly Henson.

"He used to be on commercials," said older brother, Nolan. "That's how he got to be a CEO."

"So what?" cried Herb Jr.

"Well," spoke Herb Sr., "that's a marvelous achievement."

"Whoopee-do," said Herb Jr., with a major streak of sarcasm.

"How would you like to go to bed without dinner, young mister?" barked Holly.

"Smokin' flake farts, mom!" protested Herb Jr. "You wouldn't do that, now, would you?"

"I certainly would, if you don't find some respect soon," Holly warned. "This poor attitude you have toward American heroes is pressing on my nerves."

"Sorry," said Herb Jr. in a very perfunctory manner.

"Well then, kids," said Herb Sr., wanting to change the subject. "What do you say, let's talk about next summer's trip to The TV Commercial Hall of Fame."

"You know," admitted Herb Jr., "I don't get off on those commercials like you guys do."

"What do you mean, 'get off?'" demanded Holly. "That sounds like a drug high or something. Oh, Herb, what are we going to do with Herb Jr. He's making me nervous!"

"See what you did now?" reprimanded Herb. "You made your mom cry! Here, here, dear," he said to Holly, while patting her on the shoulder. "He'll be good now, won't you, Herb Jr.?"

"I'll be good."

Holly then pulled Herb Sr. off to the side. She whispered, "We need to get little Herb some help before he gets himself into trouble by questioning more prominent entities, like our wonderful corporate government."

"Now don't you fret, dear," said Herb. "I'll think of something."

76

PRIME REAL ESTATE

HERB AND HOLLY HENSON entered The Baby Factory, where the women who were artificially inseminated could unload their burden. The two companions were to be assigned their sixth child on this blessed day, October 11, 2098.

A big sign with raised letters at the entrance read: "You Know What They Say About Money? Money: The Seed of All Joy."

"As you know, folks," said a tall, gaunt figure of a man, "sex and religion only interfere with the great capitalist endeavors. That is why we are proud to present you with Horatio, your sixth child via artificial insemination."

Holly loved and kissed the infant, then set him in a baby buggy furnished by The Baby Factory.

Lots of blue and red inks imbued the child's skin. Little Horatio resembled a baby pirate.

"Oh, we're really excited about it," assured Holly. "Do we still get a tour of the facilities?"

"Why, yes, of course. Just follow me. By the way, my name is Albert." The lanky man bowed slightly, then ushered the happy family around the corner to the main part of the plant. "Room A100 is where the women give birth. We won't disturb them. And Room B100 is Circumcision Services. And upon completion of the circumcision, the child is immediately tattooed in Building C right over here."

A conveyor with baby beds strapped into place and babies also strapped into each bed moved slowly down the line.

"The babies themselves are beforehand administered a soporific concoction so that they will not move during the application of the laser tattoos. When the conveyor stops beneath the laser gun, the design is almost instantly burned into the skin. The quick action of the laser and the soporific effect of the medication combine to minimize discomfort to the infant.

"The different stations, or stops, on the conveyor allow for the application of the laser on different areas of the body. So, there are numerous stops, including one for the forehead (prime real estate), two for the cheeks, one for the chin, two for the neck, etc. Finally, a vitamin E salve is applied by an electronic swabber device to help with inflammation and healing."

Albert continued: "First, the forehead tattoo, which is awarded to the Primary Corporation of the parents' choice. Then the cheeks are tattooed for the Secondary Corporation, and then, the chin is tattooed for the Tertiary Corporation. All chosen by you! Little Horatio underwent this procedure yesterday, as you can see. Then we have the add-ons to forearms, biceps, thighs and ankles."

"Marvelous colors!" exclaimed Holly. "And the designs seem to be healing nicely."

"Yes, these coloring lasers are designed by the Brazier Laser Company out of New York. And, again, as you see, we like to work rapidly to minimize discomfort."

"That's very thoughtful," noted Herb Henson.

The babies rolled down the conveyor like boxes of flakes on a GAFC assembly line. Different colors of babies and tattoos. According to descriptions on the line, the lighter-skinned babies would receive a higher stipend, since the skin designs stood out more on white flesh. Many claimed that that was an extension of racial bias from past times, but corporate government officials denied it.

"It's a matter of visibility," explained Albert, as the babies rolled off the line into a healing room. "Of course," he added, "multiple bids come in for each newborn. The parents can either select the highest corporate bid or choose one of their own favorites. That, you've already done. The corporation that wins gets to place its name on the birth certificate, any life insurance policies, or other such contracts, besides having their beautiful corporate colors imbedded into the skin.

"Both a lump sum and a monthly stipend will be paid to the parents promptly, the monthly payments extending until the child reaches age eighteen, at which time the payment goes to the child him-or-herself for the rest of its life, unless, for one, the child commits a misdemeanor, in which case the monthly stipend is reduced by a fractional amount to be decided by the courts, or two, the child commits a felony, in which case the monthly stipend is cancelled altogether."

Albert added: "And here is the Brazier Laser Company's pledge: 'With our modern-day tattoo machines, the process is streamlined for the benefit of the baby!'"

77

SAVED BY THE SERVER

CHEESEBALL POINTED his handheld mind-scanning intelli-phone add-on at the woman he thought was the slippery culprit, and it almost instantly detected a lie.

These nifty devices, often referred to as MTDs, or Mind Tracking Devices, simulated an instant polygraph and were, therefore, not entirely accurate and not admissible in court. But also like a polygraph, they could be used to warrant further investigation or clear a suspect. They were a part of every lawperson's intelli-phone implant extension.

"Young lady, you're lying," said Cheeseball, licking his lips then wiping them with the back of his hand.

"I'm not," the girl exclaimed. "I don't even know that guy." Tears began to drip from both eyes, a trick she had learned in assassin school. Not even the best television actors could pull off that stunt.

"So, you're telling me, Elizabeth Atkins, that you have no idea who Archibald Stevens is?" "No idea. That is correct." Of course, Elizabeth Atkins was in reality Anika Patel with fake identification. "What about him?"

"He was murdered," said Cheeseball. "And the main suspect looks like you."

Then, knowing that the officer would scan her head again, she consciously, deliberately voided her mind, another trick she had learned in spy school.

Cheeseball again pointed the mind scanner at her. "Do you swear that you do not know of Archibald Stevens?" he said.

"I swear I do not know of him," said the girl.

This time, it registered nothing. She had successfully thwarted the thing. "Now I'm going to read your DNA with this IDS device," he said.

The first thing to appear on the screen was the following advertisement: "IDS—Instant DNA Sleuth—a portable detector for DNA. Immediately senses and deciphers DNA evidence by touch. The user simply presses the suspect's skin or other surface with the sensor end of the device and they get an instant reading. The device then checks the DNA against the National Database and the screen identifies the person, his or her traits, any "wanted" status, etc. You just make contact with the item and automatically reap the results."

In Anika's case, the device could not read the database. "Server unavailable," read the message on the screen.

"So much for modern technology," remarked Cheeseball. "Alright, you can go. You're damn lucky that the computer is down. But if I see you again, I'll bust you for breathing the wrong way. Now get the hell out of here."

Off Anika went toward the horizon, leaving Cheeseball and his partner, Calvin, to make jokes and talk about the weather.

"Boy," said Cheeseball, "how'd you like to mount that skinny ass?"

Calvin speculated, "It'd be like screwing a praying mantis."

"Well, speaking of small creatures," added Cheeseball, "I once boned an Italian girl who forgot to shave her legs that day. It was like havin' sex with a tarantula."

78

REVERSE RECALL

ZIGGIE PENNED another short but bolder piece for the *Clandestine Journal*, the underground news source for resisters, as follows:

In 2025 America embarked on a tour of authoritarianism. By 2040 the purveyors of this tyranny had managed to implement a wicked plan that mandated that the beginning of time would commence at that point. Everything before 2040 would be erased. All records and documents before that time would be obliterated. Why the corporate sludge did not make 2040 the year 0 or the year 1, no one can know. But the rotten bastards succeeded at instilling fear in the populous by barring mention of pre-2040 events.

They could prohibit discussion of such things but they could not stop memories. Memories are forever, as long as they are passed on. To ban discussion of memories they persuaded people to spy on one another.

The 2040 Plan, as they called it in dark corridors of the United States Capitol, outlawed all criticism of the plan itself and any mention of the multi-pronged freedom that we once enjoyed.

Our mission must be to confiscate the hard-nosed concepts

of The Plan and make ashes of them— at least in our minds. It must start with a degree of resistance and an enlightened attitude toward replacing what has been lost. Let us reverse the process of recall. Let us create realities out of memories instead of the other way around. And if you have never tasted freedom before, that is, if you are too young to have memories of pre-2040, just ask a friend to share. I assure you that the first sample will delight you.

    —ZW

When certain officials in the corporate government learned of the recalcitrant Ziggie's letter, they seethed at the daringness of the direct reference to 2025. He was clearly approaching the Ten Most Wanted List territory top spot. Autocratic-minded capitalists howled and paced circles around the imaginary effigy of Ziggie's existence burning in the breeze.

He became a marked man.

79

AN AFTERNOON ON THE FARM

THE COOL BREEZES of autumn began to nudge their way into Domino and all parts north of Indianapolis. Ziggie wondered where he would go when the ponds froze over and the holiday lights went up. Alfi had told him to see Ned Pagorski and that destination inspired him to go south back into Indiana, but his long-run plans remained in limbo.

"I reckon I'll just hop on one of those boxcars stacked with boxes of flakes and ride it on down to Florida," he mumbled in a low voice, mimicking a cowboy in an old movie he had once heard his grandpa describe.

Cowboys were forbidden in the New America, he knew, as the Old West was well before 2040.

Ziggie, now quite scruffy and unkempt, sat on an old worm fence spitting at pebbles and trying to avoid the splinters that wanted to poke him in the buttocks. He scooped up a small stone and threw it at a bent tin can. A wisp of dust kicked up and just as quickly disappeared in the playful breeze.

"Damn slobs," he whispered, "can't they clean up their own messes?"

Just then a farmer in overalls drove up in a red all-terrain vehicle. "You know yer on private property?" he asked in a matter-of-fact voice.

"No," answered Ziggie, "sorry." He stood up and began to walk slowly toward the road upon which he came. "Didn't mean nothing by it," he said respectfully.

"You lookin' fer work?" asked the burly farmer. Coincidentally, he spoke with the same kind of southwestern accent Ziggie had just mimicked.

Ziggie stopped and turned back toward the farmer. "Yeah," said the unemployed pipefitter, "I can use some work."

"I tell you what," said the farmer, "you gather up the hay bales from this here field, stick 'em in the back of that truck over there, haul 'em to the barn over yonder, and stack 'em neatly inside, and I'll pay you a hundred fifty bucks."

"Where's the truck?" asked Ziggie.

"I'll take you there. Hop on!"

"It's a deal!" shouted an exuberant Ziggie.

On the ride to the truck, the farmer introduced himself as Elmer and asked: "Where were you headed?"

"Over to see a man in Newton County," said Ziggie.

"Well, you don't have far to go. Newton County starts right past that long grove of trees down yonder," said Elmer, as he pointed down the road.

So, Ziggie spent his Sunday afternoon in the isolated hay field of Mr. Elmer.

Why those northern ranchers idolize hillbillies to the degree that they even talk like them, I'll never know, thought Ziggie, *but they sure are friendly.*

When the work was completed, Ziggie sat on the back of the all-terrain vehicle and waited for Elmer to come out of his house, which was just up a little knoll about a hundred feet away. Soon, Elmer came out, inspected the stacked hay bales in the barn and walked toward Ziggie. He removed a small wad of money from his overalls and handed it to Ziggie, who did not bother to count it.

"Gonna be dark in a half hour," said Elmer.

"I was wondering . . . you think I could sleep in your barn for the night?" asked Ziggie.

"You'll be gone in the mornin'?" queried Elmer, the left side of his face twitching in the red glow of the sinking sun.

"Be gone by daylight," assured the fugitive.

"Sure," said Elmer, "I'll see if I can't fetch you somethin' to eat. My wife makes a mean sandwich."

Soon, Elmer brought a basket and a blanket out to the barn. A grateful Ziggie thanked him and settled in for the night. The tired, lonesome worker gratefully wiped a tear from his eye. He dared not allow Elmer to see it.

That night Ziggie gazed upon the stars. He had almost forgotten how the panoply of lights could be seen outside the city smog zones. The stars gleamed like a million electric spiders waiting in their webs for some errant bug to stumble their way. A theatre of heavenly doom in the palm of darkness.

The mechanisms of industry did not care. They buzzed and coughed wherever a dollar could be made. Oblivious to the electric spiders, and the great vault of blackness behind them, the little towns that dotted the countryside and hosted the industry, plugged away at becoming major profit centers. But for one night, at least, Ziggie relished the quietude of the rural surroundings. It was a golden moment, yet Ziggie felt lonely. Lonely as a train whistle on a dark frozen prairie.

Gradually, Ziggie's thoughts shifted. For a while, he pondered his condition. Running back and forth between Chicago and Domino, he longed to break the chain. Part of him desired to slip away and travel south, but another part of him wanted to remain with the familiar.

He tossed about his earthen bed as if something had

planted a bug in his brain. The vexations and tribulations of a mobile, secretive existence stormed through his weary mind. Rambling and galivanting around his head, as if to mimic his condition, random thoughts teased and taunted him, while his unsettled heart bounded around in his chest.

Only death, thought Ziggie, *could deliver relief. Oh, to turn to dust. Would it not render my problems obsolete? Would it not vanquish my anguish? There I lay, a speck of my former self.*

With that thought, he slid into a restless sleep.

80

PENTHOUSE PAT

TODD SWINDELL, on a business trip, had booked the penthouse on the top floor of the fabulous Winnington Hotel in downtown Chicago. His underlings smuggled in a high-class call girl—one of few left in the profession—named Pat, who wore a glittery $4,000 Joque Monet gown and a pair of $2,000 Cantrelli luxury designer boots and, of course, a billion-dollar Miss America smile.

Corporate executives could get away with this business, but worker bees could not. Well, it turns out that Mr. Swindell was a little heavy-handed with the young lady and she made a queen-sized stink about it in the upper corporate circles.

Brock Bonebanger, a professional wrestling thug turned exercise-machine mogul with a soft spot for petite blonds, heard about it, and when he saw Todd Swindell in the elevator of Fritz and Meyers' Department Store on Chicago's Magnificent Mile, he punched the spindly flake boss in the nose, giving him a pair of black eyes and a bloody schnozz and causing quite a stir on the fifth floor.

"You waz a little rough with my friend der at the Winnington Hotel," growled Bonebanger.

Before the cops came, Bonebanger had departed with a

warning that Swindell best not say anything. The battered CEO told the cops that he stumbled and went down on his face, then Swindell's subordinates whisked him away. As he was escorted out of the door, he leaped into a chain of unabashed cursing like he was going to whip Bonebanger's ass the next time he saw him. Several of Swindell's entourage snickered.

But a few weeks later embarrassment galore was the prevailing mood when Bonebanger, as emcee, greeted the cringing flake master at a Festival of Healthy Living at the historic McCormick Place on the beautiful lakefront of Chi-town. Swindell quivered like a nervous noodle the entire night through.

Swindell did not feel comfortable with all of the glitzy types at the Festival of Healthy Living, just like he did not fit in at Fritz and Meyers' Department Store. He was a down-home flake boy. He could not wait to get back to his mahogany desk at Flakes Alive Incorporated.

Swindell's mind slipped into a whirlwind of disorder. Todd Swindell thought, *I'm going to make a hit list and Bonebanger is going to be top meat. Hmm, I wonder if Tory is ready to join the Flake Wars? Maybe, but Bonebanger is not a part of the Flake Wars. Tory could probably take care of Bonebanger, though, I'm pretty sure. No, don't get him involved with this. What about Anika? She could silence that big dumb hard-ass. That muscle-bound fraud.*

81

AROMA ZONES

FENCES, houses, cars—there were so many ads painted on these objects that one could scarcely tell an ad for margarine from an ad for a table saw.

Ad overkill, Ziggie reckoned. *The bombardment of such ads kills the beauty of the thing that contains the ad.*

Indeed, the fugitive had reason to make such an observation. You drive down the street and you do not see a house. Your tired eyes instead see a staggeringly strange assortment of cola ads, hot dog ads, exercise equipment ads, toaster oven ads on some dizzying rectangle in the shape of a house.

You drive down the freeway, and it is so thickly checkered with billboards that one can barely see nature. And, of course, all of the trucks and cars broadcasted ads from their bodies.

Go up in an airplane and you see giant ads carved into the cornfields and covering the rooftops.

The world was one gigantic array of advertisements!

Attacking the eyeballs is one thing; attacking the eardrums is another. Everything you hear is steeped with advertising. Even funeral music is now laced with commercial sound bites. You begin to feel like a laboratory test dummy pelted with cornball advertising.

And, by golly, they even figured out how to make commercials of smell. Giant odor generators, standing side by side with fast food restaurant billboards on the highways, emitted scents to drive by. A sign depicting kids eating Yummy Burgers emanated the smell of Yummy Burgers for fifty square yards. Everyone who passed the sign on the various highways could experience the aroma, and these areas became known as "Aroma Zones."

Out of a hundred cars passing through the Aroma Zone for Yummy Burgers, advertisers guessed, twenty of the occupants might be conditioned or triggered to stop at a Yummy Burger stand at some later hour. Ten occupants might insist on immediate Yummy Burger satisfaction by heading directly to the nearest Yummy Burger restaurant. So, the olfactory receptors were now a legitimate target for ads. Aroma ads. There were mini-aroma ads at bus stops, tanning booths and ATM stations.

Computer ads had gone bananas. Every time you Open, Save, or Rename a file, you had to hear a fifteen-second ad. In fact, every click of a mouse button now had a pop-up ad.

From the moment you crawled out of bed, you became ad-drunk. And by the time you got ready to go to bed, you were ad-hungover. The corporate wheels kept turning at your expense.

Sale alerts, louder than tornado warnings, popped up in your intelli-phone-toting head without advance notice. You were one walking sales sponge. Loud, haughty, trampling, intrusive sales ads torpedoed you wherever you shall go.

All of this since they basically gutted the Federal Communications Commission (FCC) back in 2048.

After The Big Seven hollowed out the FCC, they banned all books that contained anything critical of America or its rulers. Then, they relaxed rules against corporate lying in 2050. For the previous ten years (in reality, much longer) the corporations utilized lying and fraud in allowing actors and actresses to portray doctors and so forth. It was a capitalist-normal lie.

But now lying was so pervasive that companies could make completely false claims about the effectiveness of their products. By 2055 The Big Seven had dismantled most of the regulatory agencies.

Then they overhauled the consumer protection agencies. Soon they began fortifying security agencies, enabling them to listen in on all phone calls, giving incentives to children who monitored all adult conversations to turn in their parents for misbehaving, even planting cameras and microphones in public restrooms.

Corporations lost regulations; individuals lost rights. As the years wore on, the rules wore in.

82

WHOLESOME FAMILY HENSON

"OH HERB," said Holly, while opening the mail, "here's some exciting news! We have been chosen as the host family of a new wheat flakes commercial. 'Herb and Holly Henson Happy Flakes Family will portray the Hensons hopping through hula hoops as they eat bowls of delicious Great American Flakes Corporation's Sweet Wheat Flakes, fortified with vitamins and protein for extra energy and without saturated fats, cholesterol, or glucose!'"

"How did we get chosen for that?" asked a bewildered Herb.

"I entered us into the contest, dear. It just said to send in this prepaid cardboard entry slip with your name and address and a photo of the family! I cut it right off the box!"

"Hmmm. Perhaps this is our true calling," noted Herb, his face glowing with adoration for his lovely wife.

"Oh Herb! We've done it! We've made the bigtime!" Holly continued reading the letter. "Let's see, 'compensation will consist of $40,000 plus a year's supply of Sweet Wheat Flakes for the entire family!' Oh, darling, I love you!"

"Love you too, honeybird," replied an anxious Herb.

"Get this," Holly read on, "'the company will also

provide brand new pink pajamas for the whole family that we can take home when we are done shooting. It will be filmed right here in little Domino at the GAFC studios in the basement of the company headquarters.' And get this: 'If we get the commercial finished in twelve hours or less, we get a free trip to Hawaii to learn from the real hula hoop professionals!'"

"This is sounding better by the minute," exclaimed Herb.

Holly continued: "There's no script. All we have to do is smile while eating our cereal. Just smile like the Great American Family that we are!"

"When is this studio session?" queried Herb.

"December 2nd," said Holly. "They say with trick photography they'll have us hopping through hoops as we eat breakfast. Yes, all we have to do is eat and smile, like we always do, at the studio's kitchen table."

———

On the day of filming the family bristled with exhilaration. For weeks the neighbors had inundated them with questions. Now, the day had come, flashing Hollywood fame.

Of course, eight-year-old Herb Jr. engaged in his usual antics, this time pinching the butt of beautiful Samantha, the programming guide, an otherwise garrulous gentlewoman with high standards and great tolerance. As soon as the startled woman turned around, Herb Jr. acted as if nothing happened. But she did not say anything to anybody. *Maybe she liked it,* suggested Herb Jr. to himself.

The stage crew was quite friendly, the makeup took long hours to put on, and the filming was tedious but easy. They spent five or six hours sitting at the kitchen table and just smiling while they ate their flakes.

If this is show business, thought little Herb, *they can cram it. My commercial career ends here.*

But what if the commercial becomes a blockbuster? I could force myself to do this a couple of hours a day for big money, he thought, *and lots of women (since the executives get to have women). Maybe become a producer or director? I could see it now: "Herb Henson, King of Commercials!" I wonder how it would be? "Spread out you ignoramuses, let Herb take over! Hey you, dog shit for brains, get over there. Ms. Tight Titties, you over here! Herb is going to shoot a commercial. Snap to it!"*

83

NED'S MEMORIES

ON A TIP FROM ALFI, Ziggie made his way to Ned Pagorski's bunker, an underground residence the host had dug out on his Indiana property.

Alfi had given Ned a heads-up regarding Ziggie looking for a place to stay. So Ned watched through the monitors for his camera's outside the hideout in waiting for Ziggie; and a good thing it was, for the bunker was hidden so well that the fugitive could have never found it. In a clearing among a small grove of maple trees, near some shrubs and bushes, the opening, a veritable trapdoor in the wilderness, did not seem especially inviting, but Ziggie badly needed rest.

Ned, a sinewy figure with long gray hair and a balding top, stepped outside when he saw Ziggie on camera and waved him forward and through the entrance.

"According to an overzealous government, you done a bad thing, son, but nobody here is gonna belittle, criticize, or judge you," he said. Ned wore a big furry gray mustache that moved with each syllable he uttered.

"Yeah," agreed Ziggie, whose hair had also become quite shaggy, "it seems that defacing a corporate logo, even if it's on your own skin, brings a penalty of indefinite enslavement. The offended corporation gets to own you. I've got to remain hidden from the authorities as best I can."

"Well, old Alfi sent you to the right place, sir. I don't think anyone followed you. You see, this is a stop on the modern-day Underground Railroad, son."

"Thank you so much, Mr. Pagorski."

"Call me Ned."

"Thanks, Ned."

"It's a constant battle with these bastards, I know," said Ned. "If you want to cling onto anything from the deep past, you're gonna be on the run all your life. If you conduct yourself in any impudent manner toward their world of lies or one of their can't-do-no-wrong corporations, you risk your freedom. Well, we won't keep you here long. You gotta remain on the run."

"I just don't want these guys," announced Ziggie, "tellin' me what to believe."

"Well," noted Ned, "you're one of the few smart ones. Most American dummies just fall right into place. You have a certain type of personality, though. You question things, which is good, son."

"Some things I have merely heard about," said Ziggie. "Other things I can remember. Some bits of the past, I found in my own attic. The only thing that is clear is that their artificial world is predicated on lies, fairy tales and denials."

"How old are you, Zigmund?"

"Fifty-two years old."

"Well, I'm seventy-four. And I remember before 2040. Of course, they're hopin' my kind will perish soon. Cause when there's nobody left who lived before 2040, that makes it easier for them to deny earth's existence before that time. They don't want anyone to know about the Civil War, The Great Depression or the Civil Rights movement . . . on account of people might get ideas about a new Civil War or a return to the Welfare State that sprouted from the Depression or how women and minorities fought for their rights. They don't want you to get any ideas. No, they want you to think that it has always been this way . . . the way it is now."

Ned led Ziggie down to a quiet room that seemed to have all the amenities of the modern world. There was a television, a stereo, and a CB radio. In an adjoining room were all the utensils of a modern kitchen. The only drawback: it was dark, as there was no sunlight. But Ned had wired the place generously and installed all of the plumbing and lighting. The kind old man had worked construction for twenty years, then worked at the steel mill for twenty more years. The walls were solid concrete. Some rooms had paneling over the concrete.

Ned Pagorski went on: "You see, I remember when it began, Zigmund. A couple of ultraconservative presidents, and, well, things tightened up. Freedoms vanished. They drew up a plan. A plan for total capitalist control. First, they came up with the Project 2025 scheme. Then, fifteen years later, they doubled down and came up with the 2040 Plan. By January of 2040, there would be no more political parties. And, sure enough, when that day came, they implemented their hard-nosed plan. And it has been all downhill from there, Zigmund, all downhill."

"Yes," said Ziggie, "I know a little something about all of those events. My grandpa left behind stacks of old newspapers and magazines, you know."

"Like I said," repeated Ned, "I remember when it began. Prisons, it was deemed, were not conducive to capitalist efficiency. To solve America's prison problem and better serve the corporation, judges began sentencing convicted souls to work hard labor at the various company headquarters or in one of the company's factories. That was right around The Great Cleanse of 2040. Scrubbing toilets, mopping and polishing floors or whatever special duty the company might assign them.

"You see, a murderer would get a three-to-twenty-year sentence serving a corporation. And, after 2040, maybe sometime about 2043, they began permanent ankle bracelet implants, so there was no way to get out of it, less'n you cut your own leg off. The logo tattoos started in about 2045, and for defacing one, as I see you have done, the penalty grew harsher and harsher."

Ned's eyes glistened with an almost forgotten tone: the tone of reminiscence. He continued: "I tried to resist one of their mandatory tattooings once, and they said they would force my son into eternal corporate service if they couldn't get me under the laser. So I had to give in. It wasn't a purty sight, but I saved my son a lot of misery and damnation."

Ned wiped a tear from his eye. "Yes, I remember it all. I recall a time when people avoided TV commercials. There was such a thing as a 'movie.' Now they only show short clips of films, and the people don't want to see 'em."

The old man jumped from memory to memory, but he made lots of sense. Ziggie sat amazed by his anecdotes, his fond and not so fond recollections. "Why, I remember when presidents were still elected by the people. You didn't have to be a TV-commercial actor or a CEO of any corporation to be president. I recall when ever'body had his or her own religion. At least in America they did. Now they've replaced religion with CEO worship. And, by golly, I remember when you could hold and caress a woman . . . and not be punished for it."

Poor old Ned began to drool as he said this. "You could enjoy real human flesh. Now, if you get an erection, you gotta tuck it 'tween your legs and hope it goes away before someone reports you."

Ned poured Ziggie some coffee and carried on. "The boys

at the bar used to say, 'authoritative capitalism is comin' to get us all.' And, boy, they was right."

Ned began to weep, and Ziggie put his hand on the lonely old man's shoulder to try and comfort him.

"I had a good job," Ned continued. "Not a capitalist slave-show act, but a real job making good money . . . and a beautiful gal named Sally. We would watch the moon slowly move through the night sky—and, yes, fondle each other a bit before you know what. It was amazing. But now it's all gone. Buried behind the countless ages."

"The one thing they cannot kill, though, is nature," a fired-up Ziggie asserted. "Wavy amber blankets of grain; flowery fields of red, blue and yellow; star-speckled skies of heavy purple; foamy seas of aqua green; busy brooks teeming with fish; rows of cattails swaying in the breezes; mountains studded with icecaps."

"Well," warned Ned, "they may not be able to annihilate it, but they can surely put a huge ugly dent in Mother Nature. They are blotting out all of these beauties with dollar signs in their moist eyes. The plow, the scarifier, the grader, the crane, the bulldozer will all play a part in the obliteration of beauty, if the human will allow it. With a most voracious zest for enter-prise, these shiny utensils will steadily carve away at nature until little is left to savor."

Ned paused to scratch his head. "Don't let the bulldozer feast upon nature, son. I'm too old now. But you are still young enough to make a difference. Don't let them do it."

84

THE WEALTH BUG

WHILE THE WEALTH Bug had happily infected the country, lavishing the upper class with enormous riches, the majority of people found it difficult to celebrate financial gains since inflation had knocked them out of any true running for an increase in affluence. Some were only a coin's throw from a Crate Camp.

While the population increased by fifty percent between 2040, "the beginning of time," and 2098, the poverty level had more than tripled. The Great Capitalist Experiment had certainly rendered some "dirty rich," while many others struggled to maintain their lower middle-class status. All of the built-up 401(k) wealth allowed many to mentally distance themselves from the poverty bubble, but their liquid assets in the form of bank and credit union accounts barely treaded water.

Yes, the free-market economy had boomed over the past twenty years and many 401(k)s bulged with mighty before-tax savings, company matches, capital gains and dividends. But for all this glory, the poor and homeless numbers swelled, graduating many tent cities to Crate Camps. That represented the measure of gain for the poverty-stricken citizens of the country.

All the cheering, all the boasting, and all the celebratory

yahooing over the market's seemingly endless upturn engendered only a limited number of true asset-gloating billionaires and some middle-class, satisfied hangers-on. The lower-class citizens had no 401(k)s to brag about or were too income-limited to invest in the 401(k)s they did have.

So, while many caught the Wealth Bug, only a small percent could attain anything resembling real wealth.

85

AN INTERVIEW WITH ANNIE DE LUCA

ANNIE DE LUCA toiled assiduously trying to solve the elusive formula for the No-Sog flakes.

A portrait of Syd Waverly rested upon Annie's desk in the laboratory at Flakes Alive Incorporated. She missed her old colleague but was grateful to have been picked as his replacement, the lead lab tech at Flakes Alive.

One mysterious night, as she diligently searched for the seemingly magic recipe, Detective Hung Cho Lee was buzzed into the lab by Human Resources. Annie was working alone that night, and HR had given her a heads-up.

"Ms. De Luca?" inquired Hung.

"Yes," replied Annie, "what can I do for you?"

"I am Detective Lee. Do you mind if I ask you a few questions?"

"Why certainly, Mr. Lee. Sit down please."

Detective Lee set himself down on a steel folding chair next to Annie's desk. He wore a look of grave determination on his countenance.

"Have you ever heard the name, Cliché Bob?" he asked.

"No, I don't think so."

"He works—er, worked for your competition, GAFC."

"Oh, is he the one who was murdered on the golf course? A terrible thing, Mr. Lee. My God, a terrible thing." Annie had a grievous tint in her eyes.

"At the golf course, yes."

"Oh dear, that poor man." A look of despondency appeared on the young lab technician's face.

"Indeed. Do you know anyone in your company who may have known him?"

"No sir, I cannot think of anyone," replied Annie in a most earnest manner.

"What about Twinkle Deshpande," asked the detective. "Have you ever heard of her?"

"I'm afraid I'm not much help, Mr. Lee. I'm sorry."

"You're working on a new project, I understand."

"Well, actually, it's a kind of ancient project, Mr. Lee, if you're talking about the formula that would produce the longed-for No-Sog, Stay-Crisp flakes, sir. We have a couple of new ingredients to try, er, well, chemicals, that is, but no luck just yet."

"Indeed, I am talking about that formula," said Detective Lee. "Ms. De Luca, are you aware of anyone attempting to spy on you?"

"Oh, goodness, nobody that I'm aware of. Have you talked to HR . . . and Todd Swindell, the CEO?"

Annie thought for a minute, then revealed a strange instance that had occurred a couple of months before. "Um, actually, there is one thing," she said. "On one occasion a guy from the Great American Flake Company named Cecil Weatherspoon asked me out to dinner. And I met him at Fat Sam's Steakhouse. But as soon as I discovered that he worked for our competitor, I broke off the relationship."

"Did you divulge any company secrets?"

"Oh no. I would never do such a thing, Mr. Lee. Never, never! You see, I reported it to HR."

"Good girl," noted the keen detective. "Now then, have you ever been—and this is a very important and private question Ms. De Luca—instructed, asked or compelled to spy on an employee of a competitor?"

"These are beginning to be tough questions, Mr. Lee." Annie was a bit coy about such information.

"Yes, and I need the full and unadulterated truth, Ms. De Luca."

"Well, sir, once I was asked to meet with Cecil Weatherspoon and pick his brain."

"You mean, after you had already broken off the communication with Weatherspoon?"

"Yes, HR and Todd Swindell both wanted me to call him back and have another dinner date. Swindell wanted me to ask Cecil certain questions, like how far along they were with their experiments regarding the No-Sog recipe."

"Did you do it?" asked Detective Lee with a very curious face.

"Yes, I did it" replied Annie, as she looked down to the floor. "But then Cecil got suspicious of *me*. So, it didn't work out so well."

"Do you have a list of the questions you were supposed to ask?"

"I have some rough notes," admitted Annie, "but HR would fire me if they found out that I gave them to you."

"HR will never know . . . 'cause I'm not going to tell them."

"This puts me in a dangerous predicament, Mr. Lee. HR would fire me for giving you the notes. And you will arrest me should I refuse to hand over the notes."

"I tell you what," said Lee, "we'll get HR permission for

you to hand over the notes." He called HR to get permission to look at Annie's notes, but he got a recording.

"I'll just make a copy for you," said Annie, who had changed her mind. "We don't need to bring HR into it." Flipping through her notepad, Annie found the page of notes and made Detective Lee a copy.

"Thank you," he said. "Now there's just one more thing. Can I get a sample of your hair?"

"My hair?" questioned Annie, now a bit alarmed. "What for?"

"Well," he explained, "I found a strand of hair outside of the crime scene where Syd Waverly lost his life. I have a hunch it came from Twinkle, but I'm looking to rule you out."

"You mean I'm a suspect?" Annie asked, with a shaken voice. "A murder scene? Me?"

"No," assured the detective, "you're only a person of interest, Ms. De Luca."

That assurance, however, failed to defuse Annie's building tension.

"If you had no part in the transgression, Ms. De Luca, you will be cleared very quickly."

"OK," agreed Annie, "but for anything beyond this, I think I might need the presence of an attorney."

The bewildered chemist allowed Detective Lee to pluck a strand of hair from her head, and the two parted ways. Lee returned to his office in the Domino Police Headquarters building and issued a BOLO for Twinkle Deshpande after the lab compared the two hairs and determined that Annie's hair was not a match.

86

THE BABY FACTORY

THE BABY FACTORY'S purpose was to harvest babies from test tubes and birth human clones.

The former method of adding to the population worked quite well, and with a little genetic engineering they could learn how to make the *perfect* baby. Of course, when the word "perfect" is bandied about, as in the case of the "perfect family" or the "perfect situation," the human mind must be in its most guarded state, for such things can never live up to their billing. Almost always, the perfect this or the perfect that has a fatal flaw. Something bad happens. Indeed, the use of "perfect" becomes an omen.

So it is recommended that we desist from the use of the word "perfect" and, perhaps, substitute the phrase "the best human" or "the best situation." But the baby must not learn bad things from the world around it, so the Baby Factory and the National Laboratory dreamed up the idea of a baby being exposed to a stable environment, with little or no negative stimuli to pervert the thinking of the child.

Select children to be raised by the corporation in conjunction with the Baby Factory and the National Laboratory became the secret target for the mighty tycoons of industry.

Living in a vacuum with pristine surroundings would specially nurture those with high intelligence quotients.

A program known as the Accelerated Corporate Development Curriculum (ACDC) arose out of the need for ultra-studious, high potential corporate citizens. Only the choicest intellects could participate. In an immaculate environment with no ill thoughts to be inculcated into the subjects' eager minds, the children might represent the ultimate corporate machine cog. This sterile world would generate the dedicated decision-makers for the future good of the corporation and the entire planet.

The select children would be exposed to no history of the Christian Crusades nor the Third Reich nor even the Manson family nor the scene at Guyana, as is the case for any young person, nor World War One nor any other human-created messes on the planet, but just pre-cleansed facts and anecdotes. Mind-reading intelli-phone implants would monitor the thought process in order to produce, as much as possible, ultra-clean specimens for the New America.

Only the best would be shaped and molded for at least sixteen years of specialized school training.

Early on, the corporate conglomerates realized that some of the lab specimens who graduated from the program, and were then exposed to the flawed scenarios of real-world environments, became petrified with shock. Some did not recover. Others remained chronically ill.

But those who survived the shock and adapted to the problems of society became the choicest of mortals, unperturbed by anything negative, unblemished by the faults of mankind, and unmoved by human wrongdoing. They existed only to make good choices for the corporation to which they were assigned and whose logos they wore on their saturated skin.

If the child's mind was bruised in an early phase of the

program, no effort to *unbruise* it could succeed, and so the child was expelled from the program and absorbed into the usual life.

The students had no exposure to the opposite sex; no exposure to vice of any kind; no exposure to policing, fragility or weakness in any degree. With the new Cyclops intelli-phone, "One Eye On The Mind," trademark R, the Corporate Gods, in the form of chief executive officers, would have total monitoring rights over each specimen.

No family would be assigned these specimens; they went straight to the corporations that helped to nurture them. They were extremely fine-tuned specimens and only a handful survived the rigors of the ACDC learning process unblemished.

87

THE END OF DEEPAK

ANIKA PATEL WAS LIVING TEMPORARILY in one of her father's motel rooms, a musty kitchenette on the south end of the building on US Route 41 twenty miles north of Domino. She tried to explain to her friend, Deepak, that she did have feelings for him, but the Attachment Code and Passion Code and Intimacy Code all forbade any sexual relations between the troubled pair.

"But, my love, who will ever know?" inquired Deepak.

"They have ways of finding out," reasoned Anika. "Some way, somewhere, someone will tell. I don't want to ruin my career."

"We cannot stand in the way of love, my dear," pleaded Deepak.

"Deepak, you are torturing yourself. You should go back to India and resume your career there."

"I would not go without you," said the distressed man.

"But the Intimacy Code," protested Anika.

"I'm tired of codes and rules and taboo relationships. Can't we just be tender?"

"We can't . . . we mustn't," warned Anika.

"I do not want to sustain myself in this fragile condition, Anika."

"Then," said Anika, "I'm afraid we must part ways, my dear Deepak, else the government will find out, and that will be the end of us both."

"No!" cried Deepak, "I cannot let it end this way. I *must* have you."

"I'm sorry, Deepak, but I must ask you to leave."

"Well then, there's only one thing I can do."

With that said, Deepak lifted a .38 caliber pistol from his waistband and shot himself in the side of the head. Instantly, he collapsed in silence, leaving a massive display of gore, consisting of blood, brain tissue, and bone fragments behind. Slimy veinous materials stuck to the walls. It was a most dreadful scene. Anika had seen death before, indeed, had caused death before, but never dealt this closely with a loved one's death. Especially such a sloppy death.

"Oh, Deepak, my love," Anika bawled. "Look what you have done to yourself. What will I tell your mother?"

The young, Indian American damsel shuddered with grief, as she called 911. "Ouch! It hurts, I know. Maybe in the next life, my darling, Deepak."

88

TORY'S TRIP

TODD SWINDELL, CEO at Flakes Alive Incorporated, brought his spoiled son to Bickner Laboratories for a clinical sampling of LSD.

Tory Swindell was sixteen years old and got just about anything he wanted. Now he was to try the hallucinogenic wonders of pure liquid LSD. The youth suffered from mild depression and anxiety and was ready for alternative medicine, so he dared his father to take him to the Drug Lab, where he could legally dip into the kaleidoscopic realm of mind-bending substances.

The first thing Tory noticed after a tiny drop had disappeared on his moist tongue was the little buzzy bugs crawling up and down his spine. Then voices began to echo throughout the facility and the bellyful of butterflies stimulated his stomach and bowels. Now the tracers set in and everything that physically moved left a fading tail of the image behind it.

All things stationary began to move. A footrest seemingly crept across the floor. The walls breathed in and out. Lights had magnificent halos. Colors were intensified.

Then, when the full effect of the drug encased the spirit, everything became funny. One laughed at anything—another person's demeanor, another person's aura, until the tripper's face was literally aching with muscle flex. At this point Tory almost drowned in his own mirth. Thus, this may be the culmination of the entire trip.

Eventually, the laughing died down, along with the nervous stomach, and then the most colorful part of the journey sets in, as the hallucinatory binging commenced. Everything read like a moving tapestry. Molecules intermingled with other molecules. All the tiny loops in the carpeting danced in circles. Incredible sights and sounds overflowed from the sensors of the mind, from the thought channels.

The blue veins in people's faces and necks stood out fantastically, and, if one experienced a bad trip, these faces could be hideous. Strange thoughts raced through Tory's mind, bouncing through the labyrinths of the brain. Corny images fired off in his thought tunnels like blasts from a row of cannons. Missiles soared through Tory's head.

Then he had a vision of his deceased grandmother dancing down a grocery store aisle wearing a long dress and tennis shoes. She was bouncing a beach ball, dodging the other customers who were trying to get the ball away from her. All of a sudden, she wore combat boots. A chain of daisies crowned her head and she sported a bushy mustache. She dribbled around the people, left the aisles, and exited out the front door and into the parking lot, where she disappeared.

Tory closed his eyes. The colors swirled in his head. In a grove of cherry trees, a giant frog with sunglasses and a martini rode a unicycle while rapping a Halloween song in Chinese. All of these various thoughts entertained Tory in the space of a few seconds, so one could only imagine the multitudinous images that sprang from his overactive mind over, say, an hour's time.

Finally, Tory was asked if he would like to partake in some marijuana. He agreed.

A whole other fantasy world germinated. The colors re-intensified, the movement grew heavier. Illusions, mirages seemed to multiply exponentially. His mind dabbled for hours in the lights and sounds. Eventually, drowsiness slowly crept in. The skin felt oily. The smile muscles relaxed, their soreness diminishing.

On coming down from his fantastic high, Tory was provided a warm shower and a massage. A drug was administered to inhibit the oncoming erection, to dull the sexual appetite, which is usually voracious by this time.

The experience imparted upon the young man a different angle from which to view the planet. He had conducted himself amiably among the medical staff and the laboratory personnel. The whole experience soothed his nerves over the next couple of days.

89

A HOLOCAUST OF SOUND

A COLD, heavy rain with hailstones pelted the door of Ned's underground bunker. Down below it sounded like a machine gun. Ned and Ziggie sat at the kitchen table, sipping coffee and reminiscing about past events in their lives. The bright kitchen lights belied the fact that the room was underground. Ned would never pass as home decorator, though, as the refrigerator was brown, the stove was green, and the microwave was white. The rumbling of thunder above added to the war effect, sounding like bombs dropping nearby.

"Is there no Heaven nor Hell?" Ziggie Wexler waxed philosophical. "The seven CEOs forbid our discussing it, yet here we lie in limbo, with our tails up our asses and our minds full of fog."

"I was never much for religion," remarked Ned Pagorski, "but it seems to me that a man ought to have a choice."

"I remember the word 'sex' used to mean something besides whether one is male or female," said Ziggie. "It was something almost magic, something wonderful beyond description. Now it is lost to the ages, to us servile procreators."

"Well," reasoned Ned, "it used to be an act. A mighty fun

act!" Ned lit a pipeful of cheap grass. "There was nothin' like that itch to be inside a woman you were intimate with. And then, the explosion of love."

"Yes," added Ziggie, "perhaps the same kind of magic that music used to invoke. Unlike this cacophony of nonsensical noises they call music today."

"Today," Ned added, "there's no substance to music. It ain't good for nothin' but TV commercials. And when it does have melody, it sounds like somethin' a child would write. Little dainty ditties—whatever happened to the three-minute song? It's all twenty-second jingles to sell somethin.'"

"Yes," agreed Ziggie, "gone are the days of artful musical passages, rebellious lyrics, and daringly out-of-bounds syncopation. Blue notes, folksy ballads, and roguish rock have all vanished. Pissed away into the cold wind."

"Yep, music is only used to sell things now," lamented Ned.

"It used to be—even for a bit after The Great Cleanse—that rock music swelled with angst, mind-blowing forays into other musical styles, and daredevil lyrics," Ziggie groaned. "Why, there was a band that I heard about—The Rolling Stones, I think their name was—who had sharp, dark lyrics and an ultra-funky sound—maybe the greatest of all rock groups ever. They're long gone now and so is good music in general. Now it's all powder-puff bathtub hummers. It used to be that rock music in commercials was taboo, unless the rock star was dead. If you wanted to be taken seriously, you wouldn't allow your music to be played in commercials. Now, radio and TV commercials are your only avenue to success in the industry."

"There was such a thing as jazz and classical," said Ned. "And in America, rock music had the Boston sound, the San Francisco sound, and the Texas sound. Now it's just the American sound, and, boy, is it wimpy." The tired old man scratched his head. "Woe to the bygone days of headphones and listening to a full album side of psychedelic rock. I tell ya, it's a genuine holocaust of sound."

90

A FALLING STAR

THE TINIEST SPECK of DNA was harvested from Chad Scandalman's golf club, which Detective Hung Cho Lee, who had gotten a search warrant, found in a shed behind the dead CEO's mansion.

Even soaking the driver in the bathtub could not rid it of all its DNA. And, given the modern expanded capabilities of DNA detecting equipment, the slightest speck of DNA could be detected. The DNA matched that of Cliché Bob!

Investigators now knew that GAFC CEO Chad Scandalman, may he rest for the ages, attacked Bob with great malice and killed him. But why would he do such a thing to his own employee? You just cannot combat the late twenty-first century DNA identifying technology; yet it could not uncover motive. That was still a detective's job, and Lee, of course, knew of Bob's disloyalty to GAFC. Anyway, these findings exonerated Flakes Alive Incorporated CEO, Todd Swindell, and his sneaky scouts, of the murder of Cliché Bob.

But what about Scandalman's death? Did Swindell order that? Lee spent many tedious hours poring over the notes and thoughts connected with that saga and just could not locate evidence enough to generate a potential courtroom winner.

Meanwhile, the BOLO for Twinkle Deshpande engendered some results. Captain Doris McElvy, working diligently on the Zigmund Wexler case, just happened, in riding with one of her officers, to pull over a woman for driving with only one taillight. The woman gave a fake name, but the officer applied an Instant DNA Sleuth to her skin to expose her identity, and what he found was exciting. It was Twinkle Deshpande!

When the wanted assassin was hauled in for an interview with Detective Lee and it was found that her hair matched the hair found outside the crime scene, she was arrested for the first-degree murder of Syd Waverly.

But doggone it, who killed Scandalman?

91

SMILE!

HERB HENSON, fresh off of having a spark up his ass at Spittoon Alley, dropped off a few foodstuffs at a Crate Camp near his house.

With permission of the state, he had recently raised money for, and sponsored, the installation of a drinking fountain at the camp. He even brought his fourth-grade class to observe the misfortune of others and to learn how to share. The entire population of the Crate Camp adored Herb and his wife, Holly.

But neither of the philanthropists ever questioned why so many citizens were living in bottomless poverty. Why the capitalist economy requires that a huge portion of the populace live in mud and filth.

Why there must be a drab and dismal lower-class Crate Camp in existence. There should have been a puzzle to ponder, but the two happy-go-lucky citizens would not think of questioning the lopsided system. The two humanitarian donors just agreed with whatever The Big Seven or its mountain of subsidiaries shoveled their way.

The Henson family model shone brightly against a backdrop of failed government policies and corporate malfeasance.

They never talked back. They never coughed up any type of backlash to a political or social boondoggle. They always exhibited their big white teeth, whether smiling in the face of joy or doom.

On one occasion, the school treasurer, Tomas Torrez, squandered half a million dollars on personal items, such as a shiny new car, kitchen appliances, and a brand new intelliphone extension for each member of his family. The school was underwater with debt, yet Herb Henson beamed with delight. He came home from work on the night that the scandal was exposed and told his wife, "Things will take care of themselves . . . a brighter day lies on the horizon."

And his wife, Holly, facing a torrent of bad behavior by most of the children in her care, grinned with a sunny outlook, simply telling Herb that "the top of the glowing rainbow will soon follow."

Even when one of their assigned children died from leukemia, the couple, through all of their misery and without the crutch of religion, mind you, smiled at the wake and funeral as if something wonderful was about to occur. One just could not break through the seemingly molded smiles.

The corporate universe touted the pair as the "Model Couple." No sex, no religion, no sports, no complaints.

92

CORPORATE SERVITUDE

LIFE in the bunker could get mighty boring, conversation being one's only friend, unless, of course, one enjoyed watching a pitiful parade of TV commercials, or listening to a silly barrage of cellphone-implant advertisements. Outside, the day glowed with plentiful sunshine; deep inside the underground home, calmness dominated the scene. The two new friends sat in the living room and played a game of poker.

"I remember," said Ned Pagorski, "when they commenced to emptying out the penitentiaries.

One by one the prisoners came before Judge Gillespie. You see, I worked as a part-time bailiff."

"I seem to recall those days," said Ziggie. "I was quite young at the time, so my memory isn't really sharp."

Ned continued. "The honorable judge would announce the conviction: 'Gordon Mendelson, you were convicted of armed robbery and sentenced to twenty-two years of confinement in the Tamms Penitentiary. You have served eight years with good behavior. I now sentence you to serve the remaining fourteen years as a laborer for the ZYX Corporation. With continued good behavior, Mr. Mendelson, you will serve ten of those fourteen years in corporate servitude. Will a representative from that corporation please step forward and state your name and job title.

"'Janice Murdoch, Human Resources Specialist for the ZYX Corporation, Your Honor.'

'Ms. Murdoch, you are now permitted to escort Gordon Mendelson to his workstation at ZYX Corporation. His chip (electronic ankle bracelet) has been implanted, Ms. Murdoch, and he shall present no trouble toward you or your company. Let it be known to the court that Mr. Mendelson has been transferred.' 'Thank you, Your Honor,' said Mr. Mendelson. 'One more piece of business,' said the judge. 'Let it be known that Mr. Mendelson shall serve the ZYX Corporation dutifully and honorably or face a maximum penalty of death as prescribed by the court.'"

"That's an awful stiff sentence," said Ziggie.

"Yep," assured Ned, "that's pretty much how it went. My uncle served a year for Woodward's Grocery Market, scrubbin' floors, cleanin' toilets and doin' odd jobs for old man Woodward. All for stealing a tomato."

Ziggie wondered what they would do with him, should he be caught.

As if Ned Pagorski was reading Ziggie's mind, he announced the following supposition: "They would probably stick you in a coal mine or a limestone quarry hammering rocks into smaller pieces. Hard labor for sure, since they don't like those who speak out against the government."

"I guess I just can't get caught," said Ziggie.

93

INDICTED!

ONE STORMY AUTUMN DAY, Todd Swindell received by certified mail an indictment for murder and corporate malfeasance, indicating that he must appear before a grand jury.

"I have to appear on November 2, 2098 at the county courthouse, goddamnit!" He said this to the fly guts on his office window. Swindell scooped up the cup and golf ball he was playing with and heaved it against the back wall of his office. With one swoop of the hand, he knocked everything within reach off the top of his desk.

"Fuck!" he shouted, then kicked the wastepaper basket, knocking it over on the floor.

His secretary, Dalia Habib, knocked at the door and opened it a crack. "Is everything alright, Mr. Swindell?" she asked timidly.

"Don't worry about it. Everything is fine."

That goddamn Detective Hung Cho Lee, thought Swindell. He's like a bad case of the clap—just hanging around and making my life miserable. Why don't I snuff him out? Eh, it's too late. I already got the indictment. I wonder what kind of evidence they have? What the fuck can I do? Goddamnit, it's all downhill from here.

Todd sat in silence. He brooded over his fate. The trajectory of his life had gone wayward.

Quickly, he opened the top drawer on his desk and grabbed a bottle of Dream Eruption Formula XX. The reliable formula, he knew, would make him unaware of everything, at least for a brief period.

94

ZIGGIE TAKES FLIGHT AGAIN

BOOM! *Boom! Boom!* "It's the FBI! Open up or we're coming in!"

Boom! Boom! Boom! They pounded on the trap door to the underground quarters. Ziggie woke up startled.

Ned Pagorski rushed into the room and gave Ziggie instructions: "Go through that red door! It leads to an underground tunnel! The tunnel will let you out in the woods . . . well back from my old house! Hurry!"

"But what about you?" asked Ziggie.

"Don't worry about me! I've had my turn at life and it's nothin' to live for at this point. Save yourself. Now get! Run!"

Ziggie, always ready for an escape, grabbed his bag and beat it out the red door and through the tunnel. Ned let in the FBI, accompanied by Captain Doris McElvy, who immediately handcuffed the old man. The tunnel led Ziggie about fifty yards to an opening in the center of the forest, out of sight to the cops.

Ziggie ran through the forest and came out on Indiana Highway 55 near a four-way stop. He jumped on the back of a semitrailer and rode it out of the area to the north. Other drivers were staring at him hanging from the back of the truck, but no one reported him. When he jumped off of the rig, he ran to an old barn to hide in long enough to slow his heavy breathing. For now, he was clear.

But, before long, he galloped through the fields, most of which had been harvested, and did not stop for a good hour. He soon ran into a stream and hid on its bank. He was headed north again, back toward Chicago.

Poor old Ned, he thought. *The old man gave himself up for me. There is a streak of goodness yet left in the modern world. There is something to live for, after all. But now where shall I go? I cannot stay here for long.*

Ziggie took out a fresh biscuit, provided by Ned, and chewed it while he contemplated where to turn. *If I could make it to New York, maybe I could get lost in the throngs of people. Got to find out which railroad tracks belong to the New York Central Railroad. No, New York is too cold. If I'm going to remain up north, I'll just head back to Chicago. I could try the guy Isabella told me about up on Armitage.*

Let's see, he thought, as he pulled out the paper with the address: Robert Casey, 17611 Armitage Ave. *Or I could just say fuck it all and take a train down south.*

———

"Pagorski, you're in a heap of shit," an FBI agent assured him. "Yeah," shouted Pagorski, "well *you're* a heap of shit!"

"We're looking for Zigmund Wexler," barked Captain McElvy. "Is he or was he here?" "Never heard of him," sounded Pagorski.

"Our intelligence says he is here!"

"Well, your intelligence must have come from a gumball machine, you ugly pieces of shit!" The agents bowled over the old man and searched every pocket of his below-ground premises.

They used Instant DNA Sleuths to uncover traces of Ziggie.

"See here," said McElvy, "we've already caught you in a lie. We found copious amounts of Zigmund's DNA in your rooms already!" McElvy trained her fiery eyes on the prisoner. "We know that Zigmund tried to extricate himself from his entanglements with his financial overseers, but our government has a stranglehold on them. And now he has zero chance of getting away. You might as well tell us where he is."

"This is not the way America was meant to be," moaned a handcuffed Ned.

95

MORE ODDS AND ENDS (FROM THE NOTES OF ZIGGIE)

CORPORATIONS CONSIDERED BODY PARTS, especially the forehead, as prime territory for tattoos and brands (brands paid even more compensation). The specific body part was known as the "living flesh billboard."

Bangs, of course, were not allowed in order to keep the forehead tattoo visible. Nor were beards allowed, as they obscured the chin and cheek designs. A proposal to mandate the shaving of all heads in order to increase tattoo real estate was being considered by Congress.

The tattoo shop traveled the same road as the caboose—utter extinction. A few basement amateurs remained. Most corporate tattoos were done by doctors with lasers these days.

———

Individuals with bad credit were remanded to a sort of concentration camp until they could pay their debts. This setup was akin to a debtor's prison of old. Upon a third offense people with bad credit were eliminated.

———

Big Pharma instituted psychotropic drugs for everyone to ingest upon birth. These were mood enhancers, meant to motivate kids to accept a life of hard work.

———

For musical acts the main goal no longer focused on achieving a Top 40 Hit, but upon writing a jingle that could be used in a television commercial. For writers, the main goal no longer focused on creating a best-seller but on inventing a lively one-liner that could be used in a television commercial. Art shows were now rehearsals for television commercials.

———

As has already been stated, traditional gods were outlawed. If you desired to worship, look no higher than a deceased CEO at your place of employment or at another company. These CEOs embodied gods of all former religions. Your current CEO should be regarded as next to godly. If your company was new and did not yet have a dead CEO, you were granted permission to worship a character in your favorite TV commercial, that is, a potential future CEO.

Worshiping capital, that is, buildings and machinery, such as an overzealous employee might do, was strictly forbidden, for capital should be valued as the means of performing your work, not the supreme deity itself. CEOs once hired or voted in were conditioned to worship themselves, while worshiping other CEO entities. Once the physical body died, they became sacred or hallowed to other people. The legal corporation, however, must be conceived as a godly enterprise. So, even though the buildings and machinery of the corporation must not be worshipped by themselves, as part of the corporation on paper these instruments were regarded as holy.

What type of heaven would the CEO Gods furnish? An industrial heaven? Maybe a heaven with hoses, belts, gears, wires and conveyors? Or would it be an information-age heaven? A heaven with computer screens and dashboards with switches and blinking lights? Surely, it could not be a heaven with nature. Maybe it would be a heaven where CEOs rule with whips and chairs to fend off we the beasts?

———

When deviant behavior went mainstream somewhere in about the 1960s (forbidden territory, only familiar to top executives), society became decimated in the view of the corporate worshipers and tended to wallow in its own poison until 2040, when The Great Cleanse commenced. Conservative stake-holders and figureheads then began the arduous task of setting tight rules and clean standards. They knew only one thing: that capitalism would thrive with the onset of the most rigid princi-ples. And there, authoritative capitalism began.

———

Marketing gurus continued to feast on every drive for a new slogan. Slobbering over each other for every glimmer of a new corporate advertising scheme, they nudged their way toward the top. By 2098 a new wave of slogans had emerged from the bowels of the flake companies. "Feed on Our Flakes; the others are fakes," said one. "Make no mistake; try our flakes," said another.

———

"The corporation," once said Ziggie, "was invented to remove human feeling and emotion from decision making, asset building, and profit taking. After all, the corporation is patterned after Mother Nature, and Mother Nature has no feelings. This Mother Nature nurtures and devours without care. And the capitalist gorilla does the same. Build 'em up; knock 'em down; repeat process. Gobble, gobble, spit, spit. Capitalism conveniently removes the human element of blame. And when the layoffs begin, no human dimension exists to take fault, absorb guilt, or yield sympathy."

———

Beginning January 1, 2099, HR Bill 87329 becomes law. For saying or writing anything negative about the corporate government, one's Social Security would be stripped.

96

ANOTHER LONELY SOUL

AS ZIGGIE HIKED north up the old Monon Railroad right-of-way through Munster, Indiana, he came upon a man walking south from Chicago.

"Wha's up?" queried the southbound party, an African American man wearing a fake leather jacket and a blue knit acrylic stocking cap.

"Hey man," said Ziggie, "I'm just headed up to Chi-town. Got a lead on a job. What about you?"

"Headed to Indianapolis," said the stranger. "Hey, you wouldn't happen to have a spare dollar, would ya? I haven't ate a damn thing all day."

"I got some quarters." Ziggie reached into his pants pocket and pulled out six quarters. "Maybe you could get a doughnut or somethin'."

"Damn, thanks man. I'm famished."

"If you're hungry now," added Ziggie, "I've got three biscuits. I'll split 'em with you."

"I'll jus' take one to hold me over." The man gratefully accepted the biscuit. "Where 'xactly you goin', man?"

Ziggie pulled out the piece of paper Isabella had given to him and showed the address to the man.

He looked at the paper and said, "17611 Armitage? Naw, man, you don't wanna go there. I jus' come from there. They got busted by the Feds, man."

"Busted? For what?"

"For hirin' felons and rebels, man. They's some dudes who was wanted an' shit."

"How'd you get out?" asked Ziggie.

"Yo, man, I wasn't wanted. I'm jus' homeless, ya dig?" The man squinted into the sun. "I mean, I don't like the way this country bein' run either, but I ain't no felon 'r nothin'."

"So, how did you get hired on?" Ziggie wondered.

"Oh, you don't have to be no criminal, 'r nothin'. Know what I'm sayin'? If you po', they let you in. I was homeless, so they gave me a job. Then, when the Feds came, I didn't have no job no mo'."

97

GET JEFFREY GEBHARDT!

AS SIXTEEN-YEAR-OLD TORY SWINDELL approached the front door to his house, he could hear his dad guffawing like a certifiable lunatic. "What's so funny, dad?" he asked when he entered the premises.

"It's these crazy commercials! They make 'em so goofy these days that I almost piss my pants in laughing over them! They are far more sophisticated than they used to be! I get a real kick out of 'em! And you know, since writers quit working on movies, which nobody wants to see anymore, all of the world's best writers are writing commercials now!"

Tory set his schoolbooks on the living room table and addressed his dad with a new topic. "Some kid asked me if I wanted to buy some Cinnamon today."

"Cinnamon? Oh, that must be that new drug I heard about. Stay away from it. It's not approved by the Food and Drug Administration or the Drug Lab yet. It could have anything in it—battery acid, arsenic, dogshit—you just don't know."

"Yeah, I wouldn't mess with it," assured Tory.

"Well, I feel rejuvenated, son. Do you want to go for a pizza?"

"Sure."

"Let me set up the video recorder. There's a new Flakes Alive Incorporated commercial on today. I don't want to miss it. The guys down in the filming studio said this'll be a great one!"

"How so?" asked Tory.

"It's something about a baby kangaroo jumping into a swimming pool. Crazy stuff."

"In a corn flake commercial?" asked the young man.

"Yep!"

Just then, the phone rang. Todd Swindell picked it up. Tory used the restroom.

"Sir," announced a somber voice, "the lead man in the popular new GAFC commercials is a guy named Jeffrey Gebhardt. We can isolate him at Dueling Donuts, where he gets coffee every morning on his way to work at the GAFC studios, where they are making yet another commercial."

"Alright. Tell your guy it's a go!" said Swindell. "Silence that sonofabitch!" Then, he whispered, "Get rid of the bastard. Do away with him, you hear? I can't stand that face-fucking grin and that obnoxious cackling he does."

"Aye, aye, sir."

"I'd like to stab that fucker with one of my swords. Right in the goddamn vocal cords! Better yet, chop off his dick and shove it down his throat. That will shut him up. A sword for a sword!"

Todd Swindell hung up the phone.

Tory, who came in from the restroom, asked, "Do away with what?"

"Never you mind, son. It's just business. You shouldn't be pokin' around my business, son. Now, let's go grab a pizza."

When the father and son arrived back at home with the pizza, Todd Swindell could feel the rage bubbling up inside him, for a commercial featuring Jeffrey Gebhardt, now a targeted man, came on the TV.

This prick, thought Swindell, *has the gall to ride a corn flake into outer space. That was my idea back in 2092, and the studio folks downstairs rebuffed it. They said that flying flakes and space age comedy might prove too nonsensical to sell many flakes. I told them "The kids get to fly on a flake, as if it were a magic carpet. What's the harm in that?" They just thought we weren't ready for it.*

And now here's this cosmic orbiting jackass using my commercial idea. And he's so handsome and all the kids adore him with his big fat smile—it makes me sick. I just want to puke at the sight of him. That no good, chintzy little cocksucker stole my concept! Just look at that grinning half-wit. I want to stomp on him! What a common thief. Hmmm, it was probably the low-lives in GAFC marketing that planned this. Oh well, he's too damn popular anyway. And too damn pretty. I want him gone! The kids just love this little bitch, with his lovely face and his golden grin. I can't wait till he's eliminated.

98

BALLOON BUFFOONS!

WITH ALL OF these Capitalist Crazy killings going on, in addition to the usual street-thug murders, which themselves were a product of the free market, the world went balloon loony.

Deflated balloons fell out of the sky the way leaves fell off trees in the autumn season. With corporate citizens slaughtering each other in waves, balloon companies feasted on mourning families who loved to release the rubbery floaters into the atmosphere upon their loved ones' violent deaths.

Behold the spread of Capitalist Craziness as the disease wraps its arms around the American populace. Go down into the lakes and streams and even ocean bottoms and uncover the deflated remains that fell back to earth. Tiny, nonrigid, rubber, plastic, and cloth bags of gas polluted the planet and reflected the soaring murder rate of America when they lost their air.

The world looked on in astonishment.

"Dear, what are we having for dinner tonight?"

"Deflated balloons."

"Mmmm. Chewy, rubbery, deflated balloons. I must be the luckiest man on earth!"

99

A LETTER OF ACTION

ZIGGIE WROTE his latest letter to the *Clandestine Journal* on paper towels from a truck stop restroom.

Masquerading as good corporate citizens the Capitalist Crazies have knocked off competitors' employees, as well as employees within their own companies. They have wiped out workers both for business purposes and personal reasons. The disease hits hardest in the most competitive situations, as when two companies are neck-in-neck in sales volume or reputation, or in situations where one company is underperforming against expectations. The personal feuds occur when undue pressure is applied to a worker to move faster or when several employees compete for a job or promotion.

A stadium-full of talent has been lost to the various industries affected by these atrocities. Only a more subdued form of competition can ease such tensions as those that bring about murder in the workplace. Should we march into the 22nd century under such stressful circumstances, civilized society cannot survive.

I have decided to back off society—to exit, stage left. My fellow citizens you need not be so drastic, but find a peaceful way to resist the heavy constraints enacted upon us by the mighty corporate apparatus. Remember, non-violence is always the right way.

Here are some ways you can resist:

- *When competing head-to-head with someone for a higher position, back out and let the other person have it.*
- *Write anonymous letters to this journal.*
- *Turn on a trusted friend to this journal.*
- *More to come.*

—ZW

The above letter infuriated the law enforcement personnel of Northern Indiana and the FBI. They redoubled their efforts to find the daring outlaw. And they renewed their endeavor to track down the location of the *Clandestine Journal's* Chicago press.

ANNIE DE LUCA routinely prepared batches of cereal at work, then brought them home to test. For each batch she employed a different chemical blend.

One Tuesday evening, the kitchen at the De Luca residence exploded with exhilaration.

"I got the fucking formula!" shouted Annie De Luca. "I found the motherfucker! I found the motherfucker!"

Her companion, Anthony Valentino, rushed into the room, where five bowls of milk and flakes sat in a row atop the kitchen counter.

"The flakes stayed crisp for twelve minutes, two minutes longer than the minimum requirement for No-Sog flakes and more than enough time to eat a bowlful! I did it, I did it!" Annie jumped up and down with jubilation.

"That's wonderful, dear!" shouted Anthony.

Then Annie jumped on Anthony and seduced him. They embraced, stripped off their clothes and began madly making love on a small mat on the kitchen floor. At first, Anthony made a futile attempt to resist, but Annie had his pants down before he could fully congratulate her.

"The rules," Anthony weakly protested.

"Fuck the rules!" shouted Annie amidst a series of heavy moans and sighs. "Let the mighty corporation come and get us! Uh, ah, ooohhh baby!"

Annie groped and fondled and gouged with her fingernails and yelled in what sounded like speaking in tongues. Her head bobbed back and forth and her hair flew in circles as she contorted herself in a dozen positions. The enraptured No-Sog Queen then gave a whoop that shook the whole kitchen as they furiously reached climax on the cold, hard floor.

Annie sexed Anthony's brains out, but poor Anthony still could not achieve a proper erection. He had No-Sog flakes but a slouching penis. Annie enjoyed it anyway. She moaned and quaked, *ew*'d and *ah*'d until her pretty little face puffed up and grew red as a Devil's butt. She rode Anthony as if he were a bronco, and when she orgasmed—one, two, and three times—the neighbors were pretty sure the entire apartment building shook. Annie soon completed herself for a fourth time and lay on the floor, gasping for air, and mumbling "I did it! I did it! I did it!"

The moment Annie had completed, and Anthony's worried worm had retreated, his guilt surged most unromantically.

"If anyone finds out what we were doing," fretted Anthony, "we're doomed. I'll be castrated!"

As soon as her breathing returned to normal, Annie called FAI headquarters and explained her accomplishment. Within a half hour a limousine pulled up to her front door. First, a second test was conducted by other lab personnel to verify the results of Annie's achievement. All of the bigwigs met at the office that evening and showered Annie with praise and gifts. This was the discovery that would propel Flakes Alive Incorporated to the top, overtaking GAFC and earning the much sought after Best Flake Award.

A great Tuesday evening celebration at the office ensued. Annie got to meet the big boss, Todd Swindell. "I am honored to meet you, sir," she gasped. Soon, the photographers and reporters took over.

Todd Swindell sat in his office beaming with joy. He hoped to soon clean off the fly guts from his office window, as soon as FAI could surpass GAFC in sales.

Some taste testers complained of "fossilized flakes," the things were so hard, so the lab quickly came up with another chemical to reduce the hardness. It was a balancing act of chemicals, but the flakes soon became perfect.

101

HAMMERING PAGORSKI

"YOU'RE a dinosaur of your day, Pagorski. A shadow of a forgotten time."

The contumacious Ned Pagorski bawled, "You bastards will never take it out of me. You can fuss about it, haul me into the fiery pits of hell, but you'll never make me forget. I remember milkmen and popsicle peddle carts and Whip 'n Chill and twenty-five cent packs of baseball cards (Grandpa Pagorski owned an antique shop before The Great Cleanse). Goddamnit I remember movies and Saturday matinees and Jamaican reggae and tossing the football in the front yard with my dad. You've drained all of the fun out of life, you stinking money hoarders. You took it all away, and for what? The almighty one-thousand-dollar bill."

Ned Pagorski wrestled with his handcuffs for a moment, then continued: "And my grandfather— God rest his aching soul—remembered Roger Maris and Mickey Mantle and Walter Payton and Joe Montana. My great grandfather remembered the Cuban Missile Crisis and Watergate. And his great grandfather remembered stagecoaches and dusty taverns and public squares and bobbing for apples and . . ."

Again, Ned struggled with the handcuffs. "Confounded

handcuffs. Take these damn things off! They're too tight!" He paused for a minute, then carried on: "You've robbed us. Robbed us of everything sacred. Taken it all and left us with silly commercials and asinine ads! Filthy bastards!"

"Process him for elimination," announced a voice over an intercom.

"Process me, you cowardly pricks." The old man spat on the floor. "C'mon you slimy tongued bitches!"

"Just give in, Pagorski. Things will go so much easier."

"Eat my banana snot. You fucking sanitizing wastrels. Your world sucks!"

"Open door 7A and let this cantankerous asshole get out of my sight," announced an officer at the Newton County jail. "Prepare him for elimination."

"I know it all, you yellow bellies. My great-grandfather remembered Nehru jackets and platform shoes and bell-bottom pants and even miniskirts, all things you paranoid swine deleted from history."

The iron door slammed and the iron lock clicked into place, but the ornery Pagorski was not yet finished.

"Your mama sucks cock warts, you ugly bitches! I hope your family drowns in the Devil's cesspool!"

102

HARVESTING DELUSIONS

ZIGGIE HOPPED through the countryside like a scared ground squirrel. A tinge of desire to give up and serve his time had planted itself in his breast, but he ran anyway.

His thoughts centered around his childhood. Finally, he slowed down to a walk. Ziggie remembered Domino before the big cereal companies moved in. It was a peaceful and pleasant little village, where everyone knew each other. He recalled secretly playing cowboys and Indians in the prairie where I-63 now sprawls.

He used to cut across that same prairie on his way to school back in the 2050s. He and his friend Jason Siebert used to go down to the little pond by the now-forgotten lumber company, down to the old railroad switchyard and look for frogs. Then, they might play a game of throw-it-up-and-hit-it with a thin plastic bat and a whiffle ball, both pretty much outlawed today.

He might head up to old U. S. Highway 41 and count the different cars that drove past. He would wave to the semitruck drivers and they would almost always wave back, and the most enthusiastic of them would toot the big horn. Life was so simple in those days. But now he had to remain on the run, looking for side doors to duck into for a moment to reestablish a steady breath, then moving on.

He thought about bussing tables at Fred's Hi-Way Café during his late teens and then his first day at work as a Local Union 4521 pipefitter. He thought he had come into riches when he saw his first paycheck. So what if he scoffed at a few customs and traditions, eschewed a few common beliefs about the corporate government's role in modern society? He had learned to keep those thoughts inside. He worked hard and got along just fine with everybody. Now he thought about his fateful decision to cover up his old corporate tattoo. He knew he would do it again, should he have it to do over.

Memories of Alfi and the colorful music he played for Ziggie flooded his mind. And visions of good old Ned Pagorski, the one who would allow no corporate-sponsored, doctored memories to confuse his sturdy mind. Ned saw things as they really were, not how the corporations wanted you to remember them or perhaps forget them altogether. He was as honest as Mother Earth—sometimes brutally so. A genuine spirit of old, a champion of truth. Not a believer in falsehoods, not a buy-in for the cellphone-sucking modern-day American public, not a sponge for the cover-ups and denials like most of the sad population had become.

That is why Ziggie could not give up. He *had* to keep going in the name of Ned.

Guys like Ned and I, he thought, *would never allow anyone or anything to roll us up into the Big Lie. To roll us up and put us on a train car to the corporate government's fictional hell. We know that freedom once existed, and it did not just roll around in our skewed minds as a maybe or a possibility, that liberty rang from every bell on the planet, and no goddamn corporate cellophane plastic wrap could hide the individual expression due us.*

The rest of society can run and hide in their company games and picnics, but we will be here cheering independent thought when you return. Ned and I will wait with a dose of knowledge yet unstirred. Waiting to pass truth on so that somebody, somewhere, someday, can break out of these corporate chains and fight against the tired lies.

Somebody has got to do it. It has got to be us.

Time melted onward like the gritty body of Ziggie plowing along the old angular vestiges of Indian trails that made up the modern country roads. He knew his destiny was about to meet him, and his long struggle for truth would soon dissect its final lie.

———

Somewhere, in a tiny room sits a quiet boy peeling away the delusions as if they were cobwebs covering a passageway to veracity. Somewhere a plain vision of what can be will snatch a girl from her muddled circumstance and deliver her a clear view of what one can accomplish with just a pinch of truth, a sliver of reality. A palpable truth for the ages. Just as before. Before lying came into vogue.

103

FROM APEX TO GUTTER: AN AMAZING DAY FOR TODD SWINDELL

TODD SWINDELL FELT LIKE A YO-YO.

Back and forth he would go, revisiting agonizing fear and invigorating ecstasy. He was of course elated that FAI was on the verge of overtaking GAFC for the top spot in flake sales, but with Detective Hung Cho Lee hounding him for answers in the deaths of Archibald Stevens and Jeffrey Gebhardt, he was frantic with fear and anxiety.

Mounting pressure on Todd Swindell, in fact, nudged him closer to a psychotic state, a Capitalist Crazy outburst that might echo through the corroded corridors of corporate America. Detective Lee had pestered him into seclusion, though he still had to orchestrate the operations of Flakes Alive Incorporated. So, he avoided the law as best he could, even though he fretted over his impending capture.

While autumn painted the trees yellow, brown and red, Swindell appeared pale and slightly disheveled. He had bitten his fingernails almost down to the bone. Just when he felt like burying his head, he received a strange letter.

I know you did it, you skinny snake. You snuffed out Archibald Stevens, then Jeffrey Gebhardt. You will pay for this, you sniveling little milksop. Savor your final days of freedom, you pathetic bitch. They are coming for you.

—*Anonymous*

Panic rushed over Swindell, ran up and down his spine like the puck in a high striker, strength tester, carnival game. Now the bell rang and he became feverish with stress. His fiery mind howled like a lone coyote trying to gather the pack, his frozen hands managed to squeak into activity.

Kill Hung Cho Lee, his brain squawked. And it grew louder in his mind. "No! No!" he said out loud in the confined office.

Soon he began to itch. His entire body itched with dread. He could not stop scratching his chest and arms. He felt the pang of diarrhea coming on. He began biting on his index finger in frustration. Then he pounded his desk with his closed fists. He finally looked up at his window, where the guts of his trophy fly lingered and, somehow, he began the process of settling down and reclaiming his racing mind.

From those dried up fly entrails he garnered a thin slice of confidence and let it grow between his ribs. And it grew until he absolutely exuded fearlessness. He soon felt brash and even cocky. What kind of magical powers rested with that brown smear on the window? He had a mysterious desire to call Detective Lee on his intelli-phone and tell him—no, dare him—to "come on! Come on you shuddering little cockroach! Come on and let's see what you've got!"

He was ready to grab his phone and do just that when his secretary knocked softly on his door. "Yes? Come in." Todd's sandpaper voice exuded newfound confidence.

"Mr. Swindell," said the excited secretary, "I have some-thing very important to tell you!"

"What's that, Dalia?"

"For the first time ever, FAI has surpassed GAFC in quar-terly sales!"

"Hot dog! Are you kidding me?"

"No, Mr. Swindell, I wouldn't kid about something like that. Here's the sales comparison charts for August 2098, released by Saxon and Wagner this morning."

"Whoopie!" shouted Swindell.

The marvelous news catapulted Todd Swindell into what may have been the last wonderous, dreamy state of his lifetime. He had conquered the beast, laid it out flat like a bulldozed tree, and delightfully pondered the status of being on top. The taste of rigid flakes, the exuberance of sitting at the pinnacle of flake sales, the suddenness of Scandalman's demise, and the so-far fruitless search by GAFC for a Scandalman replacement all coalesced to bring jubilance to Swindell and his FAI comrades, to serve the FAI and its customer community the topmost cereal on the planet.

Swindell truly reveled in the spotlight as the greatest flake-maker for all the ages. The amazing afterglow of the revelation could only be compared to the rapture following the first-time for sex, which Swindell had not realized since he was a pimply teenager back in 2036, but no, no, mustn't go there.

Alarm bells rang in his mind. *Warning! Stay away! Stay away! There is no 2036!*

For a moment he had forgotten about the harassment of Detective Lee. But a sharp pain in his chest reminded him of the dreadful hunt for his soul, the so-far absentee guilt that had now finally emerged in his soul. And just then, Todd Swindell knew that he was Capitalist Crazy! Quickly, he glanced at the fly remains streaked across his office window, just long enough to gather some more courage.

"Call everyone to the atrium for a celebration!" he instructed his secretary, Dalia Habib. Soon it was announced over the intercom system and everyone gathered for a brief, happy speech by the otherwise stress-saddled CEO.

Again, he forgot about his troubles.

"Ladies and gentlemen," announced Swindell from a raised podium, "I am proud to announce that we at Flakes Alive Incorporated have embarked on a new era in the cereal business. An era of newfound leadership. Newfound success. We have worked hard to achieve this success. We struggled almost endlessly through tough times—a terrible recession, a horrific war—to get where we are now. And just where are we? Well, I am tickled to announce that FAI now stands at the top of the heap. Starting today we are the number one company for flake sales!"

The occupants of the atrium exploded with exhilaration. Clapping, cheering, and all-around wowing reverberated throughout the halls of the newly crowned flake company.

"And I would like to add—"

Suddenly—what's this?—Detective Hung Cho Lee stepped up to the podium and held out his hand for the microphone, which Swindell refused to give him. Mr. Lee took his other hand and reached behind for his handcuffs. Another officer grabbed the microphone from Swindell's trembling hand and switched it to the "off" position.

"What—what are you doing?" protested Swindell. "Not in front of my people . . ." His words trailed off as he was cuffed.

"Mr. Todd Swindell, you are under arrest for the murders of Archibald Stevens and Jeffrey Gebhardt." The detective began reading him his rights, as the entire atrium fell into silence. In fact, the silence of the place was so deafening that a most eerie pall fell onto the stunned employees. Finally, a collective sigh emanated from the crowd as if it were one massive human being who suddenly realized it had been shot.

Then the skinny CEO made a desperate call to the audience. "Candace!" he yelled, "will you please wash the bug guts off my office window! Look in the upper left corner, and you will see them!"

"Ah, yes sir, Mr. Swindell," said an embarrassed Candace, the cleaning lady.

It seemed that the interrogation of Lady Weasel had delivered forth a mountain of evidence against Swindell. The gaunt, nervous woman apparently squawked like a flock of geese. She made a deal with prosecutors and received full immunity.

104

COCKTAIL REMEDIES

THE TEDIUM in the absence of entertainment grew on the working stiffs until they knew not what to do with themselves during their leisure time.

A weak-streaked 80 percent of the population became hypochondriacs and pill poppers. Aspirin and cold-remedy makers could barely keep up with the demand for their products. Eye drops and topical creams and ointments for this or that passed through the barcode readers at the checkout counters like flocks of geese flying south for the winter. Overanxious shoppers snatched lotions and salves, lip gloss and hemorrhoid creams, sinus sprays and vitamins, from store shelves the way a starving dog devours its food.

Big Pharma grew into Humongous Pharma as the bored population flexed its sturdy consumer muscles and gobbled pills for every known ailment. Pharmaceuticals comprised a disproportionate share of the grocery bill. America was addicted and Humongous Pharma wallowed in giant pools of cash.

One pill's side effects led to another pill to ease those effects and the second pill needed further pills to offset its negative effects until one whopping parade of pills saturated the linings of the stomach. To relieve the nagging stress of everyday job pressures and sales competitions, folks needed not one pill but a cocktail of pills to even approach normality in the workplace. Tensions built up without a means to ease them. One could walk in circles like a trapped animal to obtain some kind of succor. Mounting pressures with no mechanism for release wore on people's minds until some type of seismic explosion had to occur.

By then, one was fully in the grip of Capitalist Crazy.

105

TWINKLE ACQUITTED

THOUGH SCIENTISTS COULD DETERMINE that the single, rootless hair found by Detective Lee on the front porch at the Syd Waverly murder scene had a high probability of being Twinkle Deshpande's, they could not say for sure.

Besides, the hair being discovered outside of the crime scene made it impossible to prove that the owner of the hair had murdered Mr. Waverly inside the premises. Even if the hair had included the root, which would yield the DNA, it was still a shaky case. The hair could have blown in from anywhere. And the jury saw it that way as well, for they acquitted the young Indian American woman.

Twinkle's enlivened family cheered with joy, while Detective Hung Cho Lee scowled. The courtroom soon cleared and the excitement moved outdoors. A thousand questions bombarded the young assassin.

"Twinkle," asked Ms. Flaharty from CZBN television, "were you surprised at the verdict?"

"Not really," glowed Twinkle. "I expected all along to be acquitted."

Twinkle then moved away, first to Los Angeles, then to Miami, never to be seen again in the Chicago area. Since both

Chad Scandalman and Cliché Bob were deceased, only Cecil Weatherspoon could introduce new evidence to incriminate her, but he was too involved with his retirement problems for Twinkle to be concerned with him. Twinkle did correspond with her cousin, Anika Patel, learning that Anika's father had purchased three more motels and that Anika's companion, Deepak, had given up his life to sorrow.

Detective Hung Cho Lee was ripe from disappointment. In fact, he was incensed that he could not dig up enough evidence to support his theory that Twinkle was the hit woman. Once his anger subsided, he languished in the doldrums of dispiritedness for several weeks after the acquittal.

PRESS OF THE CLANDESTINE JOURNAL DESTROYED

THE FOLLOWING story was presented to Midwesterners as a *Clandestine Journal* news release special:

On December 17th, 2098, the corporate government whose men and women had been working feverishly to uncover the whereabouts of the Clandestine Journal's operations in Chicago, found and destroyed the printing press. This comes 261 years after Elijah Lovejoy, famous abolitionist, had his press annihilated for the third time in Alton, Illinois. Lovejoy was killed in the brutal riot that ensued.

Corporate government officials isolated the computer systems that controlled the press, and the press itself, at a secret location on Division Street on the north side of Chicago. As a gesture of raw authority, they not only deconstructed the machinery but condemned the entire building.

Fortunately, the Clandestine Journal had an auxiliary press waiting to be utilized at another location in the Chicago metropolitan area, where this issue was printed. And before this issue even hits the streets, the machinery has been moved again in order to elude the truth destroyers.

OASIS MOTEL

ZIGGIE, his hair now bushy and wild, decided to head south again.

He found his way to St. John, Indiana in Lake County. A blizzard had ambushed the town on a cold, windy December morning. The steady snow gave way to several bursts of the white stuff, which made walking miserable. Ziggie trudged along I-63 for two hours before he reached town, where he followed the exit onto the old highway, US Route 41. A dilapidated mom-and-pop motel, recently bypassed by the I-63 expressway, served as a welcome stop.

Once inside, Ziggie stomped his feet on a "Welcome to the Oasis Motel" mat to get off the snow on his wet shoes. He immediately inquired about a room.

"I've got a room for one with a queen bed for $136." The chubby motel clerk sported a brown mustache and a fading Cedar Lake Energy & Appliance Company tattoo on his forehead. He chewed on the end of an unlit cigar.

"A clean room?" asked Ziggie. "No bugs?"

"No bugs."

A thoroughly frustrated Ziggie said, "Just a moment . . . I've got a commercial." Whenever the intelli-phone implant decided to interrupt one's privacy with an automatic commercial, he or she had no choice but to pause their conversation and allow it to play out.

Tabitha ate a bowl of Flunky Flakes and had no energy. John ate a bowl of Flimsy Flakes that grew soggy within two minutes. Karen, however, munched on a bowl of Flakes Alive Incorporated's No-Sog Fortified Flakes and stood ready to challenge the world!

"OK," said Ziggie, "got that out of the way."

"But I was about to say, sir, the room won't be available till twelve o'clock noon."

"I'll take it," said Ziggie. "Is there a coffee shop near here?"

"The Shamrock Café is just across the old highway."

While counting out $136, Ziggie thought no one would recognize him in this dingy old motel. He handed the cash to the clerk and realized he only had $12 left.

"Checkout time is tomorrow morning at eleven o'clock."

Ziggie crossed the highway and had a cup of coffee at Taylor's Café. He pulled a notebook from his backpack, which he had set down on the seat next to him. He scribbled a short note for the *Clandestine Journal*, stuffed it into an envelope, and used his last stamp. Then he finished his coffee and set out for the post office down the street.

The snow had piled up to about six inches but seemed to have tapered off. The sparkling snow looked so beautiful on buildings and awnings, thought Ziggie, but so ugly where cars had driven through it and turned it to gray slush. Scraping shovels and whining snowblowers began to pierce the heavy air.

When Ziggie dropped his letter in a mail container inside the post office, he was struck by a 10-Most-Wanted poster containing ten pictures, one of which was Ziggie himself. In a fit of angst, he pried-off the thumbtack that held the thing in place with his long fingernails, stuffed the poster in his back-pack, and looked around to make sure nobody had seen him.

In a panicked flurry, he hurried back to the motel to contemplate his next move and get some rest.

THE HENSON FAMILY—ALL seven of them—went to the Commercial Theatre in the River North section of Chicago.

"Choose a category of commercials, Herb Jr.," said Herb Sr. The choices included Forgotten Gems, Commercials with Animals, and Modern Commercials.

"I'll take Commercials with Animals," said young Herb. "Maybe we can see how animals have sex—er, rather, procreate."

"Herb Jr.!" cried Holly Henson. "That's enough! Where are you hearing this stuff?"

"Tommy Esparza . . . at school," said little Herb. "Ya see, his grandpa, old Jorge, tells him this stuff on account that he's ninety-two years old and remembers it from his youth."

"Well," Holly remarked, "we'll just have to talk with grandpa Esparza. He shouldn't be telling children about this stuff. It's abrasive and probably untrue, and I don't want to hear another thing about it."

"No! Don't call Grandpa Esparza! You'll make me look like a rat!"

"Your behavior needs a major adjustment, young man," hollered Holly. "You talk like a gangster!"

At intermission the family went up front to buy some good-ies. Herb Jr. got some Rainbow Nubs candy and a cola. The rest of the clan got popcorn and cola. When they returned to their seats, Herb Jr. remarked, "These little nubs remind Grandpa Esparza of colored nipples."

That was about all the parents could endure. Within two weeks of this nasty verbal display, among other transgressions, the intractable Herb Jr. was placed in a reform school.

"More and more each day Herb Jr. gets like your cousin, Ziggie Wexler," said Holly to Herb Sr.

"I know," said Herb, "he seems destined—like a mirror image of Ziggie—to go on the run. I don't quite know what to do. Maybe reform school will help him."

FALLEN ANGEL

"HELLO, HERB?" said Ziggie Wexler over the phone.

"Who is this?" asked Herb Henson.

"It's your cousin, Ziggie."

"Ziggie? I heard you're on the run. I don't want no trouble, Ziggie."

"Herb, please, I just need a little help. I'm running out of money and I thought you might be able to loan—"

Herb hung up. He had a lovely family and a good job and he could not risk helping a fugitive. Ziggie was in more trouble than he cared to deal with. Besides, Herb was completely devoted to the Latimer Diaper Company, where he did volunteer work, and its sponsorship of The Baby Factory.

Meanwhile, Ziggie ran through alleys, stomped through empty lots and sloshed through creeks, all with the growing noise of the barking hounds behind him. Finally, half exhausted and with nowhere to go, he climbed the ladder outside a Kentland municipal water tower. By the time he got halfway up the huge tank, Captain Doris McElvy announced through a bullhorn, "Come down Zigmund Wexler! We have you surrounded. There's no place to go!"

Ziggie's hands trembled. They became wet with perspiration. He gripped the ladder tighter, as he looked down toward the eager law enforcement officers.

"You can't escape, Ziggie!" hollered McElvy.

Ziggie yelled with all of his strength: "If I come down, can I serve my time and then have my pipefitter job back? And my 401(k) back?"

"What'd he say?" McElvy asked a fellow officer.

"He wants his job back."

"I cannot make any promises," said Captain McElvy through the bullhorn, "but we'll see what we can do!" Then, she put the bullhorn down and said to Cheeseball, "He's got a lot of nerve, asking for his job back."

Ziggie came out from behind the ladder and yelled, "OK, I'm surrendering! I'm coming down!"

Captain McElvy cared not what Ziggie said at this juncture. Before he could step down a single rung of the ladder, she braced her rifle against her shoulder, aimed, and fired one round at the elevated fugitive, striking him in the chest.

Ziggie flinched. It felt as if he had been kicked by a mule. He heard the shot and knew he was hit.

His chest felt heavy, as he looked down at the authorities on the ground.

"Did they really shoot me?" he asked himself. A plethora of thoughts flooded his frantic mind. *They want to kill me. Can't I just go back to cutting and fitting pipes? I've been betrayed. I didn't mean any harm. All of this for a changed ink design and a few negative comments?*

Oh, the blood feels warm, dripping down my belly. God, help me.

Even then, Ziggie was amazed, for on the threshold of death, the guilt of asking God for help, gnawed on his conscience. How could it be? "Can't . . . let them bastards . . . win."

Time was frozen, as they all looked up at him, anxiously waiting to see him drop. How cruel it seemed to Ziggie. He could no longer breathe. He was slipping into a vacuum, nothingness. Suddenly, he tilted his head and tumbled down the long ladder. The chemicals in his brain continued to react, but his visions were fading. The faces of everyone he ever knew flashed through his mind on the way down, down, down. . . .

———

The ground shook with his landing and the air cracked with the simultaneous breaking of sundry bones. He lay dead, as the state troopers gathered around his mangled corpse. They all felt satisfied with the outcome.

Captain McElvy grimly proclaimed, "Zigmund Wexler, you are no more." McElvy received a corporate commendation for apprehending a top ten most-wanted fugitive.

In a public address regarding the life of Zigmund Wexler, Captain McElvy offered her final thoughts: "Ziggie's was a world where successful entrepreneurs were disparaged as losers, where positive thinkers were beat up and scorned, and where do-gooders were constantly weighed against evil. May he find peace in death."

Meanwhile, Ziggie's final note to his brother-and sisterhood appeared in the *Clandestine Journal*. It simply read:

When the last employee benefit is stolen back by the avaricious corporation, when every last institution—libraries, postal services, and former public schools—is made into a profit-seeking corporate enterprise, when every aspect of your life is scrunched up inside a dollar, you will then know that the capitalist has succeeded in tearing out your soul and selling it on the open market.

Don't let it happen.

The march for truth must surmount many roadblocks. Shards of untruths will impinge on your power to reason; always be ready to overcome them.

Carrying the torch of truth can at times make one feel weary. I recently met a man, a teller of truth, Ned, who told me he was tired. He said: "I hear the drum beating in my heart; but every time I hear it, it slows down." Don't let it stop! Fight on!

Peace.

—ZW

It started out as a tiny stone in Captain Doris McElvy's shoe, pricking the ball of her foot, leaving her with a feeling of frustration. It soon began to gnaw on her nerves and cause her pain. McElvy's foot ached as if there were a knife poking her. She finally removed her shoe and emptied it.

And there lay Zigmund Wexler on the concrete, its dirt-filled cracks turning gray with the trickling blood. A withered warrior, deceased and bone broken, belied the animated spirit that had just ascended from the mass of flesh.

Meanwhile, Ziggie's family reeled in shock and anger when they heard the dreadful news. His mother fell to her knees and began to wail. His father hung his head and whimpered. Even his sister, Elizabeth, with whom he had grown distant, cried heavily. They knew his individualism had been crushed, his dreams scattered in the prairie breezes, his will to challenge wrongs splattered on the concrete base of a water tower.

DETECTIVE HUNG CHO LEE finally wrapped up his investigation of the Scandalman murder case. It was not anyone from Flakes Alive Incorporated at all. It was a spouse killing.

Detective Lee first found gunpowder residue on Mrs. Scandalman's hands. Then, after visiting all the pawnshops near Domino, Indiana, he recovered the gun that had disposed of the GAFC CEO. And ballistics matched the gun to the murder. Finally, a store video camera showed Mrs. Scandalman pawning the gun.

It seems Mrs. Scandalman held a serious grudge when Chad Scandalman ate all the egg salad the night before his death. The estranged pair had often fought over Chad eating all the leftovers in the refrigerator and not leaving anything for Gertrude.

"That pissed me off!" Mrs. Scandalman confessed. "That, and the SOB always masturbated," she complained. "You know, he got on my nerves, masturbating in the shower, masturbating on the freshly made bed, and masturbating on the living room recliner. I got sick of it. So, sue me!"

"Why didn't you just turn him in if you knew he was masturbating, Mrs. Scandalman?" asked Lee.

"Cause I never caught him in the act! He left dried semen on the towels, the throw rugs, even the draperies. He just didn't know when to quit. But I never saw him doing it."

Said Lee: "This is cause to arrest you, Mrs. Scandalman, even if you had not murdered your companion." The otherwise stoic housewife did shed a tear as he handcuffed her.

Cheeseball added his thoughts: "Oh how the state has tried to eliminate such behavior, to curb sexual desires and make good, honest corporate citizens out of its subjects. All in vain, I'm afraid, in the case of Chad Scandalman. All for an instant of ecstasy and a glob of goo. Why that amounts to stealing. Stealing from the corporation, Spittoon Alley, and the Baby Factory. All of his nervous energy should have been going to those enterprises! Who knows? He could have spat away the next CEO God! The sperm residue of that little nobody could be embedded in that flowered pillowcase over there!"

"Yes," said Detective Lee, "who knows what they could have done with that wasted semen."

Said Cheeseball: "Well, you know what they say:
A wad of errant bud Leaves a name in mud."

Scandalman's sins reached out in all directions like the tentacles of a giant squid. However, Detective Lee followed protocol and tried to keep Scandalman's offenses from the public. Instead of announcing his gruesome murder of Cliché Bob, or his orchestrating the murder of Syd Waverly, Detective Lee assisted in sponsoring a plaque engraved with the CEO God's heroic accomplishments over thirty years of pristine service at the Great American Flake Company.

Were he a lesser man, Scandalman, for the murders of Syd Waverly and Cliché Bob, would have been charged with first-

and second-degree murder and sent to a work camp for five or ten years. The fake bonds crime he and Cliché Bob pulled off would have cost him another ten years. Of course, if it was the other way around, the bondholder ripping off the corporation, a minimum thirty-years-to-life sentence would have been in order for the citizen culprit. Or perhaps the death penalty.

The media, however, did discover the bond scheme and revealed to the public the involvement of GAFC company stalwarts Chad Scandalman and Cliché Bob. This news report added another layer to GAFC's woes and helped to usher in the company's downfall and Flakes Alive Incorporated's rise in the flake ranks. Nevertheless, Scandalman's status as CEO God did not suffer, and life moved on mysteriously in Domino and surrounding suburbs.

111

THE BIG BRIBE

FOR THE MURDERS of Archibald Stevens, the GAFC taste tester, and Jeffrey Gebhardt, the GAFC television-commercial spokesman, FAI CEO Todd Swindell was to receive two concurrent ten-year terms of corporate servitude, the corporation to be named later, since GAFC did not want him working for them. Final sentencing was set to begin in May of 2099.

However, Todd, the master of deals, had a tremendous agreement to make, should his lawyer, Baltimore Driggs, have the wherewithal to negotiate an agreement with prosecutors. And when prosecutors found out what Swindell and Driggs had to offer, their eyeballs swelled and their jaws dropped like lead weights. Detective Hung Cho Lee, the man who gathered most of the dirt on Swindell and slipped him into handcuffs, was now implicated in the bribing of Swindell and FAI! But how could this be?

Mr. Swindell, it seemed, possessed recordings of Detective Lee demanding $300,000 to withhold information incriminating Swindell in the two homicides and, therefore, letting him walk free. Swindell had refused to pay $300,000 and was now negotiating a deal with the district attorney.

Soon, the deal solidified and Todd Swindell pled guilty to

two counts of second-degree murder. As a result, he received a total of three years of working for his competitor, the Blake Flakes Company, doing menial tasks in a most humiliating circumstance.

The far more serious crime of bribing a monolithic corporation, at least in 2098 America, earned now former Detective Lee the death sentence. Captain Doris McElvy enjoyed the experience of arresting Mr. Lee.

Cheeseball, of course, felt compelled to prescribe his own version of a penalty: "Give Mr. Lee Viagra. Once he displays an erection, tap a three-inch sliver of glass into his urethra. Lay the penis on an anvil. Next, take a hammer and smash it against the penis so that the glass breaks inside the urinary canal."

"I think we'll stick with traditional punishment, Corporal Downey," announced Captain McElvy.

112

TORY SLIPS INTO SEVERE MENTAL ILLNESS

WHEN HIS FATHER was arrested for two murders, Tory Swindell began his slide into extreme mental anguish and suffering. He was so used to his father giving him anything he wanted that he took to craziness without him. First, he wandered into the depths of isolation, shielding himself from people's "petty positions, corny stories, and silly social bickering." He allowed himself to see no one.

Then he became horribly depressed, sinking into lonely despair. Anxiety over his position in the universe also crept into his often sorrowful, sometimes pulsating mind. He sank to new lows by the hour. Soon he began to see things that did not exist, like little blue and red demons outside of the house where he lived with his mother. The demons watched him on the inside and forbade him to leave home. Then there were the polliwogs swimming around in his toilet. In his nightmares they grew into giant carnivorous frog-like monsters invading his bedroom and trying to eat him.

His mother took him to two psychiatrists who both agreed that he suffered from schizophrenia.

Delusions that everyone was laughing at him, even the two psychiatrists, drove him into fantastic episodes of paranoia. He dumped a large can of sauerkraut into his mother's aquarium and watched the fish die, because he thought they were alien spies. He lashed out at the mailman because he thought the talkative letter carrier was snooping on him. He smacked the secretary of Dr. Felix J. Bates, giving her a broken nose. He served three months in the Newton County Jail and paid a fine of $2,000 (rather, his mother paid it).

Medication seemed to help Tory in coping with his madness, but frantic episodes continued to haunt him every few days. One day he smashed a pie his mother had baked because he thought there were hidden microphones in it, as well as all around the house.

His mother tried to have him committed to a mental health crisis center, but on his best behavior during an interview, he failed to meet the criteria for derangement. Plus, the place was overcrowded and he would have to go on a waiting list. So, he returned home, boarded up his bedroom windows, and fell into a stupor, refusing to get out of bed.

He laid there like an overripe fruit for seven days. Seven days turned into fourteen days. The room stunk like an elevator full of homeless vagrants. The stench was horrendous. Finally, his mother called the nuthouse again, and this time they agreed to come and get him, though he would have to wait a day or two for an open bed. Only Tory suspected her of turning him in, went on a hunger strike, and thought a plethora of evil things.

113

RECONSIDERATIONS

THE ATTEMPTED eradication of all enjoyment seemed to backfire on the corporate government. For example, the strictest adherence to the banning of most sports (except for golf, the executive favorite) attempted to rechannel all energy toward the corporation and its work tasks. The corporate-greedy process applied too much pressure on the American worker.

The Social Science Institute, a nonprofit organization that had been stripped of its power and could only make suggestions to the government, found that amusements outside of work were essential to employee happiness, and the lack of such ulti-mately led to a decline in worker productivity. An adjustment to the balance of work and play seemed inevitable.

Yet the corporate hardnoses clung to their old philosophy that workers will do more without the interference of baseball, football, basketball, hockey, etc., so striking a balance in the lives of American workers appeared no longer to be the goal. Instead, the attainment of total control seemed pervasive in the corporate ranks. The obvious was just too much for them to digest.

Grappling with the urge to maintain dominance then is the

notion of providing some avenue for entertainment. The two ideas just did not mesh. To revive sex is to relinquish power. To resurrect baseball is to loosen control.

As was previously mentioned, the masses were so starved for entertainment that a new form of music called "brute" invited participants to beat on each other while moving to its discordant strains on the dance floor. Note that this form of brutality was no case of revisiting slam-dancing from the punk scene of the 1980s (whoops, that's a no-no!), but a full-on thrashing of an individual participant by a group of dance-floor thugs.

To reduce this type of brawling and the subsequent calling off of work due to injury, the control fiends almost had to acquiesce to some sort of sport besides golf. The capitalists were losing money, which always marks a point of action, so the capitalists had the last word on everything, hence they reluctantly legalized baseball and outlawed brute music. This marked a rare concession on the part of the corporate elite.

By abolishing sex, the corporate government made the LGBTQ community disappear—that is, return to the closet. Sexually transmitted diseases became almost unknown. Prostitution nearly vanished.

But the pressure of the corporations to legalize sex grew stronger and stronger, until, on December 15, 2098, the topic came up for a vote by the Legislature. The corporate government would reconsider the ban on sex, with a multimedia empire salivating over the possibility of selling sex once again.

The remnants of the religious elements of society will have no say regarding the decision. Of course, they were all for the abolition of sex back in 2040.

The reason for reconsideration is that too many offenders partake in banned sexual activity, and the corporate government finds it difficult to keep track of these lawbreakers.

The bill was quickly shot down, however, by the Corporate Congress, many of whom were far-right religious conservatives before The Great Cleanse. This, despite many of the Corporate Congress indulging in such secret sexual misbehavior behind closed doors.

The final solution for this great social problem was this: the rich would be able to subscribe to a program of sexual allowance by paying a sum of $2400 a year. Thus, sex would be legal for the affluent, the only sliver of the population who could afford $2400 a year for a porn channel. Sex would, therefore, become the pay-per-view product of specific entertainment establishments.

Just as baseball once had left the little guy behind by removing games from the network television markets and broadcasting them on prepay specialty channels, sex too was now available to those who could afford it.

114

BFC RISES LIKE A BULLET

WITH CEO TODD SWINDELL away on his prison visit for three years, Lady Weasel, having supplied prosecutors information on Todd Swindell's criminal activity, basked in her new position as Interim CEO for Flakes Alive Incorporated. She worked diligently to guide the flake giant through the rapids of scandal, but she would not be able to hold on to the sole position of first place in the flake sales arena.

The newest company in the race, Blake Flakes, now streaked up the charts and knocked the Great American Flake Company, still without a CEO, into third place. Isabella Blake suddenly boosted herself into a tie for first place with Flakes Alive Incorporated! Both had a stranglehold on 34 percent market share, while GAFC reeled from the permanent loss of its CEO and had to settle for a 29 percent ranking.

Isabella kept herself out of the scandals, toned down her ostentatious style, and bolted up the charts. She found herself haggling for the number one spot in the flake ranks.

Then, on January 1, 2099, Isabella's company sat all alone in first place with a 35 percent to 33 percent lead over FAI, and without even having the longed-for No-Sog formula, which, it would have turned out, Cliché Bob, before his untimely demise, planned to orchestrate a bidding war between GAFC and BFC for the prized solution. Though two-timing Bob had promised FAI the solved formula, he had intended to try and sell it to Isabella also, then conducting the transaction with the company that made the best offer.

Of course, he perished before the formula was ever discovered.

115

LADY IN DISTRESS

LADY WEASEL FELT peevish ever since FAI lost first place in the flake sales ratings. Any little thing triggered irritability. Her printer ran out of paper and she had a fit. A paper jam, easily fixable, caused her to fight through another bout of irascibility. A somewhat dissolute citizen outside of work, she was determined to conduct herself properly within the corporate walls for as long as she served as interim CEO.

She seemed bitter, like a nun deprived of sex—empty and mean. Yet her work ethic stood high. Through a sour demeanor and a saggy frame, she conducted herself admirably for business purposes. She concealed her little fits as best she knew how. Even through her often-forced smile, she radiated ambiguous vibes.

At best Lady Weasel was a loner, quite content to be a part of anything, straight or warped, normal or skewed, average or weird. This is why she fell into the plot to kill Archibald Stevens. The hounds of doom regularly prodded her. And now they hunted her.

Lady Weasel's bony facial features mirrored her sharp mind. She had a continuous dream that some worthy companion would emerge and keep her in good company for the remainder of her life. And though her career had now proven quite successful, her social life, or lack of one, depressed her terribly.

But now a new problem had gripped her: even though FAI had gotten the patent for the finalized formula for the No-Sog flakes, the company lagged behind the Blake Flake Company for most flake sales. FAI was expected to bolt into the number one position in flake sales, but interim CEO Lady Weasel failed to steer the company to the top. This caused much turmoil and friction within the company, which left Lady Weasel grieving over what she was supposed to accomplish.

116

TIGHT IS THE GRIP

THE FEDERAL AUTHORITIES soon embarked on criminal sweeps of houses and apartments of people like Ziggie.

They pressed down hard on any citizen who wrote or spoke negatively about the corporate government. Anyone who invoked the objectionable lyrics of brute music, rock, rap, or hip-hop. Anyone who espoused the philosophy to overturn the dominance of the dollar. Anyone who dared to articulate a passion for the spiritual beyond that of dead CEOs. Anyone who questioned the deity of the corporate CEOs, whether in fact or in rumor.

Tearing apart rooms. Rooms that might contain a secret blessing to research the joy of being human. They looked through personal letters, essays and poems for any incriminating detail of a longing for sexual therapy. For sexual arousal. Anything but hardline capitalist, nose-grinding work ethic. They wanted to root out defiance of all strains, once and for all. Total eradication made for the obsession of the day, even though it might take several years to accomplish.

Social collapse was imminent, they thought, if anything should escape their tenacious drive to disclose criminal leanings. Corporate collapse, they thought, would then follow. The entire country immersed itself in the chaotic, calamitous uproar. Every string had been tightened. Every screw and bolt.

And when they discovered that there were more people than they could arrest, incarcerate or eliminate, they lowered their shoulders and took a deep sigh. They knew then that they had firmly planted the doctrine of fear for resistance in everyone's mind. They had immaculate control.

Meanwhile, Captain Doris McElvy had recovered a note from Ziggie's shirt pocket. It was to be his next letter to the *Clandestine Journal*. Inflammatory and brazen, the letter put out a call to all impecunious souls to organize and take action against the iniquitous system. The letter read like this:

December 17th, 2098

This is a very general outline of a plan that must be worked out in detail by our indigent brethren.

Working out the plan must involve messengers, as no electronic traceable devices can be used.

Organize groups from the various Crate Camps numbering about 300 persons each. Identify and isolate country estates worth over, say, $2,000,000. Move in WITHOUT HURTING ANYONE and take over their possessions. The corporate government will not send in the army or National Guard to defend one rural estate. Sell their assets on the black market one at a time. Place the money into a special fund and build up the wealth of the destitute citizens. As the groups become more adept at running these operations, they will gradually target estates that are closer to the cities.

The first meeting should be held on January 15th, 2099 at the pavilion at Calumet Park, Southeast Chicago at 10:00 am. The details can then be worked out.

—ZW

LOOSE ENDS

AFTER THE FEDS raided one of her father's motels, Anika Patel fled to some unknown location overseas. Rumor said that she lived in France, but nobody knew for sure. She continued her work as an assassin in Europe, but then, growing tired of the lifestyle, she joined a circus back in India, where she permanently lost track of her cousin, Twinkle, and rarely talked to her father.

Convicted killer Alicia Gomez got three years for murdering Megan Sally but thirty years for depriving the GAFC corporation of its star marketer. In olden times she would have spent her time at the Wabash Valley Correctional Center in Carlisle, Indiana working in the laundry room, but, instead, she labored intensely in the cornfields of Central Indiana harvesting maize for the Blake Flake Company.

Solid laborers like Alicia guaranteed that Isabella Blake would remain atop the flake makers of the Hoosier State and the nation beyond.

INK-FLAVORED MEAT

THESE GLOOMY PAGES must give up one more murderous psycho, one more macabre scene.

It belongs to Tory Swindell. Already irked by his dad, who instead of showering the boy with holiday gifts as usual was serving three years in the penitentiary, the nervous substance abuser and mental cripple tried to navigate other issues as well. This included his mother pestering him to get a better job and be more like his father, the courts badgering him to pay his past-due fines, and the fact that his mother refused to give him partying money.

Young Tory bristled with anger and frustration, until the moment arrived when his derailed freight train slammed into a warehouse full of explosives, and *BABAM!*—his mind detonated.

The maniacal hellion borrowed a twenty-inch machete from his father's sword collection and lopped off his mom's head. He then thrust the giant blade into one of the eyeballs on the detached noggin, lifted the thing up, and held it over a burn-barrel fire until the meat on it bubbled and hissed. He then ripped off a piece of flesh from the cheek area and began to chew it with great wrath.

The meat of the thing tasted funny, on account of all the tattoo ink embedded in its face. But Tory munched and swallowed until he felt better. Later, he turned himself in and a disbelieving army of cops swarmed about his mother's house and the backyard burn barrel.

Adjacent to the door of mom's home office the now famous sign read, "Money: The Seed of All Joy."

119

A POST-MORTEM NOTE FROM ZIGGIE

FROM A NOTEPAD in Zigmund Wexler's backpack, the following note was discovered:

You can't kill truth; it's always there. It lives forever.

Though Ziggie would never know it, the corporate billionaires finally realized that the level of poverty had risen too high. An alarming 32 percent of the population now lingered under the poverty line. So many had crossed the threshold that it threatened the wealth of the corporate magnates, as they could not collect enough taxes from the homeless, and they realized that something must be done to redistribute some of their riches. Almost a third of the population subsisting on welfare and disability payments did not pump enough money back into the system to satisfy the moguls' appetites for opulence.

As Cliché Bob would say, "They shot themselves in the foot."

A special meeting set for 2099 was called by American leaders to address the problem.

A SOMBER DAY

ON A SNOWY DECEMBER MORNING, Hung Cho Lee succumbed to Death's wrecking crew when he underwent chemical injection near the old electric chair in the Indiana State Prison at Michigan City.

Bribing a corporation carried the death sentence, and the corporate governor of the state would not budge on the topics of granting clemency or issuing of a pardon. They made the death announcement at noon near the front entrance of the notorious prison. Detective Lee's family filed out of the prison, stunned and heartbroken. They could not believe that the proud husband and father they had so much looked up to had expired without ceremony, spending his last few hours wallowing in disgrace.

Just two weeks later, in what the state calls "Rapid Justice," Todd Swindell had completed a month of his three-year sentence for murder. The humiliated CEO cleaned toilets for Isabella Blake's flake-factory workers. The first count was dismissed. The second count was prosecuted, but the judge gave lenience on account of Todd Swindell's top position at the Flakes Alive Incorporated headquarters.

Out on Lake Michigan, the seagulls soared and the waves rolled beneath a heavy layer of clouds. The snow blanketed a strip of dunes near where the old lighthouse used to stand, watching over what was once a better America.

ABOUT THE AUTHOR

Retired IT professional, James Owens is a trained computer engineer and technical documentation specialist who earned an A.A.S. in computer programming and a B.A. in English from Purdue University.

Immensely curious about human behavior, James spent the 1970s hanging out on the streets to observe people, many of whom became inspirations for his  fictional characters. Later, he worked in cube farms at conservative insurance companies, where the idiosyncrasies of corporate personalities sparked his imagination.

James has spent the last decade reading and writing offbeat fiction about bizarre protagonists. *Corporate Almighty: 2098*, a dystopian tale about the rise of the corporation and the fall of democracy, follows his first two novels, *Animal Candy* and *Pods of Bubbledumb: A Study in Mass Depravity*.

Born and raised in an industrial suburb on the south edge of Chicago, James lives with his wife Sue and four cats in Evansville, Indiana.